"How Can I Get Through to You?"

As he spoke, Raven gripped Pat's shoulders, pulling her close. "I'm going to break down that wall you've built around yourself, Pat Lee," he said softly.

"Why?" Pat asked, a tremor running through her. It was a contest of wills, and she wouldn't allow him to overpower her. "So you can add another notch to your belt?"

Raven's fingertips trailed over her cheek to trace the outline of her full lower lip. "If that's the kind of men you knew, I don't blame you for running away."

Dear Reader:

Nora Roberts, Tracy Sinclair, Jeanne Stephens, Carole Halston, Linda Howard. Are these authors familiar to you? We hope so, because they are just a few of our most popular authors who publish with Silhouette Special Edition each and every month. And the Special Edition list is changing to include new writers with fresh stories. It has been said that discovering a new author is like making a new friend. So during these next few months, be sure to look for books by Sandi Shane, Dorothy Glenn and other authors who have just written their first and second Special Editions, stories we hope you enjoy.

Choosing which Special Editions to publish each month is a pleasurable task, but not an easy one. We look for stories that are sophisticated, sensuous, touching, and great love stories, as well. These are the elements that make Silhouette Special Editions more romantic ... and unique.

So we hope you'll find this Silhouette Special Edition just that—*Special*—and that the story finds a special place in your heart.

The Editors at Silhouette

TRACY SINCLAIR
A Love So Tender

Silhouette Special Edition

Published by Silhouette Books New York

America's Publisher of Contemporary Romance

SILHOUETTE BOOKS
300 E. 42nd St., New York, N.Y. 10017

Copyright © 1985 by Tracy Sinclair

Distributed by Pocket Books

ISBN: 0-373-09249-0

First Silhouette Books printing July 1985

10 9 8 7 6 5 4 3 2 1

America's Publisher of Contemporary Romance

Printed in the U.S.A.

TRACY SINCLAIR
has traveled extensively throughout the continental United States as well as Alaska, the Hawaiian Islands, Canada, Europe and the Orient, just to list a few of her jaunts. She does all of her writing at her home in San Francisco.

Books by Tracy Sinclair

Silhouette Romance

Paradise Island #39
Holiday in Jamaica #123
Flight to Romance #174
Stars in Her Eyes #244
Catch a Rising Star #345

Silhouette Special Edition

Never Give Your Heart #12
Mixed Blessing #34
Designed for Love #52
Castles in the Air #68
Fair Exchange #105
Winter of Love #140
The Tangled Web #153
The Harvest is Love #183
Pride's Folly #208
Intrigue in Venice #232
A Love So Tender #249

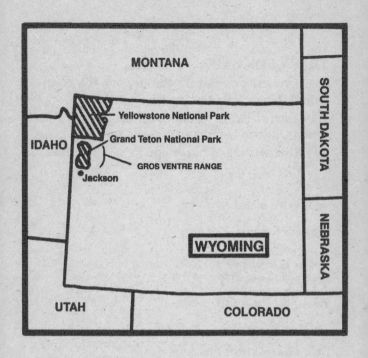

Chapter One

*P*at Lee was curled up in a comfortable chair, attempting to read. It wasn't easy to concentrate with the huge, black Great Dane trying to catch her eye. At first he had merely paced the floor restlessly, looking over his shoulder from the front door. When that produced no results he sat directly in front of her, making low moaning noises deep in his throat while fixing her with mournful eyes.

Finally Pat gave in. Unwinding her slim legs, she stood up. "You're like every other male in the world," she told the big dog, with mock severity. "All you care about is your own pleasure." She tucked the plaid shirt more securely into the waistband of her white shorts. "Oh, all right, we'll go for a walk."

The blazing sun was a ball of yellow fire in the deep blue sky, contrasting with the somber gray of the distant Teton mountain range. Outside of two hawks circling lazily in the clear air, there wasn't another sign of life. This was lonely, wild country. It was exactly what Pat had been looking for when she moved to Wyoming from New York three months previously.

It seemed longer than that, she reflected, watching Janus lope off toward a grove of trees. Was it only three months since her whole life had exploded in her face, leaving her shattered and alone? The past weeks in this majestic countryside had helped form protective layers around the pain. She no longer thought about New York—or Carl.

If Pat had found peace in Wyoming, Janus had discovered heaven. After being confined to a leash all of his life, he was ecstatic over his freedom to roam widely. Pat smiled indulgently as the dog bounded off, his graceful black shape merging with the shadows cast by a band of trees. She followed leisurely, pausing to gather a bouquet of wild mustard and blue lupine.

Suddenly the stillness was fractured by a series of screams that pierced the air like a siren. They were punctuated by frantic barking. After a frozen moment Pat raced toward the sound, crashing through the grove of trees to emerge in a small clearing. The sight that greeted her made her green eyes sparkle with anger.

A blond woman was screeching uncontrollably, clutching at the man sitting on the ground next to her. The remains of a picnic were spread out on their blanket. Janus was backing away from the hysterical woman, the hair on his back bristling as the man reached for a stout stick lying next to him.

"Don't you dare hit my dog!" Pat shouted. When his hand closed over the weapon in spite of her warning, she raced over, shielding Janus with her own body. "What kind of man are you anyway, to hit a defenseless animal?"

He hauled himself to his feet, leaning heavily on the stick which Pat now perceived was a cane. Dark brows peaked over disdainful eyes that were like gold-flecked agate in his lean face. It occurred irrelevantly to Pat that the man's pallor was surprising considering the athletic trimness of his tall, lean body.

"I had no intention of hitting him, and that dog is about as defenseless as William the Conqueror," he stated crisply.

"Who was no doubt an ancestor of yours." Pat tilted her head back to look at him defiantly. She came only to his shoulder but that didn't intimidate her a bit; nor did his powerful build or arrogant manner.

He ran an impatient hand through his thick dark hair. "Will you stop acting like the injured party? If you had any responsibility at all, you wouldn't let an animal that size race around surprising people."

"He has a right to run free. *You* happen to be trespassing." Pat scowled. "This is private property."

"In that case, what are you doing here?"

"Not that it's any of your business, but I happen to be the caretaker." She stuck out her rounded chin. "You'll have to gather your things and move on."

"You must be kidding!" His incredulous glance took in her small stature, the softly curling auburn hair around her slim shoulders, the delicate features in her heart-shaped face.

Pat stood her ground. "Don't count on it. Either you and your friend move on or I'll have to put you off."

His even white teeth flashed in a mocking smile. "Just how do you propose doing that?"

When he moved to within a few inches of her, Pat

restrained the impulse to move back. Although this man was obviously injured in some way, there was nothing of the invalid about him. His lithe, broad-shouldered body radiated power, and his square jaw showed determination.

He was quick to seize on her momentary hesitation. "Perhaps you intend calling the police?" His tawny eyes sparkled with amusement.

A surge of anger shot through her. "I wouldn't bother them with anything this minor. A double-barreled shotgun ought to convince you."

The blonde's eyes widened. "Raven, why don't you tell her—"

He motioned her to silence without taking his eyes off Pat's flushed face. "What makes you think I'd permit you to go for a gun?"

A quiver of apprehension that she didn't allow to show ran down Pat's spine. This man could subdue her easily, even in his lame state. "I wouldn't try anything if I were you; my dog will tear you to pieces. Come here, Janus!" she called sharply.

Now that the commotion had died down, the big Great Dane was investigating what had attracted him in the first place, the food on the blanket. At Pat's command, however, he loped to her side, leaning heavily against her as she hooked her fingers in his impressive studded collar.

Far from being intimidated, the man threw back his dark head and laughed. "Janus? You call your own dog two-faced?"

Pat was impressed in spite of herself. Most people merely accepted it as a strong-sounding name. They didn't know that it was the name of an ancient Roman god with two faces.

"Why Janus?" the man persisted.

"Why not?" she asked defiantly.

He chuckled. "It couldn't be that he isn't as fierce as you make out?"

It was hard to keep up the fiction with Janus wagging his tail like an oversize lapdog. Pat's full mouth curved in an unwilling smile. "You're right, he's really a softie. The only reason he barked was because your girlfriend scared him."

"Sorry about that, old fella." When he scratched the dog's ears, Janus promptly transferred his affections, licking the man's hand. "I see what you mean," he said, laughing.

Pat was of the firm opinion that anyone who liked animals couldn't be all bad. It quenched the remains of her anger. "You really are trespassing, though. After you finish your picnic, I'd appreciate it if you'd leave."

"I think it's time we cleared things up. I'm Raven Masters, I own this place. Who are you really?"

The name registered immediately, although Pat had never met her employer. She couldn't have been expected to recognize him either. Raven Masters hadn't visited the ranch since she'd been there, and the newspaper photos she'd seen had usually shown him with a helmet on. He was almost as famous for racing his own cars as he was for manufacturing them. He also made excellent copy because of his flamboyant good looks and the fact that he was a very wealthy bachelor with a penchant for beautiful women.

The reason for the cane and Raven's pallor now became apparent to Pat. She had never followed auto racing, but Mrs. Johnson, the housekeeper, had given her all the details. Raven Masters had been badly injured while test driving one of his cars recently, and had spent quite a lot of time in the hospital.

Pat disapproved of his entire life-style, but she couldn't help staring at him with interest. The man was really amazingly handsome, yet his looks were of the rugged variety, not the surface smoothness of a movie star's. A small scar over one high cheekbone gave him a slightly rakish air, and the wide, generous mouth was sensuous yet firm.

"You haven't answered my question," Raven prompted, his blue eyes narrowing slightly. "Who are you, and what are you doing here?"

Pat faced her employer uneasily. "I really am your caretaker. My name is Pat Lee."

She held her breath, hoping he wouldn't recognize the name, although there was no reason why he should. It was a very innocuous name, as her publisher and agent had been at great pains to point out.

"Pat Lee just doesn't do it," they had both remarked disparagingly, opting to use her full name, Patricia Lauren Lee.

Pat had thought it was pretentious, but she had gone along with them. Just as she had raised no more than feeble objections when the publicity department described her as a red-haired, green-eyed beauty. Her hair was actually auburn, the changeable color of an autumn leaf. And she didn't want to be celebrated as a sex symbol. Pat had worked hard perfecting her craft. She had supported herself with odd jobs, freelancing in her spare time for small newspapers and magazines while she wrote the best-selling novel that catapulted her to fame. That was all during the good times—before everything turned sour.

Raven Masters was regarding her with a puzzled frown. "I don't understand. I was told my caretaker was a man named Pat Lee."

"You're partially correct—that's my name." She acted as though it were the most natural mistake in the world.

Raven didn't see it that way. His frown deepened.

"What kind of nonsense is this? I advertised for a man—someone to plow the snow in winter and cut the grass in summer, keep the place in good repair."

"Your ad didn't specify a man," she pointed out.

"Because your cockeyed women's lib doesn't allow it. But it was implicit in the work involved."

"I can do all that," Pat declared, drawing herself up to her diminutive stature.

His disgusted look doubted it. "I'm going to have a little talk with my management firm. What did you do, bat those big green eyes at George Trimingham? He always was a pushover for a beautiful woman."

Her soft mouth thinned in anger. "I wouldn't bat my eyes, as you put it, at *any* man—not to get a job or for any other reason!"

His derisive eyes registered her anger. "I take it you don't think much of men, Miss Lee."

"That's exactly right," she replied tautly.

"An interesting subject we can pursue at a later date." His wholly masculine look was challenging. "Right now I'd like to know how you got a job you're obviously not suited for."

"I wish you'd stop saying that! Have you found anything wrong with the lawn or the flower beds? Is there anything up at the house that needs repairing?"

"I just arrived last night so I wouldn't know yet."

An unexpected reprieve came in the form of an interruption by the blond. "Oh, for heaven's sake, Raven, are you going to stand there arguing with her all day? I thought we were supposed to be having a picnic."

"I'll leave you alone," Pat said hurriedly, whistling for Janus who was eyeing the fried chicken longingly.

"How very cooperative you are all of a sudden," Raven drawled sardonically. "It couldn't be that you've run out of answers?"

"I've told you everything," she maintained stubbornly.

"Scarcely, but I suppose it will have to wait for another time."

Pat was steaming as she made her way back to the caretaker's cottage. The insufferable arrogance of the man! Automatically assuming that just because she was a woman she couldn't handle the job! It didn't take physical strength to operate an estate mower; all you had to do was sit in the bucket seat and steer the thing. The same was true of the snow plow. She was in a lot better shape than he was at the moment.

About all Raven Masters was good for was keeping that screaming blonde happy. Wouldn't you know he'd pick a woman like that? The only thing Pat couldn't figure out was why he had brought her here. When she discovered it was twenty miles to the nearest beauty shop there was going to be trouble in paradise, Pat decided gleefully.

The phone was ringing as she opened the front door. It was only hooked up to the main house, because Pat didn't need a telephone. There was no one she wanted to call or hear from.

"Can you come up and give me a hand?" Mattie Johnson sounded breathless.

"Sure, is something wrong?"

Pat and the older woman had developed an immediate rapport when Pat had come to the Circle Bar Ranch three months before. In fact the housekeeper had asked her to live in the big house after she discovered the mixup in gender. But Pat had preferred the solitude of the cottage, tactfully refusing Mattie's invitation. They had become good friends, and Pat found out that the older woman was a recent widow whose husband used to be the caretaker. All of her friends lived on surrounding ranches or in the small town they circled, so it was only natural that she stayed on. It was lonely for her, though, and she was coming to depend on Pat for many things.

"Nothing's wrong except that Mr. Masters came in unexpectedly last night," the housekeeper was explaining. "Not only that, he brought guests."

"I know, I saw her—a blonde in designer jeans two sizes too small."

"That was Miss Turner." Mattie's voice was faintly reproving. "She's beautiful."

"Ravishing," Pat commented dryly. "What was it you wanted, Mattie?"

"I was wondering if you'd help me with dinner tonight. I don't know much about serving."

"No way!" Pat's response was both immediate and definite. "Miss Turner will just have to do without fingerbowls for once."

"I didn't mean anything like that, and it isn't only for her. Mr. Masters brought two other couples too."

"Oh, Lord, they'll be all over the place." Pat groaned. "I'll probably have to keep poor Janus on a leash. How long are they staying?"

"I don't know, they just got here."

"Does he do things like this very often, bring a houseful of guests without any warning?"

"He never has before."

"They'll just have to rough it, then. It's damned inconsiderate of him to spring them on you without advance notice."

"Mr. Masters isn't like that," Mattie protested. "He's the kindest man I've ever known."

Pat raised her eyes to the ceiling, realizing there was no use arguing with her. She had heard over and over again how Raven had paid all the extensive bills for the late Mr. Johnson's last illness. Mattie was also fond of recounting his many charities, and how warm-hearted and caring he was. After meeting the man, Pat wondered if they were talking about the same person.

"If he's so kind, he won't mind that the service is less than perfect," she remarked unfeelingly.

"I don't want to disgrace him in front of his guests," Mattie answered reproachfully.

Pat bit back the sharp reply that sprang to her lips. "They can't be expecting anything too grand, Mattie. After all, this is a ranch, not a resort."

"What I'm worried about is that I won't be able to handle the kitchen and the dining room both. Won't you please help me, Pat?" the older woman coaxed.

A gusty sigh shook Pat's slender body. "Okay, on one condition. I'll stay in the kitchen and dish up the food while you wait on the lord and master."

To prevent Mattie from trying to wheedle her into anything, Pat didn't change out of her shorts when she went up to the big house that evening.

It was a comfortable, contemporary home with large rooms that looked lived in and inviting. Not at all what she would have expected of Raven Masters, but it probably amused him to play cowboy out West—although the house incorporated every convenience. His apartment in New York was undoubtedly the ultimate bachelor's pad. Pat just hoped he would go back to it soon and stop disrupting her life.

Every burner on the stove was filled with bubbling pots when she entered the big country kitchen that night. Mattie's cheeks were flushed and she greeted Pat with relief.

"Taste this chicken fricassee and tell me if it needs salt," she said anxiously.

Pat took the proffered spoon, licking her lips after

tasting the sample. "It's delicious," she pronounced, "like everything you make. What else are you giving them?"

"Soup with homemade cornbread to start, chicken fricassee with dumplings, and apple pie for dessert."

"If Miss Turner eats all that she's going to have trouble getting into her jeans tomorrow," Pat commented dryly.

"Do you think it's too heavy?" Mattie asked in sudden concern.

"No, they'll love it," Pat soothed. "And if they leave anything, I'll be glad to finish it."

The older woman looked admiringly at her tiny waist and slim hips. "I don't know how you keep that cute little figure, the way you eat."

Pat grinned. "Honest labor; it beats dieting any day."

Mattie shook her head. "It's a wonder to me how you can do all the things you do around here, a little mite of a thing like you."

"I'd appreciate it if you didn't voice that opinion to Mr. Masters," Pat observed grimly. "He didn't seem overly impressed by me today."

"I'm sure you're wrong. He was in here this afternoon asking all kinds of questions about you."

"Like what?" Pat asked uneasily.

"Oh, where you came from and what you did before, did you have family in these parts, things like that."

It didn't ease Pat's peace of mind, although surely there was nothing to worry about. She had been purposely vague with Mattie about her background. Still, why would Raven want to know about her personal life? Probably just to find out if she had any previous experience at this sort of thing, Pat tried to reassure herself.

Mattie's attention wandered to more pressing things. "Will you watch to see that nothing burns while I go freshen up and put on a clean dress?"

"Sure, take your time. I'll get the serving pieces down while you're gone."

Pat was reaching for a large bowl a short time later when she heard footsteps behind her. "That was speedy," she commented without turning around. The bowl eluded her and she stood on tiptoes, her slender body arched gracefully. Sniffing deeply she said, "Mmm, you smell gorgeous. What's the name of that cologne?"

"I believe it's called something ridiculous like Crusader, and it's after-shave, not cologne."

Raven's deep voice startled her so that the bowl fell out of her nerveless fingers. When he reached for it automatically his cane went clattering to the floor. Without its support Raven lurched against Pat, catching her off balance. They clutched at each other instinctively, and for a frozen moment she was bent back against the counter with Raven's body pressed heavily against hers.

It could only have lasted a matter of seconds, but Pat was tinglingly aware of every hard, lean inch of his taut body. They were joined from shoulder to thigh, so closely that she was in no doubt about the man's masculinity. The unexpected contact sent a shock of awareness racing through her like wildfire.

Raven swore savagely under his breath, struggling to right himself. "Did I hurt you?"

"No, I . . . it's all right." She was most unusually tongue-tied.

"It's hell to be a cripple," he said broodingly.

"But you're not! This is only temporary, isn't it?" Pat experienced a moment's compassion. She could almost feel the frustration in him.

"So the doctors say, but it's been months already."

"From what Mattie told me, you're lucky to be alive. You should leave the testing to someone else."

"I wouldn't wish this on anyone," he answered grimly. "I can't even stand up without that damn stick."

"You're just feeling sorry for yourself," Pat told him impatiently. "You ought to be counting your blessings."

"I'm glad you weren't around to cheer me up in the hospital," he remarked sardonically.

Pat's compassion dried up. "You undoubtedly had plenty of women to do that."

"Is that bad?" he asked mockingly.

She shrugged. "Not if that's what turns you on."

"What turns *you* on, Miss Lee?" he asked softly.

Pat ignored the creeping warmth that was invading her. This was exactly the kind of sexual sparring she detested. She was also less than delighted that this man, by his blatant masculinity, could make her feel like a woman again for the first time in months.

Pat gritted her teeth in annoyance. "That can't possibly be of any interest to you." She tucked her shirt more securely into the white shorts, inadvertently drawing his attention.

Raven's tawny eyes resembled a stalking tiger's as they wandered over the enticing curves under the plaid shirt. "Only my leg is incapacitated, not my . . . imagination," he drawled.

"I suggest you use it, then, instead of asking pointless questions," she snapped.

"I have been using it ever since I met you, and I still can't figure out why a beautiful young woman would want to bury herself out here in the wilderness."

"It's your ranch. If you feel that way about this part of the country, why did you buy it?"

"For a place to unwind when I need to get in touch with myself, without crowds of people around."

"Did it ever occur to you that someone else might feel the same way?"

"Meaning you? There's only one flaw in that reasoning." His eyes narrowed appraisingly on the color staining her creamy skin. "I come here to recharge my batteries, and then I jump right back into life with both feet. When you applied for the job you gave the impression that you intended it to be permanent."

Pat was presented with a dilemma. Raven wasn't too pleased over his caretaker being a woman. If she said it was only temporary, that would give him an excuse to fire her. But if she told him she was perfectly content here, he would continue with his probing questions. The long shining hair partially veiled her troubled face as Pat bent her head, looking for a solution.

Raven's expression softened. "Are you in some kind of trouble?" he asked gently.

"No, of course not!"

He was unconvinced. "Perhaps I could help if you'd tell me about it."

The very idea of Raven finding out made Pat's blood chill. She squared her shoulders defensively. "There's nothing to tell. I came to Wyoming because I got tired of the rat race in New York. Not all of us are cut out for life in the fast lane." In spite of her effort to be casual, the bitterness showed.

"Why not a small town, then?" he persisted. "Why a remote ranch where there's little chance of seeing anyone?"

"I'm not a fugitive if that's what you're implying. Are you afraid I'm going to decamp with the silver?" she demanded angrily.

The swinging door to the dining room opened before

he had a chance to reply. The blond man who came through it reminded Pat of Carl. Not that they really looked alike except for hair coloring and the small mustache. It was an intangible something, a smooth surface charm.

"Oh, there you are, Raven. I've been—" The man stopped when he caught sight of Pat. "Well, well, who is this charming sprite?"

"Would you believe this is my caretaker?" Raven asked sardonically, before introducing the man as Norman Langhorn.

"Why wouldn't I believe it? Miss Lee could take care of me anytime." Norman's inspection traveled all the way down Pat's long bare legs.

The only sign of her anger was the darkened green of her eyes. "My job is confined mostly to posting off-limit signs, Mr. Langhorn."

Raven's firm mouth curved in amusement. "That's right, Norman. She has nothing to do with the bulls."

Mattie chose that opportune moment to arrive. She frowned slightly at the little group. "Is there something I can get for you, Mr. Masters?"

"No, we were just keeping Miss Lee company," he answered easily.

"The others are all in the den having drinks," the housekeeper told him tactfully.

Raven took the hint. "I think Mattie wants us out of her kitchen." As he started toward the door Raven murmured in Pat's ear, "We'll finish our conversation at a later date."

She felt like suggesting a year from next Easter. Why couldn't he just leave her alone? What difference did her reasons for being there make? It was her life and she had a right to lead it any way she wanted. No man was ever going to tell her what to do again.

Fortunately, getting dinner on the table took Pat's mind off Raven. Mattie was a bundle of nerves and Pat had to calm her down.

"Maybe you were right about my menu being too starchy," the older woman worried. "Do you think I should serve crackers with the soup instead of my cornbread?"

"They'll love the cornbread," Pat assured her. "See if you can get them to sit down while it's nice and warm."

Mattie felt better when the guests did justice to the first course, but then she worried about the second one. "I hope the chicken didn't dry out. Maybe I should have turned the oven down more."

Pat stifled a sigh. "You're the best cook in all of Wyoming, Mattie. Will you stop wasting all your energy looking for things to worry about?"

By the time dessert and coffee had been served and cleared away, the housekeeper did look exhausted. Mattie was getting up in years, Pat reflected.

"I'll clear up," she told the elderly woman. "You go on to bed."

"I couldn't leave you with this mess."

"I don't have anything else to do. Go on now, you have breakfast to cook in the morning."

"Oh, lordy." Mattie's face was gray with fatigue. "I don't even want to think about it."

"You'll feel better after a good night's sleep," Pat assured her.

"Well, if you're really sure . . ."

"I'm sure," Pat said firmly, turning on the garbage disposal. The grinding noise stopped abruptly, replaced by an ominous hum. Pat uttered an impatient exclamation. "Wouldn't you know it would act up after I scraped all the garbage into the sink! I wonder if I overloaded it?"

"Maybe it was all those cigarette butts Mr. Langhorn emptied down there," Mattie said doubtfully.

"What!" Pat cried in outrage. "Why did you let him do a stupid thing like that? The filter tips gum up and clog the trap."

"He did it before I could stop him," Mattie answered apologetically.

Pat sighed. "Well, never mind. I'll take care of it. Go on to bed, Mattie."

Swearing under her breath, Pat went out to the utility room for a pipe wrench, a hammer, and a flashlight. As an afterthought she stuck a screwdriver in her back pocket. After opening the lower cabinet doors that hid the plumbing she wriggled underneath the sink in a half sitting, half reclining position with her long legs stretched out on the tile kitchen floor. It took a lot of pounding and all her strength to loosen the elbow joint, but she finally got it off. The gummy mess inside made her wrinkle her tilted nose in disgust.

When she heard footsteps on the tile floor Pat called to Mattie, "I thought I told you to go to bed." The noise she made thumping the section of pipe to dislodge its contents prevented Pat from hearing Mattie's reply. "Well, as long as you're here you can do something for me. Will you give me the screwdriver in my back pocket? My hands are all greasy."

As soon as the two strong hands fastened around her hips, turning her onto her stomach, Pat knew they weren't Mattie's. And when long fingers gently insinuated themselves into her back pocket, Pat was sure of the fact. The touch on her rounded bottom was definitely male.

"You're not Mattie! What do you think you're doing?" Her outrage was muffled by the cabinet.

"Just trying to help." Raven's voice held amusement. "What are you doing under there anyway?"

"Repairing the damage your idiot friend caused!" She wiggled back and forth, trying to dislodge his disturbing fingers. "Will you kindly take your hands out of my pocket?"

"It's difficult when you keep squirming around like that." He was laughing openly now. "These shorts are very tight."

They were also very brief. Pat had a sudden vivid picture of the view she was presenting. She sat up without thinking, banging her head on the bottom of the sink. The resulting thud brought tears to her eyes.

"Be careful!" Raven exclaimed, after the fact. "Did you hurt yourself?"

"Of course I did, and it's all your fault!"

Raven stuck his head under the sink, gathering Pat in his arms and carefully sliding her out. He examined her in the bright light, gently smoothing the silky auburn hair off her forehead. When she struggled to get up he said, "Lie still, I'm trying to see where you hurt yourself."

"It wasn't there, it was the top of my head."

The words were unaccountably difficult to get out. Raven's arms were cradling her in an embrace that meant something quite different to Pat than it did to him. She was terribly conscious of his arms around her, the firm shoulder supporting her head, the distinctive male scent that she already recognized as his.

Considering how she felt about him, his touch should have been repulsive, but it wasn't. Pat felt a tremor run through her body as she stared at the firm mouth just inches from her own. She was mesmerized by it, her lips parting automatically.

Raven's fingers were gently caressing now as they trailed down her cheek to curl around her chin. He tilted her face up, the concern in his tawny eyes changing to something quite different.

"It's much too lovely a head to be hidden under a sink," he murmured.

It was as though his voice released her from the spell. Pat drew in her breath sharply. What was she thinking of, letting this man hold her so intimately. She grasped his arms, pushing herself away from him.

When she saw the grease marks she'd left on his pale blue silk shirt, Pat groaned. "*Now* look what you made me do! That's all your fault too."

One dark eyebrow raised mockingly. "Do you always blame someone else for your . . . accidents?"

"If you mean clumsiness, why don't you come right out and say it?" she flared.

Raven's gaze swept her slender body and Pat only then realized that her shirt had come undone during her exertions. His appreciative eyes rested on the creamy strip of skin where her breasts curved over her revealing bra.

"I don't think you could be clumsy if you tried." As her color rose and she hurried to fasten the gaping shirt, he chuckled. "In fact the only flaw I can find anywhere is a very combative nature. You have a tendency to lash out before you're hurt."

"Better before than after," she stated grimly.

Raven's amusement vanished. "Has someone hurt you that badly?" he asked softly, his eyes searching her flushed, defensive face.

Why did he insist on prying into her life? Her past was her own business. Scrambling to her feet she said, "It's getting late. I'd like to clean up the kitchen and get out of here, Mr. Masters."

He stared up at her for a long moment. "Okay, we'll let it go for the present."

Pat was left with the frustrating knowledge that she had only succeeded in piqueing his curiosity. As he started to roll up his sleeves she said impatiently, "*Now* what are you doing?"

"I'm going to fix the garbage disposal."

"I can do that; it's my job."

He paused with the wrench in his hand. "Would you like to tell me how you learned about plumbing—in addition to all your other amazing talents?"

"Some other time," she said hurriedly. It involved her early life, and Pat was reluctant to tell this perceptive man anything about herself. He had the knack of stripping away her defenses like layers of clothing, leaving her bare in front of his amber cat's eyes.

"It looks as though you and I are going to have a marathon conversation," he observed mockingly.

She ignored that. "I already cleaned out the trap. The only thing that needs doing is to reattach the elbow joint."

"I *am* a mechanic," he pointed out.

That was like saying Einstein was a math teacher, Pat reflected, noticing the soft sprinkling of dark hair on his muscular forearms. "Well, if you don't need me for anything . . ." Her words trailed off uncertainly.

"I didn't say that." His melting smile sent a little ripple down her spine. "Perhaps we'll find we need each other."

His casual assumption infuriated Pat—along with her totally unexpected and purely physical response to his overpowering masculinity. Her green eyes blazed like emeralds as she glared at him. "I realize that you're bored and at loose ends because of your accident, but *droit de seigneur* is no longer practiced even in Europe. If Miss Turner isn't enough for you, I suggest you send for reinforcements from New York because I'm not interested!"

Her tirade produced only an infuriating grin. "You're doing it again."

"Doing *what*?"

"Overreacting. I have yet to make a pass at you. Since you seem to expect it, however, we might as well get it over with."

In a sudden movement that took her by surprise, Raven's arm snaked around her legs. Pat's knees buckled, toppling her into his lap. He caught her deftly, lowering her gently to the floor and half covering her body with his. She gasped and struggled to get up but the arm around her shoulders immobilized her while his fingers curved around her chin.

His mouth covered hers, moving sensuously over her tightly closed lips. When she jerked her head away, trying to bury her face in his shoulder, he nibbled on her earlobe. Ignoring her frantic struggles he began a sensual exploration of her inner ear, tracing all the sensitive little cavities with the tip of his tongue.

"Stop that!" She turned her head back to glare up at him. "What do you think you're doing?"

"I think it's fairly obvious," he murmured before his mouth closed over hers, catching her off guard.

His tongue entered seductively, coaxing her to share the pleasure with him. Pat's body was rigid in his arms as she fought the creeping warmth that made her want to respond. When he stroked her gently she gave a tiny moan of protest, twisting restlessly against him.

Raven's hand was warm on her bare thigh, his fingers maddening as they traced the edge of her brief shorts. He was lighting a fire she had thought was long dead, but this was like none she had ever experienced. The storm that was building inside her was an instinctive response to something she had never known in a man. This was no selfish, sexual gratification on his part, it was a mutual sharing, a desire to give pleasure as well as receive it.

The tense fingers gripping his shoulders gradually relaxed, almost of their own accord. They traced the strong column of his neck before winding through his thick dark hair.

Raven lifted his head, staring down at her with a slightly shaken expression in his tawny eyes. Stroking her cheek gently he said in a husky voice, "I knew I was right about you."

"What . . . what do you mean?"

"I was sure there was a warm, passionate woman under that prickly exterior."

Sanity returned abruptly, leaving Pat appalled at her surrender. For just a moment Raven had bewitched her into thinking he was different, but it was all an amusing game to see if he could break through her defenses.

Her cheeks were like wild roses as she scrambled to her feet. "Now that you've put your mind at rest, why don't you go back to your own kind and stop tormenting the kitchen help?"

He leaned back against the cabinet, regarding her thoughtfully. "That's a strange way of putting it. Do you find it tormenting to be kissed?"

"By you I do!"

"Raven, aren't you ever—" Suzanne Turner came through the swinging door, her words stopping abruptly as she saw him on the floor. "What on earth are you doing?"

He slanted an impish smile at Pat. "It depends on who you ask."

Suzanne hesitated uncertainly. "Well, you're needed in the living room. We want to play bridge."

Raven pulled himself to his feet, reaching for his

cane. "I guess you'll have to manage without me," he told Pat teasingly.

Her glittering eyes betrayed the anger her voice screened out. "I'll try to bear up."

Raven paused at the door, looking back with an enigmatic expression. "We'll continue our discussion tomorrow."

Chapter Two

$\mathcal{P}$at spent a mostly sleepless night following her shattering encounter with Raven. She paced the floor for long hours, reviewing her grievances against him. He was arrogant, insolent, and unprincipaled. The thing that made her the angriest was that unaccountable moment in his arms when she had felt he was different from other men. How stupid could she get! Hadn't Carl taught her anything?

Pat's mind shied away from her ex-husband the way she had trained it to, but this time she forced herself to let the past intrude. It was important to remember the bitter lesson so no man would ever take advantage of her again. Especially not one like Raven Masters who would use any means to get what he wanted.

Carl had been charming too. He didn't have the assurance or the position of wealth and authority that Raven possessed, but she had been too inexperienced at the time to penetrate Carl's phony facade. Life had been too unbelievably wonderful in those days.

It was right after her book had been published and soared to the top of the best-seller lists. Because it was her first book, everyone assumed that she was one of the lucky ones who achieved overnight success. They had no idea of the boring odd jobs she had taken to support herself, or the years of freelancing she had done, all in minor markets. Those years had been filled with as many rejection slips as acceptances, but she had painstakingly perfected her craft.

It had all been worth it when a major publisher purchased *Mourning in Autumn*. The reviews had been raves from the beginning, bringing not only money, but something even more incredible—a measure of fame. She was invited on talk shows and asked for interviews. There were invitations to parties from people she didn't even know.

Looking back, Pat wondered why she didn't realize that most of those people were merely riding her coattails. They were the sort who shone in the reflected glory of the newest celebrity, dropping one as soon as the next one appeared on the scene. How was she supposed to know that at twenty-four, though? Her own relationships had always been open and sincere.

When Carl gave her a big rush she was dazzled. For one thing, he was a distinguished-looking older man. At least, thirty-nine seemed older to her. He was handsome and sophisticated, and he seemed to know a lot of people. He took her to only the most glamorous places, never settling for any but the best table. She had just naturally assumed that he was rich, although Carl never wanted to talk about himself. Pat didn't care about his money, she just wanted to know more about the man she was falling in love with.

It wasn't until after he had rushed her into marriage that she discovered he lived by his wits. Carl put it differently. He called himself an entrepreneur.

In the first flush of marriage Pat didn't realize why he married her. When Carl proposed that he take over her finances and act as her business manager, she was glad to let him worry about the complicated contracts and royalty statements. He seemed so interested in her career, encouraging her to write and never complaining about being neglected when she became so engrossed that she worked long into the night. Pat was bitterly amused now, remembering how guilty she had felt about poor Carl.

After a suitable period he suggested that he become her agent as well as her business manager. At first Pat refused. She hadn't wanted to leave the literary agency that had shown so much faith in her, but Carl had a plausible argument for that too. He wanted to open his own agency, and with Pat for a client he could attract other name writers. Once he was launched she could go back to her old agency if she still wanted to. Pat agreed reluctantly. How could she deny her own husband a chance to get started?

Carl was very busy furnishing an expensive office. He was also tied up constantly with the new clients he signed. The only trouble was that they all seemed to be beautiful young women who had never written anything before. Nor did he ever sell anything of theirs. When Pat questioned him about it he said he was developing exciting new talent that would pay off handsomely.

The bubble burst when Pat dropped by his office unexpectedly and found Carl making love to one of his "clients" on a couch Pat had paid for.

At that moment everything joyous and trusting inside her died. It all turned to ashes—her success, her talent, her whole hypocrisy-filled life. From that day on she had never touched her typewriter. She had only brought it with her on an unaccountable whim—or maybe as a reminder.

Pat was up early the next morning in spite of her scant amount of sleep. She was filled with a restlessness that she knew was associated with Raven. He had chipped the wall she had built around herself and it wouldn't be repaired until he was gone.

After showering and brushing her long auburn hair until it gleamed like wine-colored silk, she dressed in a pair of denim shorts and a blue-and-white-checked shirt. Taking Janus's leash as a precaution against yesterday's mishap, she whistled to the big dog and went outside.

The sun was still low in the heavens, so it wasn't too warm yet. Pat breathed in the clean air appreciatively as she followed Janus out of the front gates. He loved to run along the rutted wagon-train trail that had become so imbedded in the parched land that it had survived for over a hundred years. That was one of the tourist attractions of Wyoming. Visitors marveled over the fact that covered wagons had actually traveled over this very spot.

Pat's imagination was invariably caught by it too. As she stared at the deeply grooved earth a shadowy idea began to take shape in her mind. Suppose a young woman had been coming out from the East to join her fiancé. The trip took endless months in those days. What if she became attached to a man whose wife had died on the journey? She would fight the attraction, but perhaps . . .

Pat drew in her breath sharply as she realized that the

plot for a novel was starting to germinate. She rejected the idea angrily. It was only because last night Raven had forced her to relive the past. It was all his fault with his intolerable prying. Now more than ever she was determined to stay out of his way.

The house phone was ringing when she got back to the cottage. Ignoring it, she took her car keys. Mattie had asked her to get some supplies from the village, and it was a good excuse to get away from the ranch. It was going to tax her ingenuity to avoid Raven, but hopefully he and his friends would get bored and leave soon.

When she returned with the groceries Pat took them in the kitchen door of the big ranch house. Mattie wasn't around so she hurriedly placed the paper bags on the kitchen counter. As she turned to leave a deep male voice made her jump guiltily.

"I thought you had run away again." Raven was lounging in the doorway.

Wouldn't you know he'd be lurking around? Pat scowled. "What do you mean, *again*?"

"You flew out of here pretty precipitately last night."

As though he didn't know the reason! "I wouldn't think you'd have the nerve to bring that up."

"I've been accused of many things, but never of lacking courage," he observed.

"It didn't exactly take courage to force yourself on a woman."

"Is that what I did?" he asked softly.

"Of course it is! What would you call it?"

"I'd say it was a joke that went slightly awry. We had a misunderstanding at our first meeting and you decided that I was the kind of macho male you disliked. Since I couldn't seem to change your mind I decided to live up to the image." His expression softened as he looked at her defiant little figure. "I didn't realize how—" he hesitated "—defenseless you are."

Pat shriveled inside, remembering that terrible moment of surrender in his arms. "Only because you took me by surprise," she answered indignantly, knowing that wasn't what he meant by defenseless. "I wouldn't suggest you try it again either!"

"You have nothing to worry about." Laughter warmed his amber eyes. "I'm handicapped, remember? I couldn't chase you if I wanted to."

"I'm sure you have more rewarding things to do with your time."

"I can't think of any."

Handicapped or not, Raven gave the impression of a lithe jungle cat stalking a particularly juicy prey. Pat's anger boiled to the surface. He might be her employer, but she wasn't going to put up with his baiting any longer.

"I wasn't hired as a social director, Mr. Masters. You'll have to look elsewhere for your entertainment!"

"Why are you so defensive, Pat? What sort of threat do you see in me?"

"No threat at all. I just thought it would be better if we understood each other."

"You're willing to work for me but you'd prefer to keep our contact at a bare minimum. Does that about sum it up?"

His expressionless face made Pat uneasy. If the job depended on personal favors she certainly didn't want it, but Raven didn't strike her as that kind of man. Yet he seemed determined to force some kind of confrontation.

"I don't imagine you usually have much contact with your caretaker," she answered uncertainly.

He stared at her with a mixture of annoyance and

amusement. "Don't be servile, Pat. It's a quality I detest, and it doesn't suit you anyway."

"You seem to have formed some conclusions about me too," she observed dryly.

"Only the obvious ones. Now I'd like the rest of the story."

"You have a vivid imagination. There isn't any story." It was difficult to sustain her pose of wide-eyed innocence under his penetrating gaze. Pat's long lashes fluttered in spite of her best efforts.

"I think there is and I'm going to ferret it out. You know that, don't you?"

The door opened and Mattie bustled in. "Oh, good, you brought the groceries, Pat. Lunch will be ready shortly, Mr. Masters."

"No hurry. I haven't finished my conversation with Miss Lee." The level look he gave Pat expressed Raven's determination. "Perhaps we should go in the den."

Mattie was too busy unloading the bags to notice any tension in the air. Suddenly she gave a sharp exclamation. "You forgot the bread!"

"Was it on the list?" Pat asked. Her mind hadn't really been on the marketing that morning.

"Of course it was," Mattie admonished. "Don't you remember? I even told you to get it at the bakery, not the supermarket."

"What difference does it make?" Raven asked impatiently. "We can do without bread."

"I was planning salad and sandwiches," Mattie answered doubtfully.

Before he could tell her to change the menu, Pat had her hand on the doorknob. "I'll go back and get it, Mattie. It won't take long." She was out of the door and running to the car before Raven could stop her.

By the time Pat returned from the village it was

lunchtime, so there wasn't much danger of Raven's trapping her again. But just to be sure, Pat beat a hasty retreat after dropping the bread off at the back door.

The problem of avoiding him that afternoon remained. She gave it some hard thought as she made her own lunch and gave Janus several large dog biscuits. Raven should be busy with his houseguests, yet he didn't seem to be taking his role as host too seriously. They were probably here to amuse him rather than the other way around. It would be too far to walk to the caretaker's cottage with his bad leg, and since it was the right leg, he couldn't drive. Still, Pat had a feeling Raven would manage somehow if he wanted to. The solution, therefore, was to find a place he wouldn't think of and couldn't get to.

After much deliberation Pat decided on the horse ring near the stables. The fence surrounding the oval track needed whitewashing, and what better time than this? It was far removed from the house and Raven wasn't apt to be doing any riding.

Mending and painting the fences wasn't really part of her job. The ranch hands took care of that. But Buck Henley, the foreman, wouldn't complain if she gave him an unexpected hand.

After washing her plate and cup Pat took Janus and drove to the stables. It was a long walk and she didn't expect to feel up to the return trip after the hours of work the fence would take.

The sun was at its hottest by the time she got all her paraphernalia from the storage shed. It wasn't the most ideal time for manual labor. After trotting at Pat's heels for a short while Janus retreated to the shade of a leafy tree where he settled down comfortably to watch her.

"The least you could do is suffer in the sun alongside me," she complained. "You have just as much to lose as I do if we get turned out by that macho race driver."

Janus's answer was a rapid thumping of his long tail.

"Why couldn't he go recuperate somewhere else?" Pat grumbled. "Like Australia."

Still, the mindless work was soothing. The small transistor radio she'd brought played a soft accompaniment to the back and forth swish of the brush. Time slipped by without conscious thought as the faded wood began to sparkle in the bright light.

When she reached the far turn Pat found that her back and legs were starting to protest in earnest. It was an effort to straighten up. Not only were her muscles aching, the prolonged stretch in the sun was making little specks dance in front of her eyes. A break was definitely in order.

Joining Janus under the tree, Pat stretched out on the grass with a slight groan. Perspiration had made her hair a mass of auburn ringlets, and her whole body felt damp. Pulling the checked shirt out of her shorts she unbuttoned it and tied the ends around her midriff. No one was apt to come this way and Janus would give warning if they did. With a sigh of satisfaction Pat closed her eyes. After a short rest she would go back to work.

The physical labor, coupled with her sleepless night, took its toll. In a very brief time she drifted off to sleep. The Great Dane looked as though he were napping too, but the sound of a car brought his head up. A low growl sounded deep in his throat. Pat frowned as he got to his feet but she didn't waken.

The dog raced over to the long, low convertible that slid to a noiseless stop on the dirt road. He gave an ecstatic greeting to the tall man who got out.

"Hi, big fella." Raven scratched the sensitive place behind the dog's ear. "Where is she hiding?"

After scanning the landscape Raven located Pat

under the tree. He limped over slowly, followed by Janus. When he reached the spot, Raven leaned on his cane, looking down at her and waiting for Pat to open her eyes. After it became evident that she was really asleep he sat on the grass, leaning against a tree trunk while he stared at her reflectively.

She stirred restlessly, subtly aware of being watched. Pat's eyelashes fluttered. When they finally parted she found herself gazing straight into Raven's gold-flecked, agate eyes.

Sitting up hurriedly she pushed the curling hair off her flushed face. "What are you doing here?" she demanded.

"I could ask you the same thing," he remarked with a lifted eyebrow.

"I don't know what you mean."

"Don't you, Pat?" He was looking at her with lively interest.

It was only then that she remembered her shirt was undone. Untying the tails, she hurriedly fastened herself together.

"You seem to have a lot of trouble with buttons," he observed.

Raven's amusement made her cheeks even warmer. "It's very hot and I thought I was alone." The inference was that she'd rather be.

A slight frown creased Raven's wide forehead. "You looked very enticing lying there. I'm not so sure it's a good idea with all the ranch hands around. A lot of the wranglers are transients."

"They'd have no reason to be on this part of the ranch. Besides, I have Janus."

"Your fabulous watchdog led me right to you," Raven commented disparagingly.

Janus had flopped down beside Raven, resting his

chin on Raven's thigh while he looked up adoringly. Pat experienced a moment's irritation. Janus didn't even like men. He had detested Carl, who returned the feeling wholeheartedly. Why should Janus suddenly decide to bestow his affections on this man of all people?

Pat's annoyance showed in her voice. "He isn't normally this friendly."

"Do you expect me to believe that?"

"It's true," she insisted. "He doesn't usually make up to men."

"Sounds as though he had a bad experience."

We both did, Pat thought grimly. "That could be," she answered briefly, tucking her shirt into her shorts.

Assessing her bleak expression Raven said softly, "You see, it's possible to get over a bad experience if you don't let it warp your thinking."

Pat's slender body stiffened. Was it conceivable that Raven knew who she was? Knew the whole degrading story? The tabloids had enjoyed a field day over her divorce from Carl. Was Raven playing cat and mouse with her? If that were the case she didn't have to watch her words any longer. "If that's thinly veiled advice for me, it's unnecessary."

"I'm glad to hear it. I wouldn't like to think you had anything to be bitter about," he said gently.

Did he know or didn't he? It was driving her up the wall! "Are you trying to tell me something, Mr. Masters?" she asked tautly.

"I don't think it would do any good at this point. Maybe when we get to know each other better."

"I'm an employee, not a friend," she reminded him.

"I don't know of any law that says we can't be both."

"I imagine you have enough friends."

"How about you, Pat?" he asked quietly.

Her mouth curved in a humorless smile. "I believe in quality, not quantity."

Raven's face was expressionless. "What scale do you use to weigh your friends?"

Although she knew he was baiting her, the angry words tumbled out, "Certainly not money!" She was thinking about all the wealthy party givers who had lionized her in the beginning—and disappeared when she really needed them.

"I'll buy that, but do you automatically discriminate because a person is rich?"

Pat realized that Raven thought she was talking about him. "Not necessarily, but we'd have to have something in common, whether the person was rich *or* poor."

"You mean like shared interests?" he asked innocently.

"Exactly."

"What are your interests, Pat?"

She recognized the trap belatedly. "That sounds like the kind of question men ask at a cocktail party," she replied lightly.

"And what do you answer?"

She looked at him steadily. "Usually something completely untrue."

His golden gaze never left her face. "Why?"

She shrugged. "Why not? They aren't really interested anyway."

"But I *am*, and I'm not going to settle for anything superficial." Raven settled more comfortably against the tree trunk, stretching out his long legs. "To begin with, what kind of work did you do in New York?"

Pat could see that this time there would be no convenient interruption. Also, the implacable look on Raven's face warned her that he was prepared to stay right where he was until he got the answers he wanted.

"I was a saleswoman in a department store, and I did secretarial work—things like that," she replied reluctantly. "Nothing out of the ordinary."

"You aren't a native New Yorker, are you?" He changed directions abruptly.

"No, I was born in Colorado—on a ranch as a matter of fact. It wasn't as big as this one but we did have a small herd of cattle."

"So in a sense, you've come home. Why didn't you go back to Colorado, though?"

"After my parents died my brothers sold the ranch and moved to California. There wasn't anything to go home to."

"Is that where you picked up your skills as a handyman?"

Pat's tense body relaxed. This subject was safe at least. "I have three big brothers—and I do mean big. They're all over six feet like my father was. By the time I came along my parents had practically given up hope of having a girl. They wanted to treat me like a china doll but I wouldn't put up with it. I chased after my brothers until they finally taught me how to ride and use tools, just so I wouldn't hurt myself."

As she talked about her happy childhood all the wariness left Pat's face. Raven's enigmatic gaze was on her soft mouth, curved now in a smile. "It must have been that determination that took you to New York. What were you looking for there?"

The sparkle disappeared from her green eyes. "Why does anyone go to the big city?"

"Different reasons, I imagine. What were yours?"

"I wanted to be on my own—prove that I could support myself."

Raven grinned. "With your versatility there shouldn't have been any doubt."

She couldn't help smiling back, realizing what a shock she must have been to him. "I guess you could say I've always had a lively curiosity."

"You should have been a writer," he observed.

Pat's head snapped up suddenly. There was that sly illusion again. She chose her words carefully. "I did do a little writing in my spare time."

"What did you write?"

His face showed only interest as far as she could tell. Pat watched him through her long lashes as she said, "Articles and stories, things like that."

"Did you ever sell anything?"

She had always found it difficult to tell an outright lie, even now when the occasion cried out for it. "I . . . it's a very hard field to break into," she evaded.

"I'm sure that didn't discourage you." Raven's interest quickened. "Is that why you took this isolated job, to work on a novel?"

"No!" Belatedly, Pat realized that she should have said yes. It would have provided a tidy little solution to the puzzle he was determined to unravel. It was too late now, though. She had put too much vehemence into her denial.

Fortunately it gave Raven the wrong impression. "I can't believe you'd let a few rejection slips scare you off."

Pat's nervous fingers plucked at the grass. "I decided I didn't want to be a writer." That, at least, was the truth.

Raven was silent for a long moment, staring at the shining crown of her bent head. "I'm acquainted with a few publishers in New York. If you'd like to give me some of your work I'd be happy to show it to them."

She looked up then, searching his face. "Why would you do that? I might be a terrible writer."

"That's why I can't promise anything. If you have talent, though—and so far I haven't found anything you can't do—I'd like to be of assistance."

"You don't even know me," she said slowly.

"That's not true. I know a lot about you." He took her hand, holding on when she would have pulled loose. As his thumb made lazy circles over the pulse in her wrist it started to race. "I know you can repair plumbing, that you have a hair-trigger temper, and you love dogs. That's in addition to the obvious fact that you're incredibly lovely."

She pulled her hand away abruptly. "That's what it's all about, isn't it? If I were fat and fifty, would you still offer your influence on my behalf?"

In a fury of indignation she started to get up. Raven's arm circled her waist, toppling her full length on the grass. He kept her pinned down as he stretched out next to her, propping his head on his hand.

"You're not running out on me again," he said calmly. "And since I can't very well chase after you, we'll have to do it this way."

"Let me up this minute!"

His strong hand fastened on her shoulder, gently pushing her back. "After I tell you a few things. As I said before, you are very beautiful." He surveyed her flushed face almost clinically. "I've never seen hair that glorious, changeable color red, or eyes that deep a green." His gaze moved to her rigid body. "And your . . . um . . . physical attributes are delectable."

Pat could feel a warm tide sweeping through her at his penetrating glance. She felt as though he could see through her checked shirt, through even her lace bra, to her bare breasts underneath.

"You have no right to do this to me!" she stormed, pushing with all her might against his broad chest. The thin shirt couldn't mask the hard, masculine feel of whipcord muscles lightly cushioned by a mat of curling hair. Pat dropped her hands quickly.

"I haven't finished yet. That was the good news. The bad news is that I have never before met a woman quite as conceited as you."

"What!" She stared at him in disbelief. "You must be out of your mind!" Carl had effectively taken care of any self-satisfaction she might have had.

"You're firmly convinced that my every waking thought is devoted to how to get you into my bed."

"I . . . it . . . that's ridiculous!"

"Only partially," he teased. "Some of the time I think about how to get into *your* bed."

"I don't think that's very funny," she muttered.

He chuckled. "I thought you'd appreciate my honesty."

"I have yet to meet an honest man," Pat stated bitterly. "You're like all the rest. The newest face is the one that attracts you."

Raven's amusement fled. He smoothed the silky hair off her forehead, combing his fingers through the soft curls. "I can't imagine any man leaving you for another woman. Is that what happened, Pat?"

"No! I left *him*!" she cried before she could stop herself.

"So there *was* a man involved," Raven said softly.

"All right, now you know. Are you satisfied?" Wriggling under Raven's arm, Pat sprang to her feet.

He stood up too. "I'm sorry." His low voice was gentle.

She raised her chin proudly. "You can save your pity. I survived."

"There's more to survival than just living through something," he answered quietly. "If you let this turn you against all men you'll be as crippled as I am right now—but at least I'll get better."

"Always pitching, aren't you?" she asked scornfully.

He was silent for a long moment. "You must have loved him very much."

That was the worst of it. During the long agonizing hours of introspection afterward, Pat realized that she hadn't really loved Carl at all. He was just a very clever man who had played on her inexperience, rushing her into marriage before she had time to know him. It added to her self-doubts. If she could make a mistake of that magnitude, how could she ever trust her own judgment again?

"If you're looking for the whole miserable story, forget it. You'll have to be satisfied with knowing that your side won again." She turned her back, folding her arms around her trembling body.

Raven's expression was stern as he turned her back to face him. "Is that supposed to make me happy? You're fighting the wrong enemy."

She met his gaze squarely. "Oh, sure, you're different from all other men."

"I wasn't speaking personally. I don't know what that guy did to you, but you're completing the job yourself. No one can destroy you unless you let them."

"Your pep talk is wasted, Mr. Masters. Until you showed up I was completely happy."

"I wondered last night what threat I posed to you. At first I thought perhaps you were frigid and afraid of all men, but that certainly wasn't it." His hands were unconsciously caressing on her shoulders.

Pat twisted away angrily. "That's always a convenient excuse for rejection."

"Unlike you, my ego isn't that fragile," Raven observed dryly. "I can take rejection."

He'd probably never met with any, she thought bitterly.

"When I came here I brought the real world with me, didn't I?" he continued inexorably.

"That depends on what you consider real. To you it's cocktail parties and a filled appointment book." She waved her arm at the empty landscape ending in brooding mountains. "To me this is far more genuine."

"It is if you put down your roots and make a life for yourself. But that's not what you're doing. You're using this place as a hideout to lick your wounds."

"That's not true! Just because you need people around you all the time doesn't mean everyone does."

"Your image of me is stereotyped. I couldn't stand being constantly surrounded either, but we'll let that go for the moment. What do you do with your spare time?"

"I . . . well, I read a lot, and take long walks with Janus."

The dog raised his huge head on hearing his name. After thumping his long tail a couple of times he lowered his muzzle to his paws once more.

Raven lifted a sardonic eyebrow. "That sounds like a very healthy regimen—for a woman of eighty."

"You asked and I told you," Pat said curtly. "I can't help it if it wasn't the answer you wanted."

"It's the one I expected."

She shrugged. "Then, you weren't disappointed."

"How can I get through to you?" He reached out suddenly, gripping her shoulders and pulling her close.

Pat tensed under his hands but she didn't pull away. Lifting her chin she stared back into his gold-flecked eyes. It was a contest of wills and she wouldn't allow him to overpower her even though his taut body was making her legs feel boneless.

"I'm going to break down that wall you've built around yourself, Pat Lee." The softness of his voice didn't mask its purpose. "Whether you like it or not."

A tremor ran through her. "Why? So you can add another notch to your belt?"

His fingertips trailed over her cheek to trace the outline of her full lower lip. It was a gentle caress, yet sensuous in the extreme. "If that's the kind of men you knew, I almost don't blame you for running away."

Pat forced herself to endure his touch, fighting the wave of feeling that was uncurling inside of her. "Is there any other kind?"

When he bent his head to hers Pat thought he was going to kiss her. She compressed her lips tightly but Raven merely rubbed his nose against hers in a teasing gesture. "That's what I'm going to teach you."

She drew in her breath sharply, leaning away from him as his arms slid around her waist. "It would save both of us a lot of time if you just accepted that rejection you said you could handle."

"Without even trying to change your mind?" He shook his head, smiling. "You don't know me very well, Pat."

"And I don't want to!" she cried in frustration.

"I'll remind you of that some time when you're lying in my arms," he murmured, tightening the circle around her waist.

"You'd better wait until you're better, then, because you'll have to use force," she declared fiercely.

"I would never do that." He cupped her chin in his palm, staring down at her with glowing eyes. "You're going to come to me willingly when you admit that there's a special magnetism between us, a kind of electricity that crackled at our first meeting."

"That was surprise and distrust," she scoffed.

"No, it was the thunder before the lightning." His eyes narrowed slightly. "I don't know what's going to come of our relationship, but I know it's going to be very special. I'm going to make love to you the way you deserve. I'm going to bring out all the fire and passion I know you're capable of."

His low, sensual voice and the tiny lights in his golden eyes made a ripple shiver down Pat's spine. She was tinglingly aware of every part of him, the long muscular thighs, the broad chest, the strength of the arms that held her. He would be a marvelous lover, bringing ecstasy with that sensuous mouth, that lean, taut body. Her nails dug into his shirtfront as she forced herself to remember that he was seducing her shamelessly. With a violent shove Pat freed herself from his embrace, catching him unawares.

As Raven lurched back heavily, a spasm of pain crossed his face. He reached out to support himself against a tree trunk.

"Are you all right?" she cried.

He managed a lopsided smile. "I'll live."

"Sit down for a minute and then I'll drive you home. My car is right over there. Oh!" Pat suddenly noticed the convertible parked behind her car. "Where did that come from?"

"It's mine."

"But how did it get here?"

"I drove it. I was all over the ranch until I located you."

"But you can't drive with that bad leg."

"It wasn't easy," he conceded, "and I wouldn't do it on the highway. I was half in the driver's seat and half on the passenger side."

"That's dangerous on these unpaved roads. I'll take you home in my car and come back for yours."

He hooked his hand around the back of her neck under the soft auburn hair. "You see, you're starting to care already," he teased.

She sat back on her heels, out of his reach. "Don't be ridiculous! I'd do as much for anyone who was handicapped," she added deliberately.

Raven wasn't offended, as he was meant to be. "At least my injury is good for something," he remarked lightly. "You don't have to drive me home though, just help me to my car."

In spite of all Pat's arguments, Raven insisted on doing it his way. All she could do was help him to his feet and lead him out to the road. During their slow progress Pat began to have doubts. Raven wasn't really leaning on her, he was holding her close. His arm was around her waist rather than her shoulder, and he was cradling her body against his. With every slow step her breast brushed against his chest and their hips met. It was a relief when they got to the car.

"Do you want me to follow you?" she asked doubtfully as she saw him sprawled in the middle of the seat so he could use his left foot on the gas pedal.

"To the ends of the earth," he smiled.

"Will you kindly be serious!"

His golden eyes held an unfathomable expression as he gazed back at her. "There's a strong possibility that I *am* being serious."

Pat stared after the car until it was obscured by a cloud of dust from the unpaved road. Her thoughts were in complete turmoil. She knew Raven hadn't meant one word he said to her, but that wasn't the problem. It was her own reaction to him. He was right about the thunder and lightning—for her at least. Pat knew instinctively that this man had the power to turn her quiet life upside down if he chose to pursue the course he outlined. He was undeniably more experienced than she. Would he be able to sneak under her guard with his potent virility? Her body had betrayed her before in his arms.

One solution would be to pack up and leave right now, but the idea was distasteful. She wouldn't give him the satisfaction of running away. Her only salvation was that men like Raven had a short attention span, especially when the conquest wasn't easy. If she just hung in there, he'd soon lose interest and go back to New York.

"You and I will outwit that city slicker, won't we, champ?" she murmured to the dog who stood close by her side.

Janus looked up trustingly, whining softly deep in his throat.

Chapter Three

$\mathscr{P}$at was braced the next day for a new assault by Raven. She knew that trying to evade him was fruitless, and it went against her grain anyway. She was through with running away. She purposely called the main house to tell Mattie that she was going to finish whitewashing the corral if Mr. Masters needed her for anything.

All morning she had one eye on the road, which resulted in a rather sloppy paint job. When he didn't appear Pat gritted her teeth in annoyance. He knew perfectly well that she was expecting him! Well, if he thought his little war of nerves was going to work he was mistaken. Pat ate her lunch in the shade of a tree, sharing her sandwich with Janus and telling herself she was pleasantly relieved.

It was late afternoon by the time the job was done. She was hot and tired and completely out of sorts when she got home. A cool shower refreshed her greatly. After donning a clean pair of jeans and a white linen shirt Pat stretched out on the couch to read the paper. A commotion outside captured her interest more than the news. Two cars piled with luggage were stopped just inside the gate.

Norman Langhorn, the man Pat had met, got out of the driver's seat of the first car and went to the one in back. "Try to stay behind me but if we get separated, be sure you don't miss the airport cutoff," he instructed the other driver. "It comes up pretty fast."

The two cars left the ranch, with Pat looking after them. It didn't surprise her that Raven had tired so quickly of the simple life. It was her good fortune, she assured herself. Now she could relax again and stop looking over her shoulder. Her worries about fending him off had been for nothing. All that nonsense about the magic there was between them had been as sincere as Carl's fevered protestations of love.

Janus's low growl of reminder sent Pat to the kitchen where she prepared his dinner. While he was wolfing it down she looked listlessly in the refrigerator, deciding she wasn't really hungry. The newspaper didn't interest her either. Pat wandered restlessly around the cottage, finally deciding to go up to the main house. That crew had probably left everything in a mess and Mattie would welcome some help.

She let herself in the kitchen door, calling out to the housekeeper, "Hi, I thought you might need me."

"You must have read my mind," Raven said. He was getting ice out of the freezer.

Pat's heart gave a giant leap. "What are you doing here?" she demanded.

"I was about to make a martini. Would you like one?"

"I just saw you leave," she said helplessly.

"No, you saw my houseguests leaving. It was probably very inhospitable of me, but I suggested that they'd be happier back in New York."

"Why didn't you go with them?"

He gave her a warm smile. "Because I decided I'd be happier here."

Pat clasped her hands tightly together. "That was very foolish. You're apt to be extremely bored without your friends."

"I don't think so." His eyes held hers. When the housekeeper came into the kitchen Raven said, "Set another place, Mattie; Pat is staying for dinner."

"No, I couldn't possibly! Mattie isn't supposed to wait on me."

"Nonsense," the housekeeper told her. "After what you did for me the other night? You and Mr. Masters go in the den and have a drink while I start dinner."

The older woman shooed them out of the kitchen. Somehow Pat found herself in the comfortable book-lined den without being able to do anything about it.

Raven put the icebucket on the counter of the built-in bar. "What can I fix you?"

"I . . . I'll have a glass of white wine."

He cocked a questioning eyebrow at her. "Is that what you really want? I've always wondered if people drank the stuff because they truly like it, or just because it's fashionable."

It had never occurred to Pat, but he was right. She smiled at his perception. "Actually, I think I'd like a martini."

"A sound choice." He poured gin and vermouth into a cocktail shaker. "What did you do today?"

"I finished painting the corral."

He turned to her, frowning slightly. "That isn't part of your job."

"I know, but I didn't have anything else to do. And I don't mind," she added hurriedly. "I like to keep busy."

"It prevents you from thinking?" His tone was faintly mocking. As she stiffened defensively Raven was contrite. "I'm sorry, I didn't mean to say that. Tonight we're just going to enjoy each other's company."

Pat was silent, trying to assess this new threat. She didn't trust him for a moment. He had maneuvered her into having dinner with him and she knew he didn't expect it to end there.

Raven handed her a glass. "Try this and see if it isn't the best martini on both sides of the Rockies."

She took a sip of the potent drink. "You have many talents," she commented lightly.

He leaned over her with a hand on both arms of her chair. "Like the man said, you ain't seen nothin' yet."

Pat looked down into her glass. "I'll settle for this."

"You're easily satisfied," Raven replied softly.

She raised her head challengingly. "Is this your idea of enjoying each other's company?"

"You're right." He straightened up, groaning. "And I was going to be the perfect host." He settled into a chair facing her. "From now on you'd better pick the topic of conversation."

Pat took another sip of her drink. The martini was going right to the bottom of her empty stomach, warming her pleasantly. "All right, why didn't you go home with your friends?" she asked directly. "I mean *really*."

His golden gaze was enigmatic. "I got tired of well-meaning people keeping me company day and night. I need some time that isn't planned. Also, I'd like to start doing a little work. I have an idea for a way to modify a new engine for more stress resistance."

Pat lifted her delicate brows. "I had a feeling you couldn't just sit around and do nothing."

"Is that bad?"

"I suppose not. There have to be both ants and grasshoppers in the world."

"Which one do you consider yourself?" he asked quietly.

"Certainly not a grasshopper," she protested. "I work hard." She drained her glass defiantly. "Even though it's work you don't approve of."

Raven took her glass and refilled it from the cocktail shaker. "I'm sure you're not worried about my opinion."

"It doesn't bother me but it's annoying." She took a large gulp of the drink he handed her. "Just because I don't wear designer jeans like Miss What's-her-name, I'm an automatic loser, is that it?"

"That's a category that could never apply to you." Lines of amusement creased his face. "But I'd go easy on that drink if I were you."

"Don't change the subject." Pat felt relaxed and uninhibited. "I could be just as seductive as she is if I wanted to."

"I'm sure you could." Raven was having trouble containing his laughter.

"You don't believe me!"

"I really do, sweetheart." He took the almost empty glass out of her hand and turned to put it on the bar.

"Don't patronize me!" Pat stormed. In one lithe movement she got up and followed him. Whirling him about, she clasped her arms around his neck.

"Honey, I don't think you—"

She stopped his feeble protest by pulling his head down to hers. Raven kissed her gently, his hands holding her lightly by the waist.

Her fingers anchored fiercely in his thick dark hair as she tilted her head back to stare at him with blazing eyes. "Kiss me, damn it!"

Her mouth closed over his with demanding passion, forcing his lips apart. Raven's hands tightened on her waist and when it seemed for a moment that he might push her away, Pat molded her body closely to his, moving against him seductively.

With a small groan deep in his throat, Raven's arms wrapped around her. His lips parted to admit her questing tongue, greeting it with his own. He let her lead the way, let her explore the warm depths of his mouth without taking over.

It was a heady feeling for Pat. She was in charge. Her hands wandered restlessly over the broad triangle of his back, tracing the taut muscles. But she wanted more than that. Pulling the shirt out of his waistband she ran her hands over his smooth bare skin, delighting in the male firmness that wasn't blurred by an ounce of fat.

Raven drew in his breath, arching his body involuntarily into hers. With a sudden thrust he drew her hips against his. A stab of feeling sensitized Pat's whole body. She was alive with desire, aching with need for him. Winding her arms more tightly around his neck she crushed her breasts against his chest, whispering his name over and over.

For just a moment Raven's embrace tightened. He buried his face in the fragrant cloud of her hair, murmuring, "My beautiful little darling."

"Kiss me, Raven," Pat pleaded softly, lifting her drugged face.

His hands moved to her shoulders, putting her gently away.

She looked at him in a daze, her soft mouth parting in protest. "Why—"

"You need some food, little one." His hands were tender as they smoothed her tousled hair.

The thunder in Pat's blood started to recede, leaving a chilling sense of horror at her actions. How could she have thrown herself at Raven that way? Practically attacked him actually! His rejection only added depth to her misery.

"Don't look like that, honey." He took hold of her clenched hands. "It was my fault really. I shouldn't have urged that second martini on you."

Pat knew there had been no coercion. She was solely responsible for her sordid actions. Raven knew it too. She couldn't even explain something she didn't understand herself.

Pulling her hands away she backed toward the door. "I'd better go," she muttered.

"Don't leave, Pat. You're making too much of an innocent kiss."

"One that I forced on you," she answered bitterly. "Why not tell it like it is?"

He cupped her face in his palms compelling her to look at him. "That's too foolish to refute."

"If you're trying to be kind, don't! It . . . it's insulting. I'm not a complete idiot."

"You're upset because I didn't take unfair advantage of you. Believe me, my dear, there's nothing I'd like more than to make love to you."

"Please don't!" She tried to break away but he held her firmly.

"Not like this, though," he continued inexorably. "Some day you're going to give yourself to me because it's what you really want, and it will be right and beautiful. I want you very much but I'm willing to wait."

"This will never happen again!" she cried fervently. "It was the drinks. I must have been out of my mind! I didn't know what I was doing."

Raven smoothed the petal softness of her cheek. "We all need to reach out to a fellow human being sometime. That's what you were really doing."

If only he believed that! "I guess you're right," she mumbled.

He smiled. "You'll feel better after you've had dinner."

The thought of food made Pat's stomach turn over alarmingly. "I don't think so," she gasped. "I'd better leave before I disgrace myself any further." Before Raven could stop her she ran out the door.

Back in her own cottage Pat threw off her clothes and crawled into bed. Her head ached and her stomach was queasy, but it was her memory that was giving the most trouble. She tried in vain to put the whole miserable affair out of her mind. It wasn't earth-shattering to have too much to drink. Luckily Raven realized it and there was no harm done. He already knew she was attracted to him physically, so that wasn't a big deal either.

In spite of her rationalization, Pat's fingernails bit into her clenched palms as she recalled the way she had thrown herself into Raven's arms. She groaned, burying her face in the pillow. Even now there was an unsatisfied ache deep inside her as she remembered his caressing hands and the hard thrust of his body.

The martinis were only responsible for her lack of inhibitions; the frightening thing was what had emerged. From this moment on she would have to be on her guard constantly. Raven was determined to have an affair with her. It would be a pleasant interlude to him, but Pat had a terrible feeling that it would be more than that to her, and she wasn't going to let another man mess up her life.

Pat was clearing away her breakfast dishes when the phone rang the next morning. She had awakened reluctantly, knowing instinctively that there was some reason why she didn't want to face the day. When memory came rushing back it was a temptation to pull the covers over her head and stay in bed.

Since that wouldn't solve anything she had forced herself to get up, but she certainly didn't feel like talking to anyone. Wouldn't you think Raven would have the decency to leave her alone?

Stalking to the phone she barked out an abrupt greeting. Pat was sorry for her brusque tone when she heard Mattie's voice.

"Are you all right, Pat? I was so worried when you disappeared without any dinner last night. I wanted to come down and see what was wrong but Mr. Masters said it was just a little upset and you'd be better off alone."

"Yes, I . . . uh . . . I had a bit too much sun yesterday."

"I keep telling you not to do work like that in the heat of the day," the older woman scolded.

"I guess you were right," Pat agreed weakly.

"You just lie around and take it easy today," Mattie instructed. "Come up here for your meals."

"No!"

"Now, Pat, there's such a thing as being too conscientious. Mr. Masters won't mind if you take a day off. He's a very kind man. Look at how nice he was about inviting you to dinner last night."

"I'll never forget it," Pat remarked sardonically.

Mattie missed the sarcasm. "I'm glad you're starting to appreciate him. I told you he was a gentleman. I would have called you a little later anyway, but Mr. Masters came in just now and told me to do it right away. He's waiting to hear how you are."

Pat was taken aback at this evidence of his sensitivity. He knew she wouldn't want to talk to him. It didn't please her; she didn't want to find anything good about the man. "Tell him I'm fine," she instructed curtly. "In fact you can tell him that I don't expect a recurrence of last night's . . . weakness."

"You really feel all right?" Mattie asked doubtfully.

"Couldn't be better."

"Then, do you think you could take me marketing? All that company sure left the larder bare."

Part of Pat's job was to do errands for Mattie since the housekeeper had never learned to drive. "Sure, Mattie, any time you say."

"Give me about half an hour. I just want to clear away the breakfast dishes."

On the way into town Pat questioned Mattie discreetly. "How long does Mr. Masters usually stay when he comes to visit?"

"That's hard to answer. Sometimes for only a few days, sometimes a couple of weeks. Of course with the accident, poor man, he'll probably stay longer this time." As Pat groaned inwardly she continued, "At least I hope so. He needs to get some meat on those bones, and a little sun on his pale skin."

Pat's mind veered away from that lean, taut body. She decided to change the subject. "When I was in town yesterday the decorations were already going up for the rodeo. I thought it wasn't for a couple of weeks yet."

"Well, there's not too much excitement around here," Mattie commented. "It's the big event of the summer."

"I'm looking forward to it. I haven't been to a rodeo in years. I used to love them when I was a kid."

"Mr. Masters does too. He never misses one while he's here." The older woman smiled happily. "That just about guarantees that he'll stay at least two weeks."

"Dandy," Pat muttered.

Mattie chuckled. "All the unmarried girls will be pleased—and a lot of the married ones too. Although Mr. Masters would never have anything to do with *them*," she added righteously.

Pat was getting very fed up with Mattie's concept of Raven. "Your Mr. Masters is a man like all the rest," she said disgustedly. "Surely you don't think he sits around playing checkers with all those beautiful women he takes out?"

Mattie shrugged. "Like you said—he's a man. All I know is that he would never do anything dishonorable. And when he finds the right girl he'll settle down and be a perfect husband."

"You don't honestly believe that! He'll settle down about the time that ice cubes are scarce in Alaska."

"I know him better than you do," Mattie remarked comfortably. "There's no such thing as a confirmed bachelor—just a man who hasn't found his mate."

How could you argue with such illogical reasoning, Pat thought in annoyance. "I just hope he can still do something about it by the time he finds Miss Right," she commented acidly.

The older woman wasn't shocked, as she half expected. "Don't worry about Mr. Masters," Mattie answered dryly.

No, Raven would never lose his virility—or his

potent male attraction. He would age gracefully, with silver wings in that sable hair. And women would still flock around, falling hopelessly for a man who would love and then leave them. Pat gripped the steering wheel, staring straight ahead.

After Mattie had done her shopping, lingering to chat with friends, they started back to the ranch. The gossip she had picked up in town kept her off the subject of Raven on the return trip, to Pat's relief.

He was sunning himself on the flagstone terrace when they drove up to the house. Books and papers were piled on a low table next to his chaise, and Raven was working on a clipboard propped against his raised knees. In the brief glance she cast in his direction Pat could see that he was wearing only a pair of denim cutoffs. He was always so impeccably dressed that it was a shock to see him so bare. The curling black hair on his chest that she had only glimpsed through the open neck of various silk shirts was now visible in its entirety, trailing in a tapering V down to his flat stomach.

Pat helped Mattie carry in the groceries, waiting with a sense of fatality for the familiar sight of Raven lounging in the doorway. He didn't appear, however, and Pat breathed a sigh of relief, firmly refusing Mattie's invitation to lunch.

When Raven didn't try to contact her all afternoon or evening, Pat had mixed feelings. Was he displaying the same sensitivity he'd shown that morning? Did he realize she still felt ragged from last night's encounter? That would indicate a depth of perception and kindness she didn't want to attribute to him. Raven was a man and a hunter, Pat insisted to herself. Either he had lost interest or he was pursuing some male game plan. In any case, she was happy for the respite.

The day seemed to drag, though, and the evening

was endless. For the first time, Pat was bored. After eating a light dinner and taking Janus for a long walk she returned to the cottage. Most of her evenings were spent reading, but that night nothing seemed to interest her. Pat snapped on the radio to dispel the silence that had never bothered her before. She wandered restlessly through the cottage, finding herself looking up at the typewriter that was stored on the very top shelf of the bookcase. It beckoned seductively, like Pandora's box.

"*No*!" Her rejection was explosive.

Damn Raven Masters anyway! He was the serpent in her Garden of Eden, but he wasn't going to drag her back into a life that was as phony as he was. With grim determination Pat selected a book from the bookcase.

It was late when she awoke the next morning because she had read half the night. No one was keeping tabs on her, but Pat felt guilty. She had a lot of work to do that day. The extensive lawns surrounding the ranch house hadn't been cut in over a week and they were getting definitely shaggy. It wouldn't do to give Raven something to complain about.

By the time she showered and dressed in her uniform of shorts, shirt, and sandals, the sun was uncomfortably near its zenith. Well, it couldn't be helped. Pat didn't want to risk letting the lawns go another day.

"Sorry, baby, you can't come with me," she told Janus, who followed her expectantly to the door. It was too dangerous to allow him around the powerful mower.

Pat had hoped that Raven would be busy indoors, but when she worked her way up to the house he was in the same place on the terrace. He waved and she waved back, grateful that the noisy machinery made conversation impossible. Pat glanced at him as she rode the estate mower parallel to the house but Raven seemed immersed in his work.

As she made the turn at the corner of the house and started back, a black shape came loping toward her. Janus had gotten out. Pat cut the motor quickly and jumped down, shouting at the dog. When she pointed her arm sternly toward the cottage he hesitated for a moment before making a dash for the terrace. He skidded to a stop and put both paws on Raven's shoulders, licking his face with a long, pink tongue.

Pat raced after him. "Janus, you little fiend, get down!"

"If this is a *little* fiend, I'd hate to see a big one." Raven fended him off, laughing.

"I locked him in the cottage, but there must have been a window open," Pat explained breathlessly.

"It's too nice a day for him to be cooped up."

"I have to do it when I cut the lawn."

"You can leave him here with me."

"I'd have to go all the way back for his leash," she said doubtfully.

"I don't need it." Raven stopped stroking the dog. "Janus, sit," he ordered in a quietly authoritative voice.

The Dane immediately dropped to his haunches.

Pat was secretly impressed, and slightly disconcerted. She had always considered Janus a one-woman dog. Carl's attempts at discipline had resulted in some fearsome confrontations. Of course they had cordially despised each other.

"You're quite good with animals," she commented grudgingly.

Raven gave her a melting smile. "Animals and people are very much alike. They respond favorably to affection."

Before Pat could respond, Mattie came out of the house carrying a tray with a pitcher of lemonade on it. "Good gracious, Pat, you're red as a beet. You could use a cold drink too. I'll go get another glass."

Pat felt hot and sticky and at a complete disadvantage as usual. She had pulled her long hair up and secured it at her crown but it was tumbling out of the pins now, framing her face with soft little tendrils. She swept them back impatiently, very conscious of Raven's tawny eyes assessing her.

"I know I'm a mess," she said tartly. "You might as well say it."

"Actually I was thinking of something else," he remarked absently. "Don't you ever wear anything except shorts and jeans?"

"They're comfortable," she answered tersely.

"And very becoming." His glance swept over the length of her slim thighs. "But don't you ever wear something more . . . er . . . feminine?"

"No," she replied curtly. When Raven's firm mouth curved in a mischievous smile Pat demanded, "What's so funny?"

"I was just picturing you in a denim nightgown."

The idea was so absurd that her lips twitched unwillingly. "I've never been able to find one."

"That's a relief." His voice deepened. "You belong in satin and lace."

Pat regretted lowering her guard. "I'm not the type," she said coolly.

"Even little girls enjoy playing dress up."

"They also believe in fairy tales. It's something they're supposed to outgrow—like trusting strangers," she added pointedly.

"Didn't someone once say that a stranger is just a person you haven't gotten to know yet?"

"Probably. People are always saying things that sound profound but don't really mean anything."

"You have all the answers, don't you, Pat?" he asked softly.

"I paid my dues to learn them." There was bitterness

in her voice. She stood up. "If you don't mind hanging onto Janus I'll finish the lawn."

"Where are you going, Pat?" Mattie appeared carrying a plate of sandwiches and another glass. "I fixed some lunch."

"Not for me, thank you," Pat replied hastily. "I had a late breakfast."

"What is it with you?" The housekeeper frowned. "I'm beginning to think you don't like my cooking."

"I believe it's my company she's trying to avoid." Raven's smile was mocking.

"Nonsense." Mattie couldn't conceive of that.

Janus was eyeing the food with great interest. He looked from the plate to Raven and back again, growling softly.

"Janus is more than happy to accept Mattie's invitation," Raven observed.

Pat looked at the dog with fond disgust. "Give him a tuna fish sandwich and he'll follow you anywhere."

"Too bad it doesn't run in the family," Raven murmured. "Sit down and keep me company, Pat. I hate to eat alone."

"I don't suppose you have much occasion to," she muttered sulkily. He was always maneuvering her into things she didn't want to do.

"Call me if you want anything," Mattie said before going back in the house.

"You really think I keep a resident harem, don't you?" Raven asked Pat.

She shrugged. "Does it matter what I think?"

"Strangely enough, it does." He held his sandwich suspended in midair while he stared at her with a slight frown.

Janus barked suddenly, tantalized beyond endurance.

"Behave yourself or I'll send you home," Pat warned the dog.

Raven chuckled. "Which one of us was that meant for?"

"I don't imagine you're used to taking orders," she remarked dryly.

"No, I'm used to giving them and having them obeyed. You're undermining my self-confidence."

Pat was sure that nothing could. Lying at ease on the chaise, Raven looked like the lord of the manor, in full possession of every situation. "Well, you can't win 'em all," she answered lightly.

"It won't be for lack of trying." His voice held a wealth of meaning.

Pat concentrated on her lemonade. "I thought you'd given up."

"Because I left you alone yesterday? I would have called if I thought it might help, but I knew it would only add to your misery," he said gently.

She raised her head, staring at him searchingly. Had her feeling about Raven been correct? *Was* he really an exceptionally kind man? That would make him different from most of the men she had encountered. Unless Raven was astute in his assessment of her. Had she let her experience with Carl embitter her life? Pat had never thought of it in that light.

Raven's quiet voice broke the small silence. "I'd really like to be your friend, Pat."

"Does that mean . . ." she stopped, her color rising.

"That I've given up the idea of making love to you?" he finished for her. "Not at all. But I meant what I said. Someday you're going to realize that it's not only right, but inevitable. You're going to come to me on your own terms. I won't use trickery to get you, my dear."

Pat drew a shuddery breath. If only she could believe him. If only he *were* different. This man had all the qualities she had always been looking for, Pat admitted to herself in a burst of honesty. How could she ever have been taken in by Carl? One was solid gold, the other merely cheap gilt that glittered briefly and wore off fast.

Raven watched the play of emotions over her mobile face. He leaned forward, taking her hand. "Trust me, honey. It's the first step back."

She searched his face, finding only candor. "I'll try," she murmured.

"That's all I ask." He filled both their glasses. "Let's drink to our detente. Do you think it's binding in lemonade?"

Pat felt a bubbling sense of happiness. "It has to be. I've sworn off anything stronger."

"That's good, because I think I used up all my willpower the other night."

She couldn't believe they were actually joking about it! Pat felt as though a load had been lifted from her chest. "It's good for your character," she assured him.

"Maybe, but it didn't do a lot for my peace of mind." A light suddenly flickered in his tawny eyes as they swept over her slim body. "You're not exactly lowering my blood pressure now either."

"Then, I'd better get back to work." Pat stood up in one graceful motion.

Raven caught her hand. "You're not leaving just when we're getting to know each other?"

"Don't rush me," she said softly.

Their eyes met for a long moment. Then Raven lifted her hand, kissing the palm. "Whatever you say, sweetheart. You're calling the shots."

Raven had disappeared by the time she finished mowing the extensive lawn. After she had put away the equipment Pat hesitated, wanting to go in search of him, yet curiously reluctant to take the first step. Then it occurred to her that she had to collect Janus. But the dog was in the kitchen with Mattie.

"Mr. Masters had some work to do, so he left Janus with me," the housekeeper explained.

Pat whistled to the dog and started back to the cottage, feeling a curious sense of letdown. If Raven had wanted to see her he would have kept Janus with him. Frustration threatened to engulf her. Was she falling for another line again or did Raven really mean what he said?

After showering, Pat reached automatically for a clean pair of jeans. She paused with her hand outstretched, looking at the dresses pushed to the back of the closet. After a long moment she pulled out the jeans. Anything else would be a clear signal, and she wasn't ready for that yet. This time she was going to be absolutely sure.

Pat's ears were tuned to the telephone all evening but Raven didn't call. Was that because she had asked for time? Or was he playing a clever game with her, knowing how she would react?

At ten o'clock she gave up in disgust, climbing into bed with a book.

The phone rang late the next morning. "Can you do me a favor, Pat?" Raven asked, as though nothing had ever gone on between them.

Pat's soft mouth set grimly, remembering the long hours she'd waited to hear from him. "Certainly, Mr. Masters."

He paused for a second before saying, "Will you drive me into Jackson Hole this morning? I have some business to transact."

Pat was torn between resentment and a rising sense of anticipation. It was a two-hour drive to Jackson Hole. That meant four hours in Raven's company. It didn't entail any decisions on her part either; it was strictly business.

"When would you like to leave?" She kept her voice carefully neutral.

"As soon as possible. I want to get to the bank before it closes."

Pat looked at her watch. It was a little after eleven. "I'm ready now if you are."

She changed hurriedly out of her shorts into a pair of jeans, taking only time enough to run a comb through her thick auburn hair and outline her full mouth with a touch of lip gloss.

Raven was waiting in the driveway when she drove up to the ranch house. He looked like a stranger in a lightweight gray suit, a white shirt, and a blue silk tie. The calfskin briefcase under his arm stamped him as an alien from the world she'd left behind.

"Jackson Hole is kind of informal," she remarked hesitantly, after he had arranged his long legs on the passenger side.

He grinned. "I know, but bankers aren't. I want to talk about a large amount of money, and they think a man without a tie is automatically indigent."

"Isn't that kind of silly? Anyone can buy a tie for ten dollars."

"You know it and I know it, but money men firmly believe in symbolism. It's their security blanket in a changing world."

"Well, it's a long ride so you can take off your token gesture if you want. You don't have to impress *me*."

"I'd like to," he murmured, cupping her neck under the long, silky hair.

Pat shook her head to dislodge his tantalizing fingers. "Eleven-thirty in the morning is no time to get amorous."

"What time did you have in mind?"

She took her eyes off the road to look at him briefly. "If you're going to continue on this way for two hours, I might just deposit you by the side of the road."

"You'd do that to an injured man?"

"In a minute," she assured him firmly.

"Okay, you win." Raven chuckled, settling back in his seat. "But don't think I've given up."

"I'm beginning to be convinced," she answered dryly.

"It's about time. I'll talk about the weather, even argue politics if you like, but my mind will still be on you."

"In that case, maybe I can finally win an argument with you."

"I'd say you're several up on me already," he murmured, trailing a long forefinger along her outstretched leg.

"It's a long walk back in either direction," she warned.

"I get the message." Raven's white teeth gleamed in his rugged face as he removed his hand. "What do you think of the Yankee's chances for winning the pennant this year?"

From then on the trip was a complete delight. They laughed and joked together like old friends, with the added dimension of discovering common interests and viewpoints. The undercurrent of their attraction for each other was ever present, but it merely added a fillip of excitement.

When they reached Jackson Hole, Pat dropped Raven off at the bank, where they made plans to meet later. He expressed concern about what she would do with herself while he was occupied, but Pat assured him it was no problem. She'd never been there before and would enjoy looking around.

After parking the car she spent her time leisurely

inspecting the picturesque little town. Jackson Hole was a year-round vacation spot, known for excellent skiing in winter and fishing in summer. It drew crowds of tourists, but it was an authentic Western town rather than just a resort. The wooden sidewalks echoed under the boots of genuine cowpokes as well as Eastern dudes.

Although the ranchers rode into town in automobiles, they were equally at home on horseback. The green valley surrounded by the majestic Teton and Gros Ventre ranges was dotted with working ranches, and the high country still abounded in elk, antelope, and bighorn sheep.

The time passed quickly as Pat browsed through the shops, enjoying the bustle more than she would have expected. Or was it the fact that she'd be seeing Raven again soon? Pat refused to examine her emotions too closely. Whatever the reason, she felt alive and vital.

Chapter Four

$\mathscr{P}$at was ready at the appointed time but Raven wasn't. She drove around the block several times before he appeared.

"At last!" she exclaimed, leaning over to open the door on the passenger side.

He arranged his long legs inside the small car. "It sounds as though you missed me," he teased.

"That's not why I'm glad to see you," she informed him tartly. "I drove around the block so many times the guard was starting to get suspicious."

Raven's comprehensive glance traveled over her snug shirt and hip-hugging jeans. "He couldn't have thought you were a bank robber. It's obvious that you aren't carrying any concealed weapons—at least not the conventional kind."

The purely male look in his tawny eyes made Pat's color rise. She hurriedly changed the subject. "Did you get your business over with?"

"Turn left at the next corner," he instructed, before answering her question. "Unfortunately, no. It was too late to get the information they needed from my New York bank."

"The difference in time makes things difficult, doesn't it?" Pat sympathized. "Especially when the banks close at three."

"A completely arbitrary hour," Raven agreed, sighing. "Some day we'll get those fellows into the mainstream."

Pat grinned. "About the same time you get them out of their three-piece suits."

"You're probably right," he agreed. "What did you do with yourself while I was slaving over dry facts and figures?"

An enchanting dimple appeared at the corner of her generous mouth. "I walked around downtown, flirting with handsome cowboys."

Raven raised an inquiring eyebrow. "I thought you didn't have a very high opinion of men."

"I'm not fanatical about it," she replied demurely.

"In that case, what do those cowboys have that I don't? No, don't tell me," he answered himself. "I know—two good legs."

Pat could have told him that he was more of a man with his present handicap than most men were without. She contented herself with saying, "Stop feeling sorry for yourself, the rest will do you good. You'll be back chasing girls soon enough."

Raven grinned. "It isn't the chase I'm interested in—it's catching them."

"I imagine you've bagged your share," she remarked dryly.

"Fortunately there's no legal limit," he said, chuckling.

Although she knew he was teasing her, Pat felt a rush of anger. "Fortunate for whom? The women involved might see it differently."

He looked at her rigid profile for a long, thoughtful moment. "Have you ever considered that they might have received equal enjoyment?"

The knowledge that he was undoubtedly right didn't make Pat any less resentful. It merely increased her resolve not to be one of the pack. "You don't have to present your credentials to *me*," she replied scornfully.

"I believe I already have on several occasions—at least once at your request. Turn right at the next stoplight," he continued in a perfectly normal tone of voice.

Pat was so furious at the reminder of her past weakness that she followed his instructions without question. "If you were a gentleman you wouldn't bring that up!"

His handsome face was impassive. "Hunters are known for taking unfair advantage."

Pat's anger cooled as she recalled the memorable evening when Raven could have done exactly that, but didn't. Why had she let a little harmless teasing escalate into a confrontation? "You don't have to be so sensitive," she muttered. "I didn't say you were a womanizer."

"You didn't have to." His brief answer indicated he wasn't accepting the tentative olive branch she offered. "Turn in at the next driveway."

For the first time Pat paid attention to her surroundings rather than merely following Raven's directions. Although she wasn't familiar with Jackson Hole, she knew they were going away from the main highway rather than toward it.

"We're heading in the wrong direction," she pointed out. "This isn't the way to the ranch."

"I know. We're going to the Jackson Lake Lodge."

She thought he meant for a drink, or a very late lunch. Ordinarily Pat might have been pleased, but their brief unpleasantness left her annoyed. He might at least have asked!

"It's a long ride home," she answered stiffly. "If you're hungry we can stop at a fast-food place."

"We're staying at the lodge tonight. As I told you, my business isn't completed. Since I have to be here when the bank opens, it doesn't make sense to drive all the way back to the ranch."

As comprehension dawned Pat was engulfed by fury. "How terribly convenient that we just *happen* to have to spend the night together! The next thing you'll tell me is how sorry you are that all they have is a double-bed room, but not to worry because you're going to be a perfect gentleman!" She pulled over to the side of the road, slamming on the brakes. "Well, you can just forget it, Mr. Masters! You're lucky that I don't leave you here to find your own way home."

Raven's face set in autocratic lines. "May I remind you, Miss Lee, that you still work for me—although for how long is problematical. This is exactly why I said you weren't suited for the job." When she opened her mouth he continued without letting her speak. "If you were a male employee there would be no problem."

The injustice of it drove her wild. "If I were a male employee you wouldn't find it necessary to stay overnight!"

"That's where you're wrong. The four-hour round trip is extremely uncomfortable for my bad leg. I wouldn't hesitate to tell a man we were staying the night. Since you insist you're capable of doing a man's job, I don't see how you can possibly complain."

It was a good act but Pat didn't believe him for a moment. "Perhaps because you expect different services from me than you would from a man."

Raven regarded her impassively. "You're a very beautiful young woman, Pat. I'll admit I've thought about making love to you, but it isn't uppermost in my mind twenty-four hours a day. I booked two rooms at the lodge. You can use yours, or you can drive back to the ranch and return in the morning. It doesn't matter to me one way or the other."

Her indignation faltered. If Raven had really reserved two rooms, maybe she had misjudged him. Although there was always the chance that they were adjoining—with the connecting door conveniently unlocked. There was also his contention that she was unsuited for the job because she was raising objections. If he did have to be at the bank when it opened, then it was only sensible to stay over. But suppose none of it was true?

Raven watched the play of emotions over her mobile face. "Would you mind dropping me off at the hotel while you're making up your mind? I have some phone calls to make." He sounded completely disinterested in her decision.

Pat put the car in gear, her mouth a grim line. There was no way of knowing what Raven was planning, but she was more than a match for him. It would be ridiculous to drive the long distance home, only to turn around the next morning. If he had cozy little plans for that night, let *him* be the one to be inconvenienced!

A parking attendant opened the door when Pat stopped in front of the hotel, and she got out of the car. Raven's raised eyebrow was his only comment on her evident decision to stay. She didn't put it into words either. She simply followed him to the admitting desk with her small chin thrust out.

The view from the two-story, floor-to-ceiling glass window in the main lounge drove all annoyance from Pat's mind. It was as though a master photographer had framed the ultimate picture-postcard view.

The gray, snowcapped mountains of the Grand Teton Range towered majestically in the distance, dwarfing everything with their grandeur. They formed a background for a placid lake that mirrored the rugged peaks, but softened their jagged contours. Along with the mirror images there were islands in the clear water, green oases covered with groves of cone-shaped trees, and edged with ribbons of cream-colored sand. It was so breathtaking that Pat could only stand and stare while Raven took care of their accommodations.

"John Mapleton called from the bank to reserve two rooms for me," he said. "I'm Raven Masters."

"Yes, Mr. Masters, we're happy to have you with us." The clerk's obsequious manner was partly in deference to the local bank manager, and partly a subtle recognition of Raven's own stature. "This is our busy time of year, though. At such short notice I'm afraid I can only give you one cottage."

Raven frowned, glancing at Pat who was completely engrossed in the view. "That's totally unacceptable." He kept his voice low but there was steel in it. "I distinctly stated that I needed two rooms."

"Oh, we have them for you," the clerk hastened to assure him. "But one is in the main lodge."

Raven's tense body relaxed. "That's all right, then. Give Miss Lee the cottage and I'll take the room." He turned to Pat. "Are you ready?"

"I guess so." Her eyes were dazzled. "If I can tear myself away from this magnificent scenery."

"You have the same view from your cottage," the clerk assured her. "Enjoy your stay. I'll have your luggage sent right over."

"Oh." Pat looked uncomfortably at Raven.

"We don't have any luggage," he answered without a hint of discomfort, leading Pat to wonder how often he had done this sort of thing. "Our decision to stay overnight was prompted by business."

"I see." The clerk's manner held no hint of innuendo. "Well, we have some fine shops here in the hotel if you need anything. Would you like me to make you a reservation for dinner tonight?"

Raven hesitated. "Thanks, but that won't be necessary."

As a bellman was leading them to Pat's room she began to steam. "I suppose you don't want to be seen with me dressed this way," she muttered in a low voice.

Raven raised one dark eyebrow. "You must get all your exercise jumping to conclusions."

She gritted her teeth. "It's true, isn't it?"

"We'll discuss it when we're alone," he answered firmly.

The clerk had been accurate in saying that Pat's cottage had the same breathtaking view. When the bellman drew back the draperies that covered sliding glass doors, it was like looking out at a gigantic painting. In addition to a charmingly furnished bedroom, the guest house also had an outdoor patio provided with chairs and a small table.

Pat's anger prevented her from giving the lovely accommodations more than a cursory glance. She could barely wait until the man had handed Raven his key and departed with a generous tip.

"Don't bother to make excuses," she erupted as soon as he had closed the door. "I'm not even remotely interested in having dinner with you."

"That's what I thought," Raven replied calmly. "It's the reason I didn't tell the clerk to make reservations."

"Oh, sure! The fact that this is an elegant hotel and I'm wearing jeans has nothing to do with it."

"Correct. That's just another smokescreen you're raising. You must know me well enough by now to know that externals aren't important to me." He put his hands on her shoulders, holding her when she would have twisted away. "I thought we'd agreed to be friends, Pat. What happened?"

"Nothing happened," she mumbled.

"I honestly didn't think you'd suspect me of ulterior motives when I made these reservations," he persisted. "It appeared to be the most sensible solution."

"Well, it just seemed so . . ."

A long forefinger raised her chin. "If getting you into bed was what I had in mind, I didn't need to take such elaborate measures. A midnight visit to the caretaker's cottage would have been a lot more convenient." His voice dropped to a husky note. "I've thought about holding you in my arms while you were all warm and relaxed with sleep."

Pat's lashes made feathery fans on her flushed cheeks. "Forget it. Janus would warn me if anyone tried to get in."

Raven's laughter was spontaneous. "Don't count on it; he loves me even if you don't. That big cream puff would show me the way to the bedroom."

She couldn't help joining in his laughter. "You're probably right. I don't know what spell you cast over him."

"The one meant for you." Raven's gold-flecked eyes glowed like coals. "It just got deflected."

Her mirth died as she stiffened instinctively. "Hadn't you better be finding out where your room is?"

His hands tightened on her shoulders. "Don't pull

back into your shell, Pat. You're like a wary little woodland nymph, ready to bolt at the first sign of danger. But I'm no threat to you, honey. How can I convince you of that?"

He couldn't possibly because Pat realized that the danger came partly from within herself. Raven's touch had the ability to reduce her to mindless desire. She wanted the remembered blessing of his mouth covering hers, wanted to mold her softness to the hard angles of that sinewy male body. She knew instinctively that this man could bring an ecstasy she had never known.

But Pat also knew that a brief affair would destroy her. If she ever gave herself to Raven it would be a total commitment—something he wasn't interested in. Nor was she, Pat reminded herself. Hadn't Carl taught her anything?

"I'm not afraid of you, if that's what you're implying," she said carefully. "I just don't want there to be any misunderstandings between us. It makes for unpleasantness. I'm willing to be friends, but that's *all* I'll agree to."

Raven's expression was unreadable as he stared down at her for a long moment. "Does that include having dinner with me tonight?"

"Why not?" She shrugged. "We'll find some little place in town where I won't disgrace you."

"That's hardly a friendly thing to say." The momentary rapport between them was over. "We'll have dinner in the dining room. I'll contact you later about the time."

Pat experienced a pang as she watched Raven's stiff, retreating back. She knew her barb had been uncalled for. Carl's fragile security would have been threatened if he thought her appearance reflected on him, but Raven couldn't have cared less. He was too big a man in every way to be disturbed by such nonessentials. Why had she gone out of her way to challenge him?

Suddenly Pat wanted to be a credit to Raven, even though it didn't matter to him. She picked up her purse and hurried toward the main lodge with a look of purpose on her face.

The dress shop off the lobby had some very high-style gowns in the window. It had been so long since she had worn a dress that Pat felt a prickling of pleasure as she entered.

"Can I help you?" The saleslady's voice was neutral as she assessed Pat's checked shirt and jeans.

"I need a dress to wear to dinner tonight. Something . . ." Pat waved her hand helplessly, "sophisticated, but not too sexy. It's a . . . a business dinner."

"I have some very nice coordinated blouses and skirts."

"No, I want something a little more festive. The . . . the man I'm having dinner with is quite elegant."

"I think I have just the thing."

The woman rummaged among the racks for a moment, returning with a green and white print that was quietly tasteful. The sleeveless dress had a high round neck and a dirndl skirt. The only ornamentation was in the pattern which was an exotic design of stylized leaves and vines.

"What a pretty print," Pat exclaimed.

The woman nodded. "The green matches your eyes. But you haven't seen the best part." She twirled the hanger around, revealing the back of the dress which was bare to the waist. "Isn't that a stunner?"

"To say the least!" Pat gasped. "You couldn't wear a bra under it."

The saleswoman's eyes appraised Pat's slender figure. "You don't need one. There aren't very many women who would look good in this dress, but it's just made for you."

"That wasn't what I had in mind at all!"

"Try it on anyway," the saleslady urged. "I've been dying to see how it looks on someone who can do it justice. While you're getting undressed I'll see what else I can find."

Pat went into the dressing room, amused at the woman's transparent attempt to manipulate her. She tried on the dress while she was waiting, even though she had no intention of buying it. It was completely unsuitable. It telegraphed all the signals she was trying to avoid sending, Pat told herself as she twirled in front of the mirror.

"You look adorable!" The woman was back with an armload of gowns. "Nothing I have here can even come close."

"I don't want to look adorable. I want to look . . . businesslike."

"Well, I must admit that dress doesn't fill the bill. Although it's really quite demure. You show a lot more than that in a bathing suit."

Pat gazed at her reflection regretfully. The lovely dress might have been designed with her in mind. Her high firm breasts didn't suffer from lack of a bra. The soft fabric clung lovingly to her slim midriff in front, and framed the fluid length of her back, highlighting the smooth skin that was golden from long hours in the sun.

Pat shook her head, resisting temptation. "It's definitely not right."

She tried on silk shirtdresses, linen suits, and cotton sheaths. Everything looked good on her, but nothing seemed quite right. Her eyes kept returning to the green and white print.

"I certainly don't want to influence you, but I think you're making a mistake," the saleswoman said. "Maybe it isn't exactly businesslike but it's discreet. Every now and then a person needs to buy something just for fun. I'll bet you'd get a lot more wear out of the print than you think—and a good deal more compliments."

Pat could have told her that she didn't expect to wear the dress again. This was strictly a one-shot deal. But the woman's remark about compliments struck a chord. Pat had an aching desire to appear lovely for Raven, even though she knew it was foolish. He had known women a lot more beautiful, and certainly more sophisticated. But the knowledge that he regarded her as some kind of rustic curiosity rankled. For one night she would show him that she could hold her own in his world—even though she didn't want to.

"I'll take it," she decided suddenly.

The saleswoman nodded approvingly. "You won't regret it."

While she was writing up the order Pat went next door to buy a pair of shoes. After the trauma of deciding on a dress, the sandals were easy. The only difficulty was getting used to high heels again. It had been so long. But as she pirouetted in front of a mirror, Pat had to admit that the spike heels did flattering things for her slim legs and ankles.

The phone was ringing when she got back to the cottage. As usual her key proved elusive in her capacious shoulderbag. She was breathless when she finally got the door open and raced to the phone.

"Where have you been?" Raven demanded. "I've been calling every fifteen minutes."

"I . . . I was out looking around."

"Why didn't you wait for me? I would have gone with you."

"You said you had phone calls to make."

"They weren't that urgent."

"Well, I thought—" As she turned to put her packages on the bed, something ran across the patio. Pat was startled into an exclamation.

"What's the matter?" Raven asked.

"I think a mouse just ran across my patio." She gazed out of the window, noticing a ripple of movement in the grass beyond the flagstones. "There's a whole nest of them out there!" she yelped. "Raven, *do* something!"

He chuckled. "Hang on, I'll be right down."

Pat had always prided herself on being a great nature lover, but mice weren't among her favorites. For a brief moment she wished for Janus, before dismissing the notion. He would probably be climbing into her lap. Janus's idea of hunting was finding a friendly butcher who gave samples.

While she waited for Raven, Pat hung up her new dress and put away her shoes, avoiding looking out the window. She had no idea what he was going to do about the infestation of rodents, but it made her feel better to know he was coming. In spite of all the aggravation he caused her, Raven did inspire confidence.

When his knock finally came she raced to the door. "What took you so long?"

"I stopped to get this." He held up a small paper bag.

As he started toward the sliding glass doors Pat grabbed his arm. "Don't open those! I'll have a room full of mice."

He grinned. "You can always share my room. The wildlife around here is too lazy to climb stairs."

"Is that why you gave me the cottage?" she demanded indignantly. "You knew what was out there?"

"I thought you'd enjoy them." He took her hand.

"Come on, it's cocktail time. You don't want to keep your guests waiting, do you?"

"Uninvited guests come under the heading of pests," she advised him succinctly.

Raven merely laughed and pulled her through the opened door. He took a hard roll out of the paper bag and broke off a piece.

"You're not going to feed the little varmints!" she cried.

Within seconds a small furry creature bounded out of the grass. Sitting on its haunches like a dog, it raised its tiny forepaws under its chin.

Pat's eyes widened. "That isn't a mouse."

"No, it's a chipmunk. There are hundreds of them around the lodge. Very bright little critters—they've learned to tell time."

"You're putting me on!"

Raven chuckled. "Well, it almost seems like it. After they discovered that guests return to their rooms about this time to have a drink out on the patio, they invited themselves to the party. People keep peanuts for them, or save rolls from dinner the night before."

The first chipmunk had been rapidly joined by others, all interested in the crumbs Raven was distributing. He laid a trail to Pat's feet and handed her a chunk of bread.

"Would you like to feed them?"

As she slowly held out the bread to avoid startling him, one small animal stood up on his hind legs, displaying a soft, cream-colored chest that contrasted with his tan fur. Bright black eyes were fixed unwaveringly on her as he daintily took the morsel out of her fingers.

Pat was disappointed when all the bread was gone and her visitors left too. "Talk about eat and run," she observed.

"Maybe they had another party to go to," Raven consoled her with a twinkle in his eyes.

"That must be it." Inhaling deeply, she looked out at the stunning scenery. "Isn't that pine scent heavenly? I love Wyoming. It's so quiet and peaceful."

"That quiet is deceptive. It's hard to believe there's more wildlife out there than people in the city."

"Well, that might be a slight exaggeration."

"No, it's true. Every winter ten thousand elk come to the outskirts of town to be fed when the snow covers their normal pastures. And that's just one species." He pointed to a dense stand of dark green trees in the distance. "If we had binoculars you might be able to spot a moose out there. Those woods are full of them."

"This close to civilization?"

Raven nodded. "People don't bother them. The rare sightings are the bighorn sheep. There are plenty of them in the mountains but they're very elusive."

"It's almost as though nothing has changed but the town. Wouldn't you love to know what it was like back in the old days?" Pat asked wistfully.

Raven looked at his watch. "Grab your car keys and we'll go find out."

"I don't understand."

"You will when we get into town."

It was almost seven o'clock when they reached the village and parked the car. There seemed to be an inordinate amount of people milling around the town square, and Pat soon discovered why.

Camera laden tourists who had been chattering animatedly suddenly fell silent as the sound of horses hoofs were heard in the distance. A man on a galloping black horse rode into the square, pursued by a dozen others. They overtook him with drawn guns as the tourists watched gleefully. The man's hands were tied behind his back and he was led, still mounted, to a town arch fashioned from dozens of elk antlers.

While a rope was thrown over the arch, the charges against "Clover the Killer" were read. Before the noose could be placed around his neck, the outlaw made an impassioned speech in his own defense. In a spirit of magnanimity, he was granted a chance to "shoot it out" with the sheriff. A frenzied popping of blanks rang out and both men fell "wounded."

As Clover was led away, draped over the saddle of his horse, a little boy next to Pat exclaimed, "It's just like television!"

Raven smiled down at Pat as the crowd started to disperse. "Still think you'd like to have lived in the Old West?"

"Why not? I'm a law-abiding citizen. I'd have had sense enough not to rustle cattle."

"Sometimes that's not enough. I'll take you over to the Silver Dollar bar and tell you about Cattle Kate."

The cocktail lounge that Raven led her to had a long polished bar inlaid with seemingly endless silver dollars. They gleamed in the overhead lights like shining polka dots.

"There must be hundreds of them," Pat exclaimed.

"Two thousand two hundred and thirty-one," Raven answered. "How's that for the answer to a trivia question?"

"You're a regular fountain of knowledge. Tell me more."

"First let's find a place to sit down." He grimaced. "This damn leg is giving out."

Pat was immediately remorseful. "You shouldn't have been standing that long. You're doing so well that I forget you're disabled." She stopped abruptly. "Oh, Raven, I didn't mean—"

He gave her a mischievous smile. "That's all right. I'm not handicapped in any way that really matters."

Her remorse dried up. "You're incorrigible. I don't know why I waste my sympathy on you."

He lowered himself into a chair with a grunt of relief. "Because you're a sweet, warm-hearted person under that prickly, independent exterior."

"That's a rather dubious compliment," she remarked dryly.

"Would you rather I told you what an incredibly lovely mouth you have?" His voice dropped a note. "It's shaped exactly right for kissing—except when you compress it like that."

She refused to let the conversation become personal. "I'd rather you told me about Cattle Kate."

"No, you wouldn't. She came to a bad end."

"At the hands of men, no doubt."

Raven's mischief died. It was replaced by compassion as his tawny eyes rested on the lovely face that shouldn't have had cause for such cynicism. "That's been your experience, hasn't it, Pat?"

"It doesn't matter. I've learned to live with it." Her answer was curt, discouraging further discussion.

But Raven didn't take the hint. "Have you? Hiding yourself away isn't living with something, it's refusing to face it. Do you intend doing that for the rest of your life?"

She pushed back her chair and stood up. "If you're rested we can start back. I'll get the car while you wait here."

Raven sighed. "No, I'll go with you." He got to his feet, leaning heavily on the cane.

The lines of pain in his face touched Pat as much as they annoyed her. "You don't have to put on the big male macho act for me. The fact that I have two good legs and you don't is no slur against your virility."

"I'm probably the only man in Wyoming who knows that your legs are not only good, they're fantastic." His eyes traveled mockingly over her jeans. "But don't worry, I'll keep your secret."

"Stay here," she ordered. "I'll be back to pick you up."

Pat stalked out of the bar, fuming all the way to the car. Raven was so sure he had her figured out! He refused to accept the fact that she wasn't afraid of men, just disinterested. But that was something a man like Raven would never understand—or accept. It was the age-old battle of the sexes with him. Any woman who resisted became an automatic challenge.

Pat set her small chin firmly. Raven Masters might not know it yet, but he was fighting a losing battle. No amount of compliments, neither taunts nor trickery, were ever going to make her lower her guard again.

Relations were strained between them on the way back to the lodge. Pat wouldn't have been surprised if Raven had made some excuse about dinner, but he didn't.

"Will an hour give you enough time to get ready?" There was courtesy in his voice but no warmth.

"Plenty of time," she answered coolly. He was probably wondering why she needed even an hour. "I'll meet you in the lobby."

Pat had to take a bath instead of a shower because she'd forgotten to buy a shower cap. Wrapped in a towel afterward she carefully made up her face, although all the makeup she had in her purse was a lipstick and a tube of mascara.

She regretted the lack of green eyeshadow that would have complimented the vivid print, but the result of her meager supplies was more than satisfactory. Anticipation had brought a becoming flush to her cheeks, and her eyes sparkled like emeralds in their frame of sooty lashes.

She didn't have any pins or combs to arrange her hair in the intricate style she would have liked. But after a vigorous brushing Pat decided it looked adequate— which wasn't the adjective anyone else would have used. The shining auburn fall framed her face enchantingly before curling around her ivory shoulders.

The unaccustomed preparations took more time than she had bargained on, and Pat was late. Raven was waiting in the lobby, a slight frown on his face. When she came through the door he gave her a cursory glance before looking away. His eyes returned in a startled double-take.

"I'm sorry I'm late," she said, enjoying his surprise.

"Is it really you?" He seemed dazed.

"In the flesh." She whirled around to display her smooth back.

"But how . . . where did you . . ."

"I didn't know what to do with myself so I decided to go shopping," she said carelessly. "Do you like it?" She could read the answer on his face but Pat had an overwhelming urge to hear him say it.

He cupped her chin in his palm, looking down at her with eyes that held pinpoints of light in their tawny depths. "You're the sexiest looking caretaker I ever had."

"Is that the best you can do?" she asked, disappointed.

His long fingers stroked the delicate skin in back of her ear. "I could do a lot better if we were alone."

She pulled away from his caressing hand. "I don't want you to *do* anything. You could just say you like my dress."

"I like your dress," he parroted obediently. "I also

like what's in it. At this moment I'm having trouble resisting the urge to take you in my arms right here in the lobby."

"If I'd known your reaction was going to be so unfettered, I wouldn't have bought it," she answered lightly.

Raven chuckled. "I was only being truthful. When I spring at you later I don't want it to come as a surprise."

"Could you restrain yourself until after dinner? I'm starved."

It was the most delightful evening Pat had spent in a long time. She had almost forgotten the pleasure of dining with a charming companion rather than sharing a solitary meal with Janus. Raven exerted himself to be entertaining, making her laugh and conveying the gratifying impression that there was no one he'd rather be with.

When dinner was over and he walked her back to the cottage, it seemed fitting to wind up the evening with a nightcap together. Room service provided two snifters of brandy which they carried out to the patio.

It was a perfect summer evening with crickets chirping in the undergrowth and a few night birds making sleepy noises. In the far distance the moon glistened on the snowcapped mountain peaks, and every now and then a fish jumped in the lake.

Pat was filled with a peaceful kind of euphoria. "Don't you feel sorry for all those poor souls stuck in big, crowded cities? They don't even know there are this many stars in the sky."

"Every place has something to recommend it," Raven responded quietly.

"That sounds remarkably glib."

"It's true, though. Take New York for instance," he

said casually. "You can't deny the sense of energy in the air; the feeling that something exciting is just around the next corner."

"Yes, the chance of getting mugged." Pat's glow of well being was starting to drain away.

"Now who's generalizing?"

She got up restlessly, moving to the edge of the patio, out of the light coming from the cottage. "I'd expect you to defend New York; it's your kind of town. But it isn't for everyone. You have to be hard and tough to survive."

He got up to join her in the darkness. "That's probably true of any place."

"Not like New York," she said bitterly, turning away.

Raven's firm hands on her shoulders turned her back to face him. "Aren't you confusing a whole city with one person?"

"Don't spoil it, Raven," she begged. "It's been such a nice evening."

"You're right. Tonight I saw what you must have been like." His hands tangled in her long hair, pulling her head back so he could stare down at her. "You're an enchanting lady. I won't let all of that beauty and vitality go to waste."

"You're not God! You have no right to try and direct my life!"

"I'm only trying to make you start living it, to stop being afraid of all human contact."

She was acutely conscious of his hard, lean body just inches from hers, of the strength of his long-fingered hands. A pulsing excitement that she tried to ignore started in the pit of her stomach. "I might be more impressed with your altruism if I didn't know its true purpose. Spending one night with you would solve all my problems. Is that what I'm supposed to think?"

"It might be a start."

Before she could stop him, Raven drew her into his arms. His fingers traced an erotic pattern down the tiny bones of her spine, sending a shock of awareness through her. When she flinched away instinctively, her body curved into his, molding closely to its length. The impact of his muscled loins made Pat stiffen and draw in her breath sharply.

"The man who made you like this must have been incredibly selfish," Raven said softly. "He took everything without giving anything in return, didn't he?"

Raven's arms wrapped around her bare back, his hands gliding inside her dress to cup around the fullness of her breasts. The initial touch left her powerless to resist, and when his fingers gently manipulated her hardened nipples, Pat felt a flame of desire ignite. A tiny moan escaped from her parted lips.

Raven's mouth covered hers, his tongue probing delicately with an erotic suggestion that left her clinging to him. He gratified all of her senses, urging her toward an ecstasy she knew instinctively would be like nothing she had ever experienced.

"Let me show you how it should be, sweetheart," he whispered huskily. "Let me bring you the pleasure you deserve."

She didn't have the will to stop him when he gently slipped the dress off her shoulders, leaving her bare to the waist. Raven's eyes glowed as he gazed at the pink-tipped whiteness of her breasts gleaming in the moonlight. When he leaned forward to circle one small bud with his tongue, Pat's fingers tangled convulsively in his thick dark hair. It had never been like this with Carl. Never had she felt this slow, arousing of passion that mounted so wildly she wanted it to go on forever.

Raven's lips were turning her into a pillar of fire that destroyed all her inhibitions. As he continued to caress her, Pat's shaking fingers kneaded the corded muscles of his back, tracing them down to his waist. She pulled the shirt out of his slacks and ran eager hands over the warm, taut skin beneath his belt, possessed by a primitive need to touch his splendid male body.

Raven's groan was one of pleasure. He pulled her hips against his, letting her know the strength of his desire. His lips rained kisses over her face and neck as he murmured, "My beautiful, passionate darling. You want me, don't you?"

Pat knew she could never save herself. With a supreme effort she begged him to do it for her. "Please, Raven, don't do this to me!"

He crushed her in his arms, burying his face in the scented softness of her hair. "Just let it happen, sweetheart. You don't have to fight the world anymore. I'm going to take care of you."

The words penetrated slowly into her fevered brain. *I'm going to take care of you.* That was the excuse Carl had given for stripping her of everything before betraying her. She had given up all her gifts freely—love, money, career—believing he cared about her, just as she was being seduced by Raven into a similar trap. How could she have fallen for the same line again? Raven was no different from any other man. He even used the same empty platitudes.

Twisting sharply out of his grasp, she hurriedly slipped into the top of her dress. "I think you'd better leave now."

He stared at her incredulously. "What is it, Pat? What did I say?"

She turned her back, hugging her arms tightly around her trembling body. "It isn't important. I just want you to go."

"Not without an explanation." He turned her around. "A moment ago you wanted me as much as I want you. What happened?"

"I changed my mind," she said miserably, since she couldn't very well deny her response.

"That isn't good enough." His fingers bit into her shoulders. "I want to know why"

She couldn't look at him. "Surely you've been turned down before. It's a woman's prerogative." She was very conscious of his eyes boring into her.

Finally he said, "There's a word for what you just did—and it isn't a nice one."

"Use it then if it makes you feel any better." Pat's control was slipping. The nearness of his lithe body was seducing her own treacherous one. "Only please *go*!"

His hands fell mercifully away. Even in the dim light Pat could see his expression of contempt. "Gladly. We both almost made a serious mistake."

Chapter Five

*P*at didn't fall asleep until almost morning, with the result that she overslept. The dark hours had been filled with bitter self-recrimination and renewed resolve—but also with haunting regrets. The memory of Raven's fervent caresses was difficult to banish. There was no doubt that he would have brought ecstasy. But at what cost?

As soon as she awoke and saw how late it was, Pat phoned Raven's room with a feeling of apprehension. The bank was already open; it would give him one more thing to be angry about. Because in spite of everything, she was still obligated to act as his chauffeur.

When there was no answer she was momentarily

stunned. Had he checked out and left her there? But how could he get around? A call to the desk brought the solution.

"Mr. Masters took a taxi to his appointment," the clerk informed her. "He would like you to pick him up there at eleven o'clock."

Yesterday Pat would have thought that Raven hadn't awakened her out of consideration. Today she knew it was because he wanted to spend as little time in her company as possible. It was a depressing thought. How was she going to bear the long trip home with Raven in the next seat, hating her? It was useless to tell herself it was better this way. Pat had the forlorn feeling that she had lost something very precious.

After driving downtown she accomplished a minor miracle, finding a parking place almost directly in front of the bank. Her timing was right too; Raven came out a few minutes later. His appearance didn't do anything to reassure her, however. He was wearing a frown. When Pat tapped the horn lightly to attract his attention the frown disappeared, but he still looked austere.

She went on the offensive as soon as he had settled his long frame in the car. "You didn't have to take a taxi this morning; I would have driven you. All you had to do was call me."

He looked mildly surprised. "There wasn't any point in your waiting in the car."

Pat was thrown off balance; she was expecting recriminations. "Well, I just wanted you to know that it wasn't my fault," she muttered.

His well-shaped mouth had a mocking tilt. "Why all the hostility? Are you feeling guilty this morning, Pat?"

"Certainly not!" She gave her full attention to starting the car, purposely misunderstanding his question. "I have nothing to feel guilty about. I just told you I was available if you wanted me."

He raised a derisive eyebrow. "I don't think that's a subject we'd better pursue."

Pat's cheeks bloomed like roses. "Where do you want to go now?" she asked, without looking at him.

"I'm all through. We can start back unless there's something you want to do."

"No, I want to go home."

"Too much excitement for you here?"

The one thing Pat knew was that she couldn't go through two hours of Raven's baiting. Somehow she would have to find a way to set things straight between them.

She gripped the steering wheel tightly. "I'm sorry about last night, Raven. I'm sure you think I led you on just for kicks, but it wasn't that way."

"I know," he said calmly.

She gave him a startled glance. "But you said . . . I mean you acted so . . ."

"I'm the one who should apologize." He smiled ruefully. "I'm afraid I wasn't being very objective last night."

"Neither of us meant for it to happen," she murmured. "We both just got carried away."

"In the interest of harmony I could agree with you, but we both know that's not true. I wanted you and you wanted me. Why did you retreat behind the barriers again, Pat?"

"Please, Raven! I'd rather not talk about it."

"Pretending it didn't happen isn't going to change anything. For those few moments in my arms you were being yourself—a warm, passionate woman admitting her need for love."

"Men talk so glibly about love when what they really mean is sex," she answered bitterly.

"Sex isn't a dirty word, Pat. It can—and should be—a beautiful and fulfilling experience."

"You can dress it up in any language you like. It's still just a biological urge," she said curtly. Conscious of his golden gaze appraising her set face, Pat kept her eyes straight ahead.

"If that's the way you feel, you were right to back off last night."

"Don't pretend you felt any differently! I just happened to be the one who was there."

He shook his head in wonder. "I don't know how such a captivating woman can underrate herself so inconceivably. I'm not a high school boy, my dear, aroused uncontrollably by the sight of a female body—no matter how lovely."

Pat was acutely embarrassed, remembering Raven's ardent eyes devouring her naked breasts in the moonlight. The memory of her own unfettered response was more upsetting though.

"I gather that I'm supposed to believe I'm something special. How long do men think they can get away with that same tired line?"

"Whether you're willing to admit it or not, there's been something special between us since the day we met."

"You keep saying that but it isn't true," she denied vehemently. "You're just bored and at loose ends. Under normal circumstances you wouldn't look at me twice."

"Even *your* self-esteem can't be that low. Although you go out of your way to deny your femininity, you must look in the mirror occasionally."

"I suppose some men find me attractive," she admitted grudgingly. "But I'm not your type."

"You're sure you know what that is?"

"Yes." Her soft mouth set grimly.

Even if she hadn't seen Suzanne Turner, Pat could have described her. And there must be dozens like her in New York. Glittering, accommodating females who would gaze adoringly at him and tell him how wonderful he was. That was Pat's own novelty—the fact that Raven thought she was playing hard to get. The conquest was all he was interested in.

"I'm not going to be the little plaything you use to relieve your boredom," she stated angrily.

His golden brown eyes were as hard as the agates they resembled. "And I'm not going to be the forum for your revenge—not any longer."

She gave him a startled glance. "I don't know what you mean."

"Somewhere along the line you met a real louse. I'm sorry about that but I refuse to be held accountable for his sins. If you want to think that all men are cast from the same mold, that's your problem."

"I never asked for your help." She accelerated to pass the car ahead, anxious to be free of him.

"You need somebody's," Raven muttered. Frustration etched deep lines around his mouth. "What did the guy do that was so terrible? Can't you understand that even men are human?"

"I'd expect you to be on his side," she said coldly.

"I'm *not* on his side. If I knew who he was I'd hunt him down and beat the hell out of him—without even knowing why." Raven's expression softened as he gazed at her delicate profile. "No, that's not true. I'd take him apart limb by limb for leaving you a beautiful, empty shell."

Is that what he thought she was? Pat almost wished Raven was right about her. Vacuums couldn't feel pain—or desire. "You're being overly dramatic," she said carefully. "I'll admit that I once had an unpleasant experience with a man, but it hasn't warped my life. If it eases your male pride to think that, go ahead, I don't mind." She was aware of his intense scrutiny.

Finally he said, "Okay, Pat, you win. Maybe I pictured myself as a brave knight on a white charger, freeing a beautiful maiden from her imprisonment. But if the maiden doesn't want to be rescued, then I'm just a meddlesome guy making unwanted waves." He was suddenly intent. "Is that the way you see it?"

She smiled wistfully, unwilling to make it final. "Good samaritans seldom get thanked for their efforts."

"I wasn't looking for gratitude."

"I can't give you any of the things you *are* looking for."

"Can't, or won't, Pat? Never mind, it's the same thing in your case." He reached over and covered the hand that gripped the wheel until her knuckles were white. "I have a feeling that it would have been sensational between us, honey, but the price is too high for you. You'd have to trust me, and I realize you're unable to let any man close. I honestly thought I could be part of the solution, but since I only added to the problem I'll let you alone from now on."

It was what Pat had been hoping for ever since their paths crossed, yet his quiet statement left her desolate. It was the only sensible course, however. Their physical attraction for each other was undeniable, and neither of them could keep going through the torture of denial.

Pat drove the rest of the way in a haze of misery, although Raven did his best to make it easy for her, carrying on a light conversation that carefully avoided anything controversial. He was like a well-bred guest making the best of an awkward situation. It was a relief when they arrived at the ranch.

Mattie and Janus came out of the house to greet them. Pat had called her from Jackson Hole, asking her to take care of the dog overnight.

"Did you have a good time?" the housekeeper asked.

Janus's exuberant greeting saved Pat from having to reply, and Raven concentrated on swinging his long legs out of the car.

Mattie didn't seem to notice that neither had answered. "I'm glad you got Pat away from here for a while," she told Raven. "She needs to get a little fun out of life now and then."

His enigmatic eyes held Pat's for a long moment. "Good-bye, Pat. Thanks for the ride."

"My goodness, that sounds so final," Mattie protested. "She's only going down the road."

With a hasty wave, Pat opened the car door for Janus and drove to her own cottage, Raven's farewell echoing in her ears. There was no doubt about his meaning; he had finally given up on her. Whatever there might have been between them was over.

The next week was the most difficult of Pat's life. All the joy seemed to have gone out of the world and she found herself dreading each new day. She stayed away from the main house as much as possible, going there only to do Mattie's errands. In the course of her work it was inevitable that she would see Raven every now and then, but they had no conversation. If he happened to see her he would wave and she would wave back. That was the extent of their contact.

Pat found out from Mattie that Raven's leg was improving rapidly. It was her only ray of hope. If he'd only go back to New York she would forget him, Pat assured herself. It was seeing him occasionally—plus the suspense of never knowing *when* she would see him—that kept her in this unsettled state.

Every glimpse brought a memory—Raven's deep, rich voice teasing her; his hard, lean body taunting her with its promise. A golden tan had replaced his former pallor, making him even more wildly attractive. But it wasn't just the leaping excitement he brought; Pat missed his company too. Raven could make the simplest things fun. The world took on color when he was around.

On her solitary walks with Janus, Pat couldn't help thinking what a wonderful role model Raven would be for the hero of a novel. He was just the sort of man who would have had the courage it must have taken to set out on those long wagon trail treks. And if he and the heroine, who was vaguely formulating in her mind, had met—Pat never allowed herself to explore the idea any further. It was already too intriguing and she had vowed never to write again.

One afternoon the house phone rang. Pat had just happened to return for her sunglasses; otherwise she wouldn't have been there. Since the call was to change her life, she would always wonder afterward if it wasn't fate. At the time she merely thought Mattie needed her. It wasn't Mattie, however.

"Could you come up to the house, Pat?" Raven's deep, remembered voice sent the blood rushing to her head. "I'd like to talk to you about something."

Pat's thoughts were in turmoil all the way up to the house. What could Raven possibly have to say to her? Was he going to tell her he had missed her company— as she had missed his? Was he going to suggest that they be friends again? And if he did, what should she say? No matter how tormenting, wasn't it better to leave well enough alone? In her heart Pat only hoped she'd have strength enough to choose that course.

Raven was waiting for her in the driveway. "Let's go into the den where we can have privacy," he said in a low tone.

Pat looked at him doubtfully. His voice had a conspiratorial ring, but it certainly wasn't amorous. What was he up to? She followed him warily into the den.

His first words were not even remotely what she expected. "I want to talk to you about Mattie."

Pat stared at him blankly. "What about her?"

"Has she complained to you about anything?"

"I don't know what you mean."

"I was wondering if anything was bothering her," Raven said slowly.

"I'm sure she's completely happy here." Pat's answer was swift. Surely he wasn't thinking of replacing Mattie? This was her home; she didn't have anywhere else to go.

"I know she's happy, what I'm asking about is her health. A couple of times I've found her bent over the kitchen sink. Her face was pale and there was perspiration on her forehead, but she insisted that she was all right."

It was news to Pat. She and Mattie were good friends. They talked about all sorts of things, and she *had* noticed that the other woman was a little touchy about growing older. She didn't want anyone to think she couldn't do all the things she'd always done. Pat hadn't given it much importance. She'd merely resorted to subterfuge to save the older woman work.

"Mattie isn't exactly young anymore," Pat answered carefully. "But I'm sure she can still do her job."

"You're missing the point. I'm concerned about *her*, not her performance."

Pat felt a sense of relief that Mattie's job wasn't in jeopardy. It reminded her fleetingly of the housekeeper's assertion that Raven was a kind man. "She probably gets tired—this is a big house to take care of."

"If that's all it is, maybe I should get in some extra help."

"Don't do that," Pat warned urgently. "She'd think you were trying to ease her out."

Raven ran an impatient hand through his thick, dark hair. "You two make me feel like Simon Legree. How can I convince you that I'm not about to throw either of you out into the cold, cruel world?"

Pat was more concerned about Mattie than she was about herself. "You mustn't put it on that basis," she cautioned. "Mattie has her pride. If she thought you were just keeping her on out of charity she'd quit in a minute."

Raven's handsome face wore a look of frustration. "I'm only trying to find out if there's anything wrong with her."

"Not that I know of, but I can—" A knock at the door brought her words to a halt.

Mattie's appearance created a small pool of guilty silence as Raven and Pat avoided each other's eyes. The housekeeper looked at them tentatively. "Am I interrupting something?"

"Not at all, come right in." When she continued to look uncertain Raven said, "I asked Pat up here because . . . uh . . . I'd like her to drive me into town. The city newspapers should be in and I want to check the stock market reports."

"Is that all?" Mattie's face cleared. "You two looked so serious that I got worried."

"No need to," Raven replied smoothly. "I'll walk down with you to get the car, Pat."

As Pat got to her feet she stared at the older woman closely, but there was nothing to bear out Raven's conjecture. Mattie's plump face and comfortably padded figure appeared the same to her as they always had.

"While you're in town would you bring back some of that chocolate crunch ice cream from Shedloe's?" The housekeeper gave a self-conscious little laugh. "It's sinfully rich and I certainly don't need the extra pounds, but I've had a hankering for some all week."

"Then, you should have it," Raven declared. "Life is too short to deny oneself the simple pleasures, I always say."

Pat shot a sharp glance at him but Raven's expression was bland. Still, she accompanied him with an uneasy feeling. "I guess we really do have to go into town now because of Mattie's ice cream," she commented.

"Just remind me to pick up the papers." He grinned. "There's nothing wrong with her mind anyway."

Pat grinned back. "Or her appetite." She felt suddenly lighthearted; this was the way it used to be with Raven. If only nothing happened to spoil it!

While he went to the newsstand in the drugstore, she did some errands of her own. Then they met at the ice cream parlor where Raven suggested a soda.

They sat on wire chairs at a little round marble table, and Pat felt transported back in time. That was the nice thing about small towns; not much changed. She might have been sixteen again, out on a date with her best boyfriend. It was useless to remind herself that Raven was neither a boy nor a friend, Pat's heart persisted in beating joyously as they talked and laughed over their ice cream. The illusion was shattered abruptly when they were joined by a beautiful, leggy blonde.

"I heard you were back, Raven, but I couldn't believe you wouldn't call," she pouted, giving him a reproachful glance shaded by long eyelashes.

"I've been slightly out of commission, Laura." He turned to include Pat. "Do you know Pat Lee?"

Mattie had introduced her to Laura Cameron, whose father owned the ranch adjacent to Raven's. The two women exchanged polite greetings before Laura turned back to her primary interest.

"We were all so sorry to hear about your accident." Her eyes swept appreciatively over Raven's lithe body. "I must say you don't look any the worse for wear."

"I've been getting excellent care."

"I see." A slight frown puckered Laura's smooth forehead as her gaze flicked briefly to Pat.

His tawny eyes gleamed with amusement at her misconception. "Yes, I don't know what I would have done without Pat," he declared mischievously.

"All I did was drive him around," Pat said sharply. "It wasn't really part of my job."

"I'll be happy to take over for you," Laura offered. Her lovely face suddenly lit with animation. "In fact, I have a super idea. Why don't we drive over to my place and go for a swim? It's a perfect day for it."

"Sounds good," Raven answered. "How about it, Pat?"

"You go ahead, I have work to do," she replied curtly. He knew perfectly well that she wasn't included in the invitation!

After her initial dismay, Laura voiced polite regrets, although she didn't go so far as to urge Pat. In fact she rushed Raven out to her car before Pat could have second thoughts. "Don't worry about picking him up," she tossed over her shoulder. "I'll see that he gets home safely."

Pat couldn't hear Raven's low-pitched comment, but Laura's answering trill of laughter made her hands clench impotently. Raven was certainly getting better; he was back to chasing girls. One minute he was having a soda with her, pretending he was enjoying himself, the next minute he was accepting a better offer. There was no doubt about how acquiescent that blonde would be! Not that it mattered to her, Pat assured herself. It was just that it was insulting to be dropped like a used tissue.

Pat fumed all the time she was waiting for Mattie's ice cream to be packed in a cylindrical carton and placed in an insulated bag. Raven had forgotten all about his housekeeper's request. Right now the poor thing's mouth was probably watering. Well, at least one of them had some sense of responsibility, she thought righteously.

When Pat delivered the ice cream, Mattie asked her in to share it, but she declined. "We had a soda in town. This is all for you."

"My goodness, I can't eat the whole thing by myself," the older woman protested, but she didn't seem too daunted by the prospect.

Pat spent the rest of the afternoon weeding the flower beds. Uprooting the pesky dandelions that were choking the roses satisfied her deep-seated need to destroy something. It rid her of some of her aggressions, and after a refreshing shower she felt pleasantly relaxed. Until Mattie phoned.

"Would you like to come up for dinner, Pat? Mr. Masters called to say he wouldn't be home, and I have a big pot roast."

It was what she had been expecting, but he would just have to eat leftovers tomorrow night. "No, thanks," she replied coolly. "That soda ruined my appetite."

Mattie sighed. "I wish I could say the same thing."

Pat was reading in bed when Laura brought Raven home. Her eyebrows rose as she looked at the clock. It was only a little after ten. Then her mouth tightened as the thought occurred that they might have returned to the ranch for more privacy than Laura's place offered. It was only a matter of minutes, however, until the blonde's car came back down the driveway with the radio blaring.

A short time later the phone rang. Pat's immediate

reaction was fury; it could only be Raven. Was he feeling at loose ends because his date ended early? He had a lot of nerve phoning her at this hour! Did he think she was at his beck and call twenty-four hours a day?

"Pat, it's Raven. I—"

"If you called to tell me you got home safely, it wasn't necessary," she interrupted angrily. "My only interest in you is the paycheck you sign every month."

"I'm well aware of that," he answered quietly. "I thought you'd want to know that Mattie is sick."

"What's wrong with her?" Pat cried, but Raven had hung up.

She flung on her clothes in a fever of apprehension. What could the trouble be? Mattie had been fine that afternoon.

Raven was sitting on the housekeeper's bed, talking to her in a low soothing voice. The transformation in the older woman was dramatic. She was very pale and her face was taut with pain as she clutched at her stomach.

"What is it, Mattie?" Pat gasped.

"Nothing serious." She could barely get the words out. "Just something I ate."

"I called the doctor," Raven murmured as Pat took his place. "He said he'd come right away."

Pat did as much as she could to make the other woman comfortable. She sponged her forehead with cool water and straightened out the tangled sheets. Without knowing what was wrong, it was all she could do. Mattie kept insisting it was a simple upset stomach, which Pat and Raven knew was impossible. They were both relieved when the doctor arrived.

"Well, Mattie, what's all this?" He was a calm, older man who inspired confidence. "Have you been going off your diet again?"

"Well, maybe a little bit." The words were faint with pain.

"What do you call a little bit?" The doctor was rummaging through his bag. "What have you been up to?"

"I had some ice cream this afternoon," she answered reluctantly.

"Ice cream! You know that's poison." When he saw the blank look Pat and Raven exchanged, Dr. Melton explained, "She has a gall bladder condition, you know."

"No, I didn't know!" Raven exclaimed. "Why didn't you tell me, Mattie?"

She looked faintly ashamed. "It isn't anything special; lots of people have it. Doctors just like to make a big deal out of everything."

"Oh, do they?" Dr. Melton asked dryly. "Well, this little indulgence is going to land you in the hospital—where you should have been long ago."

"It's that serious?" Raven asked in a low voice.

"It isn't life threatening, if that's what you mean. But Mattie's needed this operation for a long time. It isn't going to get any better, and if she keeps going off her diet it's going to get a lot worse."

"I've learned my lesson," she assured him. "I won't do anything foolish again."

"Until next time," the doctor commented disparagingly.

"There's nothing to be afraid of." Raven took both of her hands in his. "It's better in the long run than giving up everything you like to eat." He gave her a strained smile. "What's life without chocolate crunch ice cream?"

"But Mr. Masters, who's going to take care of you?"

"Don't worry about it. I'll manage until you're well."

Pat was grateful for his tacit promise to the older

woman that he wasn't going to replace her. It seemed to be the reassurance she needed.

Since the doctor decided that an ambulance would upset Mattie more than it would benefit her, he took her to the hospital in his own car. She was made as comfortable as possible with a pillow in the back seat of his sedan while Pat and Raven followed in Pat's car.

It seemed that Mattie was in the operating room for an eternity, although the nurses explained that she wasn't under the knife all that time. There were tests that had to be taken first, and routine preliminaries to be gone through. They went out of their way to reassure Raven. Even the stern, older ones found time to have a word with him, Pat noted cynically. She couldn't fault his behavior, though. The nurses might have hoped something would develop, but Raven was only interested in Mattie.

"I'm sure she's going to be all right," Pat told him gently. "It's a routine operation."

"I know," he answered soberly. "But she's so alone in the world."

There was something very touching about his concern. Did Raven know what it was like to be alone in the world too? It didn't seem possible, yet Pat realized that she knew nothing about him. She had been so busy defending herself against his questions that she never thought to ask him any.

"Do you have family, Raven?"

"No, I was an only child and my parents were killed in a plane crash while I was in college." His smile was wistful. "I know what it's like not to have anyone."

"But you have a million friends."

"It isn't the same." At that moment he looked very vulnerable.

Pat's heart twisted even though she knew it was stupid. Raven had a great many people who cared about him. They flocked to him like a magnet, eager to share whatever part of his life he would part with. He couldn't know what real loneliness was.

A nurse came toward them, smiling. "Mrs. Johnson is out of surgery and doing fine."

"Can we see her?" Raven asked.

"You can take a quick peek, but she's still under sedation. After you see that she's okay, I'd suggest you go home and get some sleep. She won't be welcoming any visitors until tomorrow afternoon at the earliest."

Pat and Raven tiptoed into Mattie's room to stand on either side of the narrow bed. She was sleeping, as they had been told, all pain erased from her round face. They stood there awkwardly for a moment before filing out quietly for a conference with the doctor.

"She's going to be fine," he assured them. "A week in the hospital and a few weeks of convalescence at home, and she'll be a new woman."

Pat and Raven spoke little on the ride home. They were both experiencing the letdown that comes after prolonged tension. She felt tired but not sleepy, wondering if he felt the same.

"Would you like a cup of hot chocolate to sort of unwind?" Pat asked tentatively.

"That sounds good." Raven massaged his tight neck muscles. "I'm really beat but I don't think I could fall asleep yet."

"That's why I suggested hot chocolate instead of coffee." She opened the door of the cottage, fending off Janus's ecstatic greeting. "Down, Janus! Where are you getting all this energy? Don't you know it's the middle of the night? Stretch out on the couch if you like," she told Raven. "I'll only be a minute."

She returned a short time later to find that he had taken her suggestion. Raven was lying on the couch with his eyes closed, one hand resting on Janus's head as the big dog curled up contentedly on the floor next to him. They both looked completely relaxed, as though they belonged there. Pat stared at them for a long moment, feeling a heady sense of propriety. Raven's eyes opened under her scrutiny and he started to get up.

"Stay there," she urged. "There's nothing for you to do."

He sat up anyhow, stretching luxuriously. "I think reaction is setting in. I'm so relaxed I could stay here all night."

"The invitation was for cocoa," Pat answered lightly.

He smiled ruefully. "Don't worry, I'm too tired to be any threat to you."

Pat didn't believe that for a moment. Raven was a threat—at least to her peace of mind—just by being in her living room. She carefully set out the steaming cups without comment. They sipped the hot drinks in silence for a few moments while Janus crunched on a dog biscuit.

"One thing I'm glad about," Raven said, breaking the lull. "At least I was here when Mattie got sick—not that there was anything I could do."

"You did a lot just by holding her hand. Mattie's terribly fond of you. She looks up to you, but I think she also considers you family."

Raven shook his head. "If she did she would have told me about this gall bladder thing long ago."

"Not necessarily. Some people don't like to admit to what they see as a weakness. Especially in front of someone who's so . . . so impervious."

He indicated his leg. "Surely you can't mean me."

Pat grinned. "That was an error in judgment, not in equipment."

He gave her a slow smile. "I'm glad you think my . . . equipment . . . is in good shape."

"Don't take it personally," Pat warned, ignoring the creeping warmth that was invading her midsection. "I was explaining Mattie's reaction, not my own. There's another possibility. She told me that you paid all the bills for her husband's illness. Perhaps she didn't want to be an added burden to you."

"That makes me feel even worse! If George were alive she would have confided in him, but she thought I'd consider her an obligation."

"You don't know that. Maybe George was responsible for her habit of secrecy. He might not have wanted to hear about her aches and pains."

"He was her husband!"

Pat smiled cynically. "You make it sound almost holy."

Raven's narrowed eyes were cold. "You've made your opinion of men abundantly clear, but to tar a fine man like George Johnson with the same dirty brush is downright sick. George and Mattie were married for thirty-one years."

Pat had no real doubt about the love there had been between Mattie and her husband. She had been pushed into her disparaging remarks by the tension that always developed between herself and Raven. His icy contempt made her determined not to back down.

"What does that prove?" she asked defiantly. "Just that they stuck it out."

"It's futile to argue with you, but if you'd ever seen them together you'd have recognized a true love affair."

Pat threw back her head, laughing bitterly. "How naive you are! If you'd seen the way *my* husband acted toward me in public you'd have thought the same thing." As Raven's eyes widened she rushed on. "Yes, the man who educated me so liberally was my own beloved spouse. Does that satisfy your insatiable curiosity?" Springing to her feet, Pat went to stare out into the dark night.

"Would you like to talk about it?" Raven asked quietly.

"No!" With her back to him, she hugged her body tightly to ease the pain. Damn Raven Masters anyway! She *didn't* want to talk about it, didn't want to relive the hurt and humiliation. But once the crack in the dam appeared, it widened inexorably. The words burst out of her.

"You want to know why I find it difficult to trust men? Because I know how convincing they can be when they want something. And they *always* want something," she added grimly.

"You must have been very much in love with him."

"Let's just say I thought I was."

"What went wrong, Pat? Was he unfaithful?"

"Among other things." Memories rushed back, endless degrading incidents. She stared out the window, speaking almost to herself. "The bitterest pill was finding out why he married me."

"That would be obvious to any man."

Raven's throaty voice brought her back to the present. Realizing how much she had disclosed, Pat attempted to be offhand. "You don't have to be kind. I don't take it personally anymore. Philandering husbands are a common cause of divorce."

"I have a feeling there's more to the story." He got up to join her. "What else did he do to you?"

"Isn't that enough?" She was very conscious of Raven's masculinity, and she didn't want to be. When he smoothed her hair gently she twitched away from him.

Raven's hand fell to his side. "Not to make you this frightened of human contact."

"Your timing is certainly rotten!" she exclaimed

angrily. "Even *you* ought to know that a pass isn't exactly welcome after what I've just told you."

"I wasn't trying to make one." He cupped her chin in his palm, gazing down at her. "What I'd like to do is comfort you, the way I'd comfort anyone who's been hurt."

"I don't want your pity," she mumbled.

In a sudden uncontrollable movement he gathered her tightly in his arms. "Don't you know the difference between sympathy and pity, you little idiot?" Pat stiffened instinctively, but Raven held her, burying her face in his shoulder and stroking her back gently. "Someday the wounds are going to heal, honey, and you'll meet a man who's worthy of all you have to give."

I already have! The words sprang silent and unbidden into her mind. Raven's arms were a protective shelter she had been seeking all her life. His strength and kindness were genuine. She had observed him long enough to know that. Even now when her defenses were down, he wasn't trying to take advantage of her. Or was he? The habit of wariness chilled her blood.

Drawing away slightly she stared up at him. "Kiss me, Raven," she whispered.

He kissed her forehead tenderly.

"No, I mean really kiss me." She put her arms around his neck, raising her face.

His arms released her and he put his hands on her shoulders instead. Bending his dark head, he touched his lips lightly to hers.

Pat's arms tightened as she crushed her mouth against Raven's tracing the closed line of his lips with her tongue. She molded her body the length of his muscular frame, feeling the strength of his sinewy thighs. His arms wrapped around her convulsively, and he urged her straining body even closer for a long, quivering moment. Then he groaned deep in his throat, carefully easing her away.

"I'm sorry, honey," he muttered huskily. "I didn't mean to do that."

Pat raised drugged eyes to his. "I wanted you to."

She tried to move back into his arms but he held her off. "No, you're tired and upset. It isn't what you really want." His breathing was rapid as he stroked her smooth cheek. "There isn't any doubt about how much I want you, but not this way."

Happiness enveloped Pat in a pink cloud. She was right about Raven! He was as different from Carl as two men could possibly get and still be the same gender. How had she ever questioned Raven's integrity? Pat felt the cold core in her breast melting as both her soul and her body came to life.

She looked up at him with a captivating smile curving her generous mouth. "You once told me that someday I'd come to you willingly. Will a night do just as well?"

He drew in his breath sharply. "Are you sure, Pat? I don't want you to have any regrets."

She slowly unfastened the top button of his shirt. "If you don't make love to me I'm going to regret it for the rest of my life."

Chapter Six

$\mathscr{P}$at's murmured words erased all of Raven's lingering doubts. He held her against him so tightly that she was aware of the restraint he had used before. The throbbing of his body entered her own, igniting a blaze that swept through her almost uncontrollably. Raven's mouth fueled the fire. His tongue explored the moist recess of her mouth with a hunger that corresponded to her own.

They sank down to the carpet, entwined. Raven's hands caressed her as he murmured endearments, pausing only to kiss her eyelids, her throat, the sloping curve of her shoulder. He unfastened her blouse and then her bra, looking at her bare breasts with blazing eyes. Her nipples curled into coral rosettes under his ardent gaze and he took one in his mouth, circling it with his wet tongue until she cried out in delight.

Her fingers wove through the crisp hair on his chest, clutching it tightly as the fever in her blood mounted. When she traced the narrowing V down to his flat stomach, Raven's movements quickened. He stripped off the rest of her clothes, kneeling over her to run his palms from her shoulder blades to her thighs.

"You're so beautiful, my darling. I've wanted to see you like this for such a long time," he groaned. "I knew how lovely you would be."

The sensuous feeling of his fingertips on all of her erotic zones was tantalizing. "I've never wanted anyone like this before," she gasped, arching her body to get closer to his.

"Do you know what it means to hear you say that?" he asked thickly.

Raven's hands slid under her, raising her hips so his mouth could complete the destruction his hands had started. Pat felt as though she would melt in the flame of their mutual desire. She reached for his belt buckle with trembling fingers.

He took over for her, flinging off his clothes before returning to take her in his arms. The initial contact with his hard male contours sent the blood racing wildly through her body. She dug her nails into the firm muscles of his back, moving against him with an urgency that was both pliant and demanding.

"I need you so much, Raven." The words were a whispered plea for release from the exquisite torment that was churning inside her.

"I know, darling," he murmured, gently parting her legs with his knee. "I've always known."

As he completed their union Pat clasped him tightly, filled with a sensation so electrifying that she gasped with pleasure. Raven's driving force carried her higher and higher in an upward spiral that grew more intense with each mounting thrust toward the stars. She reached the dizzying summit in a final crescendo that arched her taut body into his.

Their descent was slow and peaceful as complete fulfillment wrapped them in a cloud of contentment. Their bodies were relaxed, but Raven continued to hold her in a protective embrace, his face buried in the curve of her neck.

When she stirred after a long time, his hold tightened and he wrapped one leg around both of hers. "Don't think you're going to get away just because you've gotten all you wanted from me, woman."

Pat could have told him she would never get enough of him. Instead, she tried to match his light tone. "I didn't think you wanted to spend the rest of the night on my living room floor."

"You're right, I don't. It's getting late." To her dismay he looked at his watch. Was he going to leave so soon? Then he smiled at her, a tender smile that seemed to melt Pat's bones. "Come, my sweet, it's time we went to bed."

It was a night such as she had never experienced. Raven made love to her over and over again, until the velvet darkness turned to pearly gray. He brought her to the brink of ecstasy countless times with his kisses and caresses, then took her over the edge with his hard, lean body. They couldn't get enough of each other, and when they finally fell asleep, it was still twined together.

Pat awoke to find Raven looking at her. She was still in his arms, the way she'd been the night before.

"Hello, beautiful." He smiled and kissed the tip of her nose.

"Hello, handsome." She smiled back.

"How do you feel?" His hand stroked the length of her bare back.

She wriggled suggestively against him. "Mmm, a little more of that and I'll feel even better."

Raven laughed. "You're shameless."

"You're right," she agreed happily. "Isn't it wonderful? I didn't even know it myself."

His face was suddenly serious. "Any regrets?"

"Only one." As his expression changed to alarm she smoothed his eyebrows lovingly. "I'm sorry we wasted so much time."

"Is that all!" He relaxed, fitting her body closer. "I'm glad to hear you admit the error of your ways, but we'll have plenty of time, sweetheart."

"Not really," she said slowly. "Sooner or later you'll go back to New York." It was something she couldn't bear to think about—not now when everything was so perfect.

"That's true, but you'll come with me."

"No." She moved out of his embrace. "I'm never going back there."

His warm breath feathered her ear. "Want to bet I can make you change your mind?"

Pat knew there was trouble ahead if he didn't understand that she meant what she said. As much as she loved him, it would never work. Raven had his business in New York, engrossing work that he enjoyed. He also had friends whose interests were the same. Where would she fit in? At first, passion would be enough to hold him, but how long would it be until he started comparing her to the sophisticated women he was used to? Raven traveled in the fast lane that she hadn't been able to cope with.

"Nothing you can say will change my mind," she told him earnestly.

He chuckled. "I had a different strategy planned."

His mouth closed over hers and his hands began a seductive journey over her instantly receptive body. It didn't change the validity of her arguments, but somehow they didn't seem terribly urgent at that moment. While she was in Raven's arms, being aroused to feverish heights, the future seemed far away.

It was late when they finally arose. Pat laughingly rejected Raven's suggestion that they shower together, and he reluctantly agreed to return to his own house.

"Come back here and I'll make you something to eat," she consoled him. "You must be starved."

Raven grinned. "I'll admit that's the most exercise I've had in a long time."

"Now who's shameless?" she demanded, pushing him toward the door.

His laughter died as he took her in his arms. "Not shameless, grateful—for the privilege of making such an enchanting woman happy." He lifted her chin, looking at her searchingly. "This is only the beginning for us, sweetheart. You know that, don't you?"

Pat felt the prickle of tears tighten her throat. If only he were right. She managed a smile. "It's no time to plan our whole future. If we don't get over to the hospital soon, Mattie will think we deserted her."

Raven was vaguely dissatisfied with her answer but he had to agree. "That's true. I also want to talk to the doctor to be sure Mattie has everything she needs."

Pat drove to the hospital over Raven's protests. "You don't have to treat me like an invalid any longer," he complained. "I thought I proved rather convincingly that I'm almost fully recovered."

One part of Pat was delighted about it, the other part wanted him to remain dependent on her. Once Raven was completely fit there would be no reason for him to remain at the ranch. How would she bear it? Pat tried to ignore the pain, forcing herself to speak normally. "If you think I'm going to ride with a man who drives racing cars, you're crazy."

"I feel a lot safer on a racetrack than I do on a highway," he informed her. "For one thing, the cars are all going in the same direction."

"At a million miles an hour. Just buckle your seat belt and relax. This might take longer but at least I'll get you where you're going in one piece."

They bickered happily, feeling relaxed and secure with each other. All the tension of their former confrontations was gone.

Mattie looked very wan, although she tried to appear cheerful for them. She exclaimed over the flowers they had stopped to buy, and expressed regret over causing so much trouble.

"I feel terrible about keeping you two up half the night."

"Actually, you did us a favor." Raven studiously ignored Pat's sharp intake of breath. "You brought a little excitement into our lives."

"How are you feeling, Mattie?" Pat asked hastily.

"Like someone's been rummaging around inside me for buried treasure," the older woman answered wryly.

"You'll feel better in a few days," Pat consoled her.

"Not if I stay here." Mattie showed a flash of her old spirit. "Hospitals aren't for sick people. You never get any rest. They wake you up to ask you if you want something to make you sleep."

Raven laughed. "At least you're being waited on for a change. Enjoy it while it lasts."

"This isn't my cup of tea, Mr. Masters. I'll be glad to get home."

"The doctor says you're to stay at least a week," he warned. "And that's what you're going to do."

"But what will happen to you all that time?"

"Don't worry about a thing. Pat has turned out to have amazing talents."

She poked him sharply in the small of the back,

muttering too low for Mattie to hear, "You're going to pay for that."

It seemed that the older woman looked at them a little speculatively, but Pat didn't really mind. She felt like broadcasting her love for Raven over the radio.

They were careful to stay for just a short time. Although Mattie professed to be happy to see them, she soon looked very drawn.

When they arrived back at the ranch Raven said, "Wait while I get my shaving gear and toothbrush, and I'll ride back with you."

It was obvious that he expected to move into the cottage with her. "I don't think that's a very good idea," Pat said hesitantly. "There isn't any phone in my place. If the hospital should call they couldn't reach us."

"True. Then I'll wait while you get *your* toothbrush."

In her state of euphoria, Pat hadn't thought beyond the moment. The idea of living with Raven—even temporarily—might not be too sound. She didn't want to get used to falling asleep in his arms and waking up the same way. It was going to be hard enough to give him up when the time came.

"Maybe we ought to leave things the way they are," she said slowly.

They were stopped in front of the main house and he turned her to face him. "We've been given a gift of time, Pat. If you think I'm going to waste a minute of it, you're mistaken. We're going to get to know every single thing about each other. We're going to live together, laugh and talk and love together—and then we're going to make plans."

She knew there couldn't be any, but he was right about one thing. She had been given a precious gift. This week with Raven would be something she would treasure all her life. When he was gone and the sun ceased to shine, she would at least have memories of her own private Camelot.

It was a week that surpassed all expectation. The nights were enchanted and the days filled with joy. It was a combination of being on a honeymoon and playing house. Pat loved cooking for Raven, although it wasn't her strong point. One morning he took over, seating her in a kitchen chair and lecturing her good-naturedly on the proper way to make an omelette.

"I thought you said your brothers taught you every-thing," he commented.

"Except how to cook. Mother wouldn't let us in the kitchen."

"Did you expect your husband to be so dazzled by your skill at plumbing that he wouldn't notice the only thing you knew how to make was hot chocolate?"

It was a tribute to Raven's magic spell that Pat never connected the word husband with Carl. She grinned impishly. "No, I expected him to be so captivated by my ravishing body that he wouldn't think of food."

Raven left the stove to kneel in front of her, linking his arms around her waist. "That's called betting on a sure thing," he murmured huskily.

Pat's heart soared as she looked at this man she loved so much that it was almost an ache. She framed his face in her palms and touched her lips to his.

Raven's arms tightened as he deepened the kiss. He slid her gently into his lap without allowing their mouths to lose contact. Pat twined her arms around his neck, feeling a warm tide rising inside her.

He was lowering her slowly to the floor when the unmistakable smell of burning eggs filled the air. With an exclamation of annoyance he sprang up and snatched the pan off the fire.

Pat gave a small laugh. "That's what happens when you try to do two things at once."

He turned off the stove before coming back to draw her to her feet. "Especially when one of them deserves my full attention."

Raven's lovemaking was something Pat would never grow used to. It wasn't merely his expertise, although that was undeniable. It was the tenderness he showed her along with the passion. When he sought out all the pleasure spots of her body, stroking her until she writhed with delight in his arms, Raven's tawny eyes glowed. His one thought was to please her. She commented on it shyly, in the warm aftermath of their love.

"That's the way you deserve to be made love to." He smoothed her hair gently. "You don't know what it does to me to see you flame in my arms. You're the one who makes it so wonderful."

She had never responded to Carl this way, but he hadn't noticed. Carl's lovemaking was superficial, designed mainly for his own gratification—like everything else in his life. Since he had been the first for Pat, she had nothing to compare him to. She thought that was the way it was supposed to be.

Her long eyelashes fluttered down. "I never even knew it could be like this."

Raven's understanding look correctly assessed her thoughts. His hand curled around her chin, raising her face to his. "Don't think about him, sweetheart, he isn't worth it. Any man who takes his own pleasure selfishly isn't really a man."

Pat's eyes misted over. She traced the curve of his firm mouth with a trembling forefinger. "You're just too good to be real."

The serious look on Raven's face dissolved into one of mischief. Chuckling wickedly, he leaned over to nibble on her ear. "I thought I just demonstrated that I was *very* real. You aren't going to ask me to prove it again so soon?"

Laughter chased away Pat's tears. "Your stamina is awesome, but I think the time has come to stoke the inner man. Only this time I'm going to cook breakfast —or rather, brunch."

Raven glanced at the clock on the bedside table. "Don't bother, we'll get something to eat in town." He threw back the sheet and got out of bed, turning to look down at her sternly. "In the interests of speed we'll shower together, but I expect you to behave yourself."

"Of all the nerve! Whose fault was it the eggs burned?"

A slow smile warmed his golden eyes. "Any complaints?"

As she looked at his perfectly sculpted body, broad shoulders tapering to slim hips and lean flanks, happiness welled up inside Pat. "Not a one," she murmured.

He pulled her to her feet, wrapping his arms around her so their bare bodies were joined along their full length. "Don't look at me that way, woman, or we'll never make it to town."

"Do you really want to?" She kissed the smooth hollow in his throat.

"I thought you wanted to go to the rodeo."

"Is it today?" she exclaimed. "I've lost all track of time."

Raven grinned. "That shows I must have been doing something right."

She pinched him sharply on the bottom. "Enough of your suggestive remarks. We have a rodeo to go to."

The small town was bustling when they got there. Brightly lettered banners were stretched across the main street, and the sidewalks were lined with people waiting for the parade to start. It was the traditional opening for all rodeos, a chance for local dignitaries to preen themselves and cowboys to dress in unaccustomed finery.

At some of the big rodeos like Cheyenne's Frontier Days, called the "Daddy of 'em All," the parade is a lengthy affair. Celebrities promenade by on immaculately groomed horses adorned with ornate, silver-encrusted saddles. The men wear smiles carefully rehearsed for the cameras, and their flamboyant satin shirts and buckskin pants are both costly and pristine. Interspersed among the riders are Indians in full war paint, people dressed as early settlers, and marching bands.

The parade at Cougar Run, the small town that served the surrounding ranches, was a more modest affair. The mayor led the way, but he was the only celebrity. All the people lining the sidewalk were locals, and they returned his greeting, calling him by name. Everyone in the procession knew everyone else, making the proceedings seem like a big block party.

Pat and Raven stood on the sidelines, eating hot dogs and waving along with everybody else. They watched until the last cowboy had pranced by, followed by the small high school band, before strolling to the rodeo grounds.

The stands had filled rapidly. As they were preparing to climb to the top, someone called Raven's name.

"Over here!" Laura Cameron was waving wildly from the front row. "I've saved you a seat."

"Great," he remarked to Pat. "Now we'll be able to see better."

"Well, *you* will anyway." She stiffened as he took her arm. "The invitation wasn't meant to include me—any more than the last one did. Your little friend is trying to cut you out of the herd." Remembered indignation made Pat's eyes sparkle as she recalled the way Raven had left her to go with the other woman.

"I've already been branded." He raised her chin to look down at her with smoky eyes. "You've put your mark on me for everyone to see."

His low, husky voice teased her nerve ends, reminding Pat of what they had shared. There wasn't any doubt about their mutual passion. Raven did belong to her for this small, enchanted period of time. She smiled tremulously at him. "In that case, why are we standing here? Let's go sit in the first row."

Their tender exchange didn't go unnoticed. Laura was subdued as she introduced them to Farley Britt, the young man sitting next to her. Laura's father was on the other side of him. Raven and Dan Cameron were old friends. While they exchanged conversation over the intervening two, Pat turned her attention to the small boy next to her.

It was evidently his first rodeo and he was giving rapt attention to his grandfather, a colorful old gentleman who was explaining the proceedings. The saddle bronc riding event was just starting and the first horse was being saddled in the chute. After the cowboy dropped onto his back, the gate opened. Horse and rider exploded into the arena in a frenzy of motion. The cowboy's left arm waved triumphantly in the air while he gripped a braided rope with his right hand.

"Watch closely, sonny," the child's grandfather instructed. "He can't touch the horse with either hand, and he has to stay aboard for ten seconds."

"Wow, look at him buck!" the little boy shouted as the animal plunged and reared like a rocking horse, with the rider clinging doggedly.

"It's not the straight buckers that spell trouble," the older man advised. "It's those educated broncs you have to watch out for. The kind that change direction and spin around oftener than a pinwheel in a washtub. A rider's bottom never lands in the same place twice when he pulls one of those sky climbers."

Raven and Pat smiled at each other. "Looks as though we have our own commentator," he murmured.

"Do you think he traveled the circuit in his day?" Pat whispered.

"Could be." Raven discreetly assessed the older man's weather-beaten face and spare frame. "He sounds like he's speaking from first-hand knowledge."

The little boy's excitement mounted through the various events, calf roping, bareback bronc riding, and steer wrestling. It reached a climax when the Brahma bull riding contest was announced.

"Look at the bell under that cow's stomach, Gramps!"

"That's a Brahma bull, sonny. Some of them weigh as much as a ton."

"What's the bell for?"

"Just to aggravate him as far as he's concerned. He doesn't care much for music—or anything else either. Those Brahmas are meaner than a rattlesnake in a cactus patch."

The youngster's attention was distracted by several men in clown suits. He pointed excitedly. "Hey, look! I didn't know they had clowns at a rodeo."

"Those men are an important part of a bull riding event," his grandfather explained. "A wild bronc is willing to let bygones be bygones once he's got that pesky cowboy off his back, but a Brahma bull figures the fun's just beginning. He holds a grudge and he's always in a nasty humor. When the rider hits the dirt, the bull wants to pound him into it. Luckily, he takes out his temper on anything with two legs. So while the cowboy's trying to count up if he's got enough unbroken bones to get on his feet, the clowns distract the bull long enough for him to finish adding."

The child's eyes were wide. "What happens if the bull catches one of the clowns?"

"It isn't something their insurance companies look forward to," the older man answered dryly. When he saw the apprehension in his grandson's eyes, he added reassuringly. "That's what those barrels scattered around are for. If it looks like the bull is going to trot off with the honors, the clown makes a running dive inside the barrel. The Brahma thinks that's cheating so he punishes the barrel something fierce. It's a bit like going over Niagara Falls in a beer keg, they tell me, but at least the clown lives to tell about it—except that his ears ring for quite a spell."

Pat and Raven had both been to enough rodeos to know what was going on, but the older man's commentaries added to their enjoyment. When the show was over they expressed their appreciation.

"Just trying to teach my young 'un how courage is spelled," he answered with a twinkle in his faded blue eyes. The humor died as he spoke straight from the heart. "Other sports talk a lot about team spirit and sportsmanship, and a lot of the time that's all it is—talk. But these men practice it. They help each other and they're one hundred percent honest. That's the kind of man I want my boy here to grow up to be."

"He's right, you know," Pat commented to Raven as they watched the older man lead his grandson toward the exit. "Rodeo events aren't fixed."

Raven chuckled. "What could you offer a wild bronc to throw a contest?"

Pat grinned back. "A wild lady bronc?"

Before he could answer, Dan Cameron came over and put his hand on Raven's shoulder. "We didn't get a chance to talk much during the show, Raven. How about you and Miss Lee coming back to our place? We're going to have a little barbecue."

When Raven hesitated, Pat slipped her hand into his and answered for him. "What a nice invitation, Mr. Cameron. We'd be delighted."

On the way to the Cameron ranch Raven was still unsure. "If you accepted for my sake it wasn't necessary."

She turned her head to smile at him. "Yes, it was. I'm tired of your complaints about my cooking."

His fingers wove an erotic pattern up her thigh. "I'll admit it leaves something to be desired, but you make up for it with your other talents."

"Male chauvinist!" She captured his disturbing hand. "All you really care about is my performance in the bedroom."

Raven was abruptly serious. "Don't say that, Pat, not even in fun. I care very much about you—as a person, not just a beautiful, desirable woman."

"I know," she answered softly. It was what made him so special. Pat had never known a man so kind and giving. Her heart swelled with the love she couldn't voice.

The Cameron ranch was more lavish than Raven's spread. Extensive, manicured lawns surrounded a handsome two-story house that overlooked a large swimming pool. Not a leaf cluttered the grass, nor a weed intruded on the precise flower beds. It reminded Pat that Raven's place was beginning to look slightly unkempt. The summer sun made the grass grow like Jack's beanstalk, and she hadn't performed any of her chores lately. It wasn't something Raven would ever complain about, but it had to be done. The question was when? She didn't want to sacrifice one moment of her time with him. Pat shoved the problem out of her mind as they joined the throng around the swimming pool.

It was a very festive party. A bar had been set up at one end of the flagstone terrace, and a three-piece combo played rollicking Western music at the other end. The delicious smell of meat broiling over glowing coals drifted tantalizingly from a huge barbecue pit where a whole steer was slowly turning on a spit.

Raven was greeted with great enthusiasm by his friends and neighbors. He fit in so easily that he might have been one of them. In his tight jeans and Western shirt he could readily be taken for a full-time rancher, Pat reflected. Especially since his interest in the conversations about cattle and feed were genuine.

If only Raven would settle down here permanently. It was an idea that came out of the blue, galvanizing Pat. A tremulous hope filled her. Was it a possibility? They could have a whole life together in this peaceful, unhurried country! Excitement blazed in her eyes as she gazed up at him.

Raven looked at her quizically, aware that something was up, but uncertain of what. "Did something happen that I don't know about?"

"I just had a . . . an idea."

The corners of his firm mouth tilted. "Is that all? I have those every time I look at you."

Pat was too swept up in her delirious thought to respond in kind. "I want to talk to you later when we get home, Raven."

His face sobered. "Is anything wrong, honey?"

Her answering smile was blinding. "No, I think everything might work out perfectly."

"It already has as far as I'm concerned." His voice was a husky murmur.

They were forced to dampen their ardor when they were joined by Laura and the young man who had been with her at the rodeo.

"Laura told me that you're a race car driver, Mr. Masters. That sure sounds exciting." Farley Britt's admiration was evident.

"Actually, I build and test race cars; I don't drive them too often."

"That's even more dangerous."

"Not if they're engineered right in the first place."

"You almost got killed testing a car only a few months ago," Laura reminded him.

He shrugged. "There's an element of risk in most of the things we do. You can't play everything safe or life wouldn't be worth living."

Pat stiffened defensively. Was there hidden meaning in his words? "Putting yourself in a position where you know you can get hurt doesn't sound very sensible to me," she said sharply.

"That's because you're a woman," Farley remarked, with the superiority of youth.

"Isn't that just like a man!" Laura exclaimed in disgust. "Women are just as willing to take chances as men."

"*Some* women are," Raven agreed.

There was no doubt now that his words were aimed at her. Pat looked at him squarely. "And some women profit by experience."

"Or think they have." His eyes held Pat's. "They can also wake up one morning to find they're bankrupt."

"Do you have any idea what they're talking about?" Farley asked Laura.

Raven turned to him with an easy smile. "It's kind of a challenge I made to Pat. I want her to come back to New York with me."

"What kind of a challenge is that?" Laura looked

enviously at Pat. "I only wish someone would make me the same offer. After I finish college, New York is where I'm heading."

Her confidence struck a poignant note. Pat had possessed that same spirit when she set out to conquer the world. How long ago was it—a million years? Laura didn't know the pitfalls that could trip up the unwary, the wide-eyed young women who believed in decency and fair play.

"Why would you want to leave Wyoming? You have everything that matters right here," Pat told her, knowing it was hopeless.

"Are you kidding? There's a whole world out there. I want to experience everything it has to offer," Laura stated confidently.

"Pat considers this place Shangri-la," Raven commented unemotionally. "She thinks she'll shrivel up and die if she leaves here."

Laura had only disdain for such a notion. "She has it backward. Anyone who *stays* here needs to have her head examined."

"That's Raven's opinion too," Pat said bitterly. She must have been out of her mind to allow herself to hope for the impossible.

"I wouldn't put it that strongly," he replied slowly. "Wyoming is beautiful country and this is a good way of life."

"Come on, Raven!" Laura said impatiently. "You couldn't live here full time."

"I could if my work was here. I don't think the place matters, it's what you do there." His eyes were on Pat's strained face.

Pat was in no mood for a sermon when her dreams lay in shreds. As soon as their little group expanded and Raven's attention was diverted, she moved away.

It was an effort to act as though she were enjoying

herself, but Pat worked at it grimly. She talked and laughed with acquaintances, always conscious of Raven's unreadable gaze following her. He let her mingle by herself, though, and Pat thought the subject was closed. It wasn't until they were at home that he reopened it, and then not directly.

"You said there was something you wanted to talk to me about," he reminded her.

"Not tonight, I'm too tired." Her body was taut as he followed her down the hall to the bedroom.

"It seemed very important at the time," he remarked quietly.

"A lot of things do, and then you realize they aren't."

"I think we should talk about it anyway."

Pat's control suddenly snapped. "For heaven's sake, can't I even have any thoughts of my own? Do you have to treat me like a backward child?"

Raven's serious expression lightened briefly. "I thought our relationship was quite adult."

"Adults don't try to control each other's lives," she flared.

He put his hands on her rigid shoulders. "I don't want to control yours; I want to share it."

His gentle touch renewed her desperate hope. If it was even remotely possible that Raven was waiting for her to make the first move, Pat knew she had to do it. She couldn't give him up without trying to salvage their happiness. There was too much at stake to worry about silly pride.

"Then, stay here with me!" The words tumbled out in a rush. "We've been happy, haven't we?" she pleaded.

"Very happy. But this is only an interval." When she stiffened as though he had slapped her, Raven groaned, drawing her resisting body into a close embrace. "You know I didn't mean it that way, darling."

"It's all right," she mumbled, struggling to get away. "I always knew the score."

He held onto her firmly. "You don't honestly believe I consider this a summer fling?" he demanded.

She was drowning in humiliation. Leaning back against the strong arms that restrained her, she pushed futilely against his hard chest. "You don't have to dress it up in fancy words. We've never pretended it was anything else."

"You can only speak for yourself." His eyes narrowed on her flushed face. "Are you telling me that all you feel when I make love to you is physical gratification?"

That was a pale description of the heights she reached in Raven's arms, of the total rapture she felt when his body was wedded to hers. Just the touch of his hand made her glow, and the sight of his strong face relaxed in sleep filled her with tenderness. The love she felt for this man transcended mere physical satisfaction, but it was something he must never know. She was already much too vulnerable—something she had vowed never to be again.

Long eyelashes veiled her too revealing eyes as she murmured, "You know we're good together."

"I'm glad you admit that much," he remarked dryly. "But is that all there is, Pat?"

"What do you want me to say? That I'll give up everything and follow you like a faithful puppy dog?" She succeeded in twisting free. "Well, I won't! You can make up any reasons you like, but the plain truth is I have my own life to live. I don't need you."

His golden eyes surveyed her trembling body. "I could very easily prove you're wrong."

"All that would prove is that you're very experienced. I've already admitted that. Why can't you leave it alone, Raven? Why can't we just enjoy our . . . interlude . . . and part amicably when it's all over?"

He stared at her for a long moment, his thoughts a mystery. Then he shrugged. "If that's the way you want it."

Pat's heart plunged. If Raven cared anything about her he wouldn't have agreed so swiftly. It was a confirmation of what she already knew. Raven's instincts were honorable. He wanted to cloak their affair in polite phrases, but it was better this way—no protestations that she meant more to him than the obvious.

He smiled sardonically. "I feel as though I just completed a business deal."

Pat managed to return his smile, although it hurt terribly. "Would you like to shake hands?"

"No, I'd rather make love to you."

For once Pat wasn't receptive. She felt too destroyed by this latest encounter. "I'm really awfully tired. I think I'll go back to the cottage tonight. I have some . . . uh . . . some things to do."

He started to speak and then thought better of it. "If that's what you'd like," he answered pleasantly. "Sleep well, Pat."

"You too," she mumbled, ducking her head to avoid looking at him as she went out the door.

Chapter Seven

$\mathscr{T}$he cottage felt lonely and deserted that night, even after Pat turned on all the lights. She wandered into the bedroom and started to undress listlessly, knowing she wouldn't sleep. The decision to return to her own place had been the right one, though. She needed some time alone to shore up her defenses.

Janus followed Pat closely, his long waving tail expressing approval. At least one of them was glad to be back. Janus had been sleeping in the kitchen of the ranch house all week, where his accommodations were actually more comfortable than they were at the cottage. He had one of the long, thick pads from an outdoor chaise to lie on instead of his accustomed place on the floor at the foot of Pat's bed. But Janus was a social animal. He preferred company to comfort. He settled down with a sigh of contentment and was soon fast asleep, a blessing denied to Pat. Eventually, however, her tired mind rebelled and she slept too.

Heavy drapes kept out the morning sun. In the twilight atmosphere Pat looked very young and vulnerable. Traces of tears still stained her cheeks, and her slight body made only a small mound in the bed.

Raven's eyes were very tender as he stared down at her. With a soft warning to stifle Janus's joyous greeting, he started to take off his clothes.

Pat's eyes flew open when Raven slid into bed and took her in his arms. "Who . . . how did . . . what are you doing here?"

"I got lonesome."

"You can't just walk into people's houses and get in their beds!"

"I wouldn't want to—only yours."

Pat was having trouble sustaining her indignation with Raven's hands wandering over her body. She made a half-hearted attempt to stop him, not really wanting to. His slow caresses were having a devastating effect.

"What are you doing here?" she repeated.

Raven chuckled. "I trust that's a rhetorical question. If not, maybe this will give you a clue." After nuzzling the curve of her neck, he worked his way up to her ear which he proceeded to explore sensuously with the tip of his tongue.

Pat tried to ignore the leaping excitement that filled her. Raven really mustn't be allowed to think he could win every argument this way. Jerking her head back she said coldly, "Don't I have anything to say about it?"

"Naturally." His fingertips made maddening circles

around her breasts, tantalizing the taut tips without touching them. "But I hoped you'd say yes."

She captured his destructive hands. "You weren't this impetuous last night."

"Would it have done any good?"

The fact that it wouldn't didn't lessen the hurt. Raven had let her go almost casually. "You didn't try very hard to change my mind," she said stubbornly.

"You had worked yourself into a state where you were spoiling for a fight. It seemed only sensible to leave you alone until you'd worked it out of your system."

His calm male reasoning infuriated her. He was treating her like a child who'd had a temper tantrum! "Get out of my bed this minute!" she ordered. "I was *not* spoiling for a fight, and if I had been it was with good reason. You were the one who insisted on snipping away at me, ridiculing me in front of other people just because I favor a different life-style than yours." It didn't bother Pat that her accusations weren't really accurate. All of her pent-up disappointment came boiling out. "If you had any—"

Raven's mouth covered hers with unruffled purpose. When she struggled frantically, he merely held onto her. His lips teased at her closed mouth while his legs wrapped around hers and his arms pinned her against his bare body. Pat's struggles only succeeded in making their contact more intimate. Her writhing slowed to a measured tempo as Raven's male potency began to work its familiar magic. Instead of pushing him away, her palms spread over his chest, smoothing the wiry hair lingeringly.

"That's better." He raised his dark head to smile down at her. "If I'd wanted to argue I would have done it last night."

Pat knew she shouldn't make it this easy, but she wanted him so terribly much. "You're really sure of me, aren't you?" she asked.

He kissed the tip of her nose. "Isn't that the way it's supposed to be? Aren't you sure of me?"

"No." Her long lashes fell. "I thought it was all over last night."

"You didn't!" He raised an incredulous eyebrow. "When are you going to believe that I'll never let you go?"

It was a lovely fiction, they both knew that. But what was wrong with pretending for just a little while? Instead of answering, Pat raised her face to his, parting her lips in mute invitation.

Raven's kiss was slow and arousing. His hands caressed her body, lingering where he knew it pleased her most. She stroked him in the same way, wanting to give as much pleasure as she was receiving. Their reunion was so sweet that they postponed its conclusion, delighting in the touch and taste of each other.

But the tiny flames they lit along the way soon merged into a roaring blaze that threatened to consume them. Raven's kisses became passionate rather than seductive, his hard body demanding rather than suggesting. Pat's own need made her happy to comply. She moved her legs to accept him, raising her hips in a joyous rhythm that matched his. Their taut bodies were filled with rapture so intense that there had to be an end. It came in a thunderous upheaval of sensation that throbbed through both of them at once.

Pat floated gently to earth clinging tightly to Raven. The pounding beat of his heart seemed to enter her own body, making them one person.

After a long time Raven sighed, cuddling Pat closer and kissing her temple. "It's been so beautiful that I hate to see it end." When she looked up in alarm he hugged her tighter. "Not us, silly. I meant this idyllic time alone together." He grinned. "They're springing Mattie today."

She snuggled against him. "Couldn't you persuade them to keep her a little longer?" Pat was instantly remorseful. "No, that's mean. I know how much she wants to come home."

"It's going to be rotten for us, though. I'm not used to sleeping alone," he complained.

"You got through last night all right," she reminded him tartly.

"No, I didn't—it was plain hell. Can't you think of some good excuse for us sharing the same room? Besides the obvious one," he chuckled.

"You know better than that." She gave him an impish smile. "We'll just have to visit a lot."

"Count on it," he said emphatically, before lowering his head to hers.

Mattie's return from the hospital changed Pat's life even more than she had anticipated. It wasn't merely that she and Raven had to be circumspect. Mattie was a virtual invalid for the first week and needed a great deal of care. Pat not only had to cook for her and bring her meals on a tray, she also had to change the bed and help her bathe.

The older woman was very apologetic. "You shouldn't have to do all this for me. You'll wear yourself out."

"I never get tired," Pat assured her.

"How are you going to do your other work and take care of Mr. Masters and me too? You'll have to fix all the meals."

Pat flicked a laughter-filled glance at Raven. "Well, it

won't be up to your standards, but maybe the boss will pitch in and help. He claims to make a superior omelette."

Mattie was scandalized at the very thought. "You mustn't bother Mr. Masters! There's no reason why I can't at least do the cooking."

"The doctor said you're to stay in bed for the first week, and that's exactly what you're going to do," Pat declared, before Raven could agree to volunteer his services. "I was only joking about Mr. Masters."

"Well, I can get up for my meals anyway. That would save you some steps."

"You're to follow the doctor's orders." Raven lent his authority. "Pat and I will manage fine."

He had second thoughts in the days that followed. Pat seemed to be in perpetual motion. For one thing there were three meals a day to prepare, which she wasn't used to. Pat's own breakfast consisted of juice and coffee, and her lunch was a very light one. It would have benefited Mattie to go on the same regimen, but this wasn't the time to suggest it.

Raven's handsome face wore a look of dissatisfaction one afternoon as he watched Pat scurry around the kitchen. "Do you have to do that now? Can't you sit down and talk to me?"

"I have to start dinner," she answered briefly.

"We just had lunch!"

"I'm making a pot roast; it has to cook for hours."

"This is ridiculous!" he exclaimed. "We have to get some extra help in here."

It was the first thing he had suggested when Mattie came home. Pat gave him the same answer she had given then. "This isn't the city. You don't just call an agency and hire temporary help."

"I can hire a nurse," he said grimly.

"No, you can't. It would scare Mattie into thinking

she was really sick, and besides, she'd worry terribly about the expense." Pat knelt down to get a pot out of the cupboard. Her voice was muffled as she added, "She's feeling guilty enough."

"But I never get to see you."

With her back to him, Pat started to peel potatoes. "You're seeing me now," she answered absently, wondering if there were enough eggs for breakfast, or if she'd better go to the store.

Raven came up behind her to put his arms around her waist. "I mean *see* you." He buried his face in the curve of her neck.

Pat's wandering thoughts fled abruptly. She leaned back against him, inhaling his wonderful male aroma. "The culinary union frowns on employers harassing the kitchen help," she commented huskily.

"They'd have a stroke if they knew what I'd like to do to you."

He unfastened the top button of her shirt and then the next two, exposing the creamy curves of her breasts. After caressing them slowly, he slipped his fingertips inside her bra and captured the rosy tips that stiffened under his touch. Pat felt a shock of excitement electrify her body. It intensified when Raven kissed the sensitive spot at the nape of her neck.

"Let's go down to the cottage for an hour," he murmured in her ear.

Pat was torn between duty and desire. "Do you think it would be all right?" she asked longingly.

Raven chuckled. "I think it would be fantastic."

She turned in his arms, raising eager lips. As his head lowered toward hers there was a loud crash, followed by an exclamation. They looked at each other blankly for a moment before rushing down the hall to Mattie's room.

The housekeeper was looking with distress at the

mess she'd caused. She and the bed were both sopping wet, and a vase of flowers lay broken on the floor in another puddle.

"What happened?" Pat gasped.

"When I was trying to pour myself a glass of water I knocked over that nice little vase. I reached out to grab it, but then I spilled the whole pitcher in my lap." Her face was pinched with dismay.

"Well, don't worry about it, there's no harm done," Pat consoled her.

"You'll have to change the entire bed."

"That isn't the end of the world. While I'm getting fresh linens you can put on a dry nightgown."

Mattie pulled at the soggy mess around her midsection. "This might be a good time to take my bath. I'm already soaking wet." She glanced questioningly at Pat. "Unless you have something else to do?"

Pat avoided looking at Raven. "No, I'm free as a bird."

He swore under his breath and stalked out of the room. But what else could she say, Pat asked herself?

Mattie watched Raven's departure with apprehension. "I'm afraid Mr. Masters thinks I'm a real nuisance, and I don't blame him."

"Nonsense! Anyone can have an accident," Pat hastened to assure the older woman. "He probably has his mind on . . . uh . . . the stock market or something."

After she had helped Mattie in and out of the bathtub and made her comfortable, it was time to start dinner. Pat knew that Raven was still sulking because he didn't come in the kitchen to keep her company. Her patience with him was eroding swiftly. It was just as hard on her—harder really—but there was nothing to be done about it. Mattie would have knocked herself out for them if the shoe were on the other foot.

She summoned Raven to dinner after taking the housekeeper her tray.

"Are you going to join me, or do you have more important things to do?" he asked sardonically.

Pat's green eyes sparkled with annoyance. Surveying him coldly she said, "Don't you think you're a trifle old to be acting like a spoiled child? There are a lot of things *I'd* rather be doing too, but it can't be helped."

He sighed. "You're right of course." Pulling her into his arms, he rubbed his cheek against the softness of her hair. "It's just that I'm so damn frustrated! Catching little glimpses of you is almost worse than not seeing you at all."

Pat's resentment was fading fast. "It isn't forever," she reminded him.

"It seems like it," he insisted. "It feels like a million years since I held you in my arms all night long."

She scraped her fingernails lightly up his spine. "Will you settle for part of a night?"

"I'd settle for five minutes!" he declared fervently.

Pat gazed up seductively through long, flirty lashes. "I think we can do better than that. How would you feel about a late date? Perhaps ten o'clock—after Mattie's gone to sleep."

Raven's hand wandered down Pat's back, fitting their hips more closely together. "What if I give her a sleeping pill and come at nine?"

The evening might have dragged for Raven but it flew by for Pat. After dinner she cleaned up the kitchen and made sure that Mattie had everything she could possibly need. Instead of taking Janus for his nightly walk she sent him out by himself, ignoring his pleading eyes. The cottage needed straightening, since she hadn't had time that morning.

It would have been nice to take a warm, relaxing bubble bath, but there was barely time for a shower.

Pat was like a whirling dervish as she brushed her thick auburn hair, sprayed herself with perfume, and pulled a long flowered robe from the closet, all with one eye on the clock. She had just tied the belt around her slim waist when Raven arrived.

"Mmm, you smell fabulous." He sniffed appreciatively. "And you look even better."

Pat's flawless skin was glowing from her recent bath, and in the muted light the tiny lines of fatigue under her eyes weren't visible.

Raven gently fingered the ruffle that framed the neckline of her robe. "You look so soft and feminine."

"Unlike my real self?" she asked dryly.

"This *is* your real self."

Pat wanted to take exception to that, but when Raven's mouth closed over hers it didn't seem important. His magic was transporting her to the familiar land of enchantment where nothing mattered except this man she loved so totally.

The rapturous hours flew by as they made love with the passion that denial brings. They were both conscious of the fleeting time, and the fact that Raven would have to leave her.

"It isn't fair," he groaned. "I'll never get enough of you."

They were lying in each other's arms in the warm afterglow of love. Pat trailed her toes up and down his calf. "I just happen to be free tomorrow night," she murmured.

"I plan on being here," he assured her, slowly stroking her back. After a moment he sighed. "It won't satisfy me, though."

Pat laughed. "The last thing I expected was complaints."

Raven chuckled in response. "Pretty pleased with yourself, aren't you?"

It was said in jest, but she realized it was true. Raven made her feel like someone special. Her self-esteem that had taken such a beating was gradually being restored. In Raven's arms Pat felt cherished and secure. It was just one of his many gifts to her.

"You make me feel that way," she whispered, kissing the hollow in his throat.

"My beautiful angel." His arms tightened, and conversation was forgotten for a long time.

It was much later that Raven returned to his earlier complaint. "I don't want to wait until ten o'clock every night to see you. I want to be with you in the daytime too." He propped himself up on an elbow. "How about a picnic tomorrow? After you give Mattie her lunch we'll take off, just the two of us. I know a pretty little lake up in the mountains where the deer come down to drink, and the trout are as big as porpoises."

"You wouldn't be exaggerating?"

"Wait and see. We'll take some fishing poles and catch our dinner."

"It sounds heavenly, but I can't," Pat replied with real regret.

Raven frowned. "There's such a thing as being too conscientious. Mattie isn't an invalid. She'll survive for a few hours without you hovering over her."

"It isn't that. I have work to do tomorrow. We're having trouble with that stand of pine trees down by the utility shed. I always hate to lose a tree, but I'm afraid some of them will have to go."

"You can't mean you intend cutting them down yourself?" he asked incredulously.

"No, of course not. The pine needles are clogging the drains, though, and I have to flush out the lines or all our water will back up."

"That isn't your job," he growled. "Get somebody from town to do it."

"I already tried and they can't come out till next week." Pat had felt guilty about calling in outside help because it really was her job, but it was all academic now. They couldn't wait until next week.

Raven scowled. "I won't have you doing manual labor."

Pat had the feeling that they were treading on shaky ground. His acceptance of her in her official capacity had always been lukewarm, now it threatened to cool off completely. She tried to tease him out of it.

"It's what you hired me for—before you discovered my other attributes."

He wasn't buying. "It's time to call a halt, Pat. I've gone along with your cutting the grass and doing a lot of other things that are too difficult for you, but this is too much. I'm going to get a man in here to take over."

She sat up against the headboard, a careful distance from him. "Are you firing me?"

He hesitated. "You have enough to do taking care of Mattie and the house. I won't have you killing yourself."

Her eyes held his. "I asked if you're firing me."

"No, damn it!" He ran a square, capable hand through his hair. "God knows I'd like to! Look at you." His long fingers spanned her delicate wrist. "You shouldn't be doing this kind of work. If you weren't so blasted stubborn you'd admit it."

"And if *you* weren't so stubborn you'd admit that I've been able to handle every single thing that's come up."

"That's just the point. There have been all of these unforeseen occurrences. You can't be expected to take care of Mattie and do everything else too."

Pat was in love, but she was by no means blind. She recognized Raven's ploy. He would hire a man, ostensibly on a temporary basis, and somehow it would become permanent. After Mattie got well, that job too would disappear. With nothing to do and nowhere to go, the logical step would be to accompany Raven to New York. It was a neat plan with only one flaw—she had no intention of falling for it.

"Mattie isn't going to be laid up forever," she hastened to point out. "By next week she'll be out of bed."

"She still won't be able to handle the cooking or cleaning."

Pat made light of that. "It will be a breeze once I don't have to run with trays and help her do everything."

Raven sighed. "We both know that isn't so, but if you refuse to be sensible I don't know what I can do about it."

She let out her breath in a soft sigh of relief. "You can kiss me, for one thing. I think we've spent enough time talking about Mattie."

"More than enough," he agreed, pulling her back against him. Just before his mouth took possession of hers Raven muttered, "You've won this skirmish, my tricky little beauty, but don't think you've won the war."

It was late when he left—very reluctantly. Pat was just as sorry to see him go. She wanted to curl up in his arms and sleep for ten hours straight. Although she would never admit it to Raven, she was tired. But it was only a temporary condition. If she could just get through this week, life would be a little easier.

The main thing was to avoid giving Raven cause for complaint. She had to show him that she could handle Mattie, the property, and the house, and still have time for him. It shouldn't be too difficult if she cut out nonessentials like sleeping and brushing her teeth, Pat reflected dryly.

As her eyelids started to droop she reached for the alarm clock. Mattie liked an early breakfast. Maybe she'd fix something really fancy to show Raven how little trouble it was. Something like . . . Pat fell asleep in the middle of the thought.

When the alarm clock rang after what seemed like only minutes, Pat groaned and dragged herself out of bed. A cold shower refreshed her enough to dress and walk up the driveway to the ranch house. She was frying bacon when Raven came into the kitchen in a pair of pajama bottoms. With his broad chest bare, his hair tousled, and a light growth of beard, he looked slightly sleepy, and very, very sexy.

He put his arms around her and rested his cheek on the top of her head. "Good morning, sweetheart. You're up bright and early."

"So are you." She drew back to look at him, resting her hands on his lean hips and hooking her thumbs inside his drawstring waist. A gleam of mischief lit her face. "I've never seen you in pajamas before."

The drowsiness vanished from his tawny eyes as they started to glow. "If you'll step into my room I'll see what I can do about remedying my image."

"You just want me to burn the bacon the way you did the eggs," she teased.

"Can you think of a better reason?" he asked in a throaty growl.

"Is that you, Pat?" Mattie called from her room.

Raven sighed. "Well, so much for good ideas."

From then on Pat's day speeded up. First she took Mattie's breakfast to her on a tray, then served Raven his and poured herself a cup of coffee.

He looked at it with disapproval. "That isn't enough for breakfast."

"It's all I ever have," she assured him, wishing he would hurry up and finish.

She still had the kitchen to clean up before she could get to the major job of flushing out the water lines. But Raven had nothing pressing to do, and he was enjoying her company. It wasn't until Mattie called that she was through and Pat went to get her tray, that he left to do some work in his den. Pat hurriedly piled the dishes in the dishwasher before going out to tackle the pipes.

The late August sun was already uncomfortably warm when she started working. It was arduous physical labor and Pat didn't even have the solace of Janus's company. Since Raven had come into his life, the Great Dane was dividing his loyalties. His first love was Pat, but he also valued comfort. When she took him for walks or in the car, he stuck closely by her side. But when she did something foolish like working in the hot sun, Janus went in search of his second love, Raven.

"What can you expect from a male?" Pat muttered to herself, but she didn't really mind. The fact that Janus had put his stamp of approval on Raven was an affirmation of her own judgment.

The job wasn't even half done by lunchtime. Pat looked at her watch despairingly. If only she could have worked straight through and gotten the messy thing over with. But someone had to fix lunch, and it wouldn't do to have it be late. She didn't want to give Raven the opportunity of saying I told you so.

After hastily sluicing her face and arms with the hose, Pat hurried back to the house. Her cheeks were flame red from the sun, and her damp hair was curling in little tendrils around her delicate face.

"You look terrible!" Raven exclaimed sharply when he saw her.

"Well, thanks a lot." It wasn't exactly what Pat

wanted to hear when she was hot and tired and still had work to do.

"You know I didn't mean it that way." He put the back of his hand against her cheek. "You've been out in the sun too long, honey. You'd better go lie down for a while."

"I have to start lunch."

"Forget about lunch!" he said violently. "I'll make it."

"No, I'm fine." She glanced in the mirror over the sink and was startled by her own image. After hurriedly taming her hair by combing her fingers through it, Pat pinned a bright smile on her face. "Nothing like a little exercise to give you an appetite. I'm starving, how about you?" She hurried on without giving him a chance to reply. "I thought we'd have jellied consommé and shrimp salad with deviled eggs and home-made biscuits. How does that sound?" She groaned inwardly, thinking of all the preparation involved.

"I couldn't care less." He was staring at her with deep concern. "I'm worried about you, Pat."

"For heaven's sake, why?" She was like a perpetual motion machine, getting lettuce from the refrigerator, bowls from the cupboard, utensils from the drawer.

He reached out a long arm, immobilizing her. "Why are you doing this to yourself? What are you trying to prove?"

She looked up warily. "I don't know what you're talking about. Would you mind moving away from the stove so I can turn on the oven?"

His hands tightened on her arms. "Do you know what it does to me to see you working until you drop?"

"Please, Raven! I thought we settled this last night. If you'll just go in the other room for a little while I'll call you when lunch is ready."

He stared at her for a long moment, anger and

frustration on his face. Then he turned and strode out of the room, flinging over his shoulder, "Don't bother, I'm not hungry."

Pat's mouth thinned with annoyance. She had planned this whole meal for him. Well, let him sulk if he wanted to; Mattie would appreciate it anyway.

She was right about the housekeeper. Mattie regarded her tray with anticipation. "My, that looks good! You're spoiling me, Pat. I won't want to get out of bed next week."

"I know you better than that. You're probably itching to get back in harness."

"Not necessarily." The older woman laughed. "A person could get used to being waited on."

While Mattie was eating, Pat went in the kitchen to fix her own lunch, but it seemed like too much trouble. She made herself a glass of iced tea instead. Sinking into a chair she slumped down to the base of her spine, stretching out her legs and putting her head back. Pat's eyes were closed so she didn't see Raven appear in the doorway. It was just as well. The enigmatic expression on his face would have made her nervous.

After cleaning up the kitchen a second time, she went back to work. As the sun climbed, the temperature soared, but Pat ignored it, doggedly sticking to the job. It was late afternoon before it was finally finished. She coiled the hose and put away the heavy shovel and other equipment, feeling as though her back was permanently bent.

After a shower and a change of clothes she felt better. Her body still ached, but at least that didn't show. Raven wouldn't have cause for any disparaging remarks this time. To insure it, Pat brushed her long lashes with a touch of mascara, and outlined her mouth with lip gloss.

It didn't seem possible that it was time to prepare yet

another meal, she reflected, trudging up the driveway. At least this one was going to be simple, though— broiled steak, baked potatoes, and tossed green salad. Outside of washing the lettuce and dicing the vegetables, there weren't too many preparations. Still, there was the table to set, water glasses to fill, condiments to be put out. She had never realized how many things were involved in getting together even a simple meal.

Pat only hoped that Raven had gotten over his pique. She wasn't in any mood to deal with a sulky man at the moment. She assessed his mood warily when he came into the kitchen a short time later.

He was looking at her without expression. "Did you get finished?"

"Ages ago," she assured him brightly. "What did you do today?"

"Spent a fun-filled afternoon working," he answered briefly.

Pat smothered a sigh. Raven was determined to be difficult. "That must have made you feel righteous."

"It wasn't what I had planned."

She scrubbed the potatoes harder than necessary. "Everything can't always go according to plan."

"It can if we really want it to."

Enough was enough. Pat slammed down the vegetable brush, turning to him with flashing green eyes. "The water lines didn't happen to pick this time to get clogged just to thwart your personal enjoyment. I can think of a lot of things *I'd* rather have been doing today too!"

His face softened as he gazed at her defiant little form. "Did I figure in them?" he asked softly, caressing her cheek with the tips of his long fingers.

Her anger abated somewhat. "Of course you did. That's a silly question."

He pulled her into his arms, stroking her back until Pat felt like purring. "I missed you today. I kept picturing all the things we could be doing."

"*All* of them?" she murmured.

"Yes, that's the hell of it. I almost came out there and carried you off by force."

"I never knew you were the caveman type," she teased.

He raised one eyebrow. "That might be the best way to deal with you."

"Could you put off flexing your muscles until later? I have to get the potatoes in the oven."

He shook his head in disgust. "I seem to be way down the list of your priorities."

Raven wasn't really angry, though. His annoyance had vanished along with Pat's. They could never stay at odds for long. Their need for each other was so great that they were both miserable when they were arguing.

"I'll go choose a bottle of wine if you think you can get along without me for a few minutes," he observed mockingly.

Dinner was very festive. Pat set the table with candles and used the best china and silver. The red wine glowed in the crystal glasses, matching the warmth inside Pat as she gazed at Raven's lean, dark face across the table. It had been a long hard day, but this made it all worthwhile.

"You must be tired," he remarked.

"Not at all," she replied quickly. Giving him a seductive smile she said, "Do I look tired?"

"You look superb!" The candlelight reflected in his eyes, turning them a tawny gold. He leaned forward to cover her hand with his. "How would you like to skip dinner and let me escort you home?"

Pat's smile faltered. "I have to get Mattie ready for

bed and do the dishes." She waited for the explosion but it didn't come.

Raven merely sighed. "I'm not even going to argue about it anymore."

"I'll see you later," she consoled him. "Ten o'clock will come around before you know it."

"I doubt it. All I've been doing today is watching the clock."

He didn't let it spoil the evening though. It was a dinner like the ones they'd shared the week before. The wine made Pat feel relaxed and happy. Her only problem was smothering the yawns that kept surfacing.

After Mattie was freshened up and the kitchen cleared, Pat went back to the cottage. She was glad that she'd already showered, since the very thought of the effort involved made her groan. She did have to change clothes, however.

After stripping off her jeans and shirt she put on a pale blue chiffon gown and matching peignoir. The filmy robe fell in crystal pleats from a yoke made of delicate lace that matched the banding around the long, full sleeves.

Sitting at the dressing table she applied a more elaborate makeup, using a creamy foundation to tone down some of the damage the sun had done to her delicate skin. Subtly shaded eyeliner and green shadow deepened the emerald color of her eyes. After a finish of translucent powder and a slick of lip gloss, Pat's face looked luminous. All traces of fatigue were artfully covered.

She was through by nine thirty, with nothing to do until ten. Raven couldn't very well get away before then since Mattie would surely wonder where he was going. Neither Pat nor Raven enjoyed the clandestine position they were placed in, but the alternative was to distress the older woman, which neither of them wanted to do.

Pat went in the living room to turn on a lamp and tune the radio to soft music. She sank down on the couch, a little smile playing around her full mouth as she thought about Raven. He was so absolutely perfect —strong yet gentle, intelligent, witty, and loving. Her pulses quickened as she thought about just how loving. She could see his face on her closed eyelids, so ruggedly handsome with that straight nose, golden lion's eyes, and sensuous mouth. Pat's breathing slowed as she drifted into a deep sleep.

Raven didn't realize she was asleep when he let himself in some time later. He stood over her, drinking in her loveliness for a long moment. When she didn't move he bent down to kiss her gently.

"Wake up, sleeping beauty," he whispered.

Pat smiled in her sleep, linking an arm around his neck. As comprehension dawned, Raven sat down on the couch and stroked her body very lightly. She made a small sound of pleasure, carrying his hand to her cheek.

His eyes were very tender as they wandered over her exquisite features, lingering on her soft, full mouth. He touched the curve of her cheek almost reverently. When her long lashes fluttered, Raven lifted her in his arms and carried her into the bedroom.

He sat down on the bed, holding Pat in his lap while he removed her peignoir. She curled up against him with a soft sigh of contentment, resting her head on his broad shoulder. Raven's arms tightened for a moment as he kissed her temple.

"I'm going to take care of you whether you like it or not, my little darling," he muttered in a husky whisper, sliding her gently between the sheets.

When Pat murmured something in her sleep, Raven bent down to listen. She repeated it like a prayer. "I love you, Raven."

Fierce triumph blazed in his eyes. Just before he touched his lips to hers, Raven said softly, "I love you too, sweetheart."

Chapter Eight

$\mathcal{W}$ ithout the alarm clock to wake her, Pat slept late the next morning. She awoke feeling marvelous. Her tired body was completely renewed, and a wonderful, yet elusive dream teased at her consciousness. She couldn't quite recall it, but it had made her very happy.

Pat's well-being vanished when she looked at the clock. How could she have slept that late! Why didn't the alarm go off? As she sprang out of bed, the unaccustomed nightgown she was wearing jogged her memory—but only up to a point. The last thing she remembered was lying on the couch waiting for Raven. Had he tried to wake her and failed? Or had he realized how exhausted she was and let her sleep? Pat groaned. Either way it was a disaster!

When she burst into the ranch house kitchen a short time later, Raven was reading the newspaper. The remains of his breakfast was still on the table.

"I don't know what happened," she gasped. "I must have overslept."

"Good morning, sweetheart." His lion's eyes glowed with a special warmth. "Do you feel better this morning?"

"I felt fine last night," she replied warily. "You should have wakened me."

Raven chuckled. "Short of a cannon blast next to your ear, I don't know how I could have accomplished that."

Well, at least he wasn't angry. And more important, he wasn't going to deliver another lecture about overwork. "I'm truly sorry, Raven. Would you like another cup of coffee while I see what Mattie wants for breakfast?"

"She's already eaten. I made breakfast for both of us."

"You didn't have to do that. Why didn't you call the cottage and wake me?"

He put his arm around her waist, pulling her between his knees. Her breasts were on a level with his mouth and he nipped at one nipple through the cotton shirt. "Why would I do that? I know how to cook—when there's no one to distract me." His free hand traced the edge of her brief shorts.

"Raven, stop! It's nine-thirty in the morning."

He pulled her into his lap. "There isn't any time that I don't want you."

His muted voice vibrated with a passion that Pat shared wholeheartedly. She framed his face in her palms. "I really am *so* sorry about last night."

"I'm not. I found out something very precious." He cupped her chin in his hand, gazing deeply into her eyes. "You were so beautiful all dressed up in chiffon and lace. I wanted to hold you in my arms and just look at you all night."

"I wish you had," she whispered, twining her fingers through his thick hair.

Raven's kiss was slow and sensuous. His tongue traced the inside of her lower lip, then skimmed her teeth before plunging deeper. It was a totally male invasion that seduced her with its enticing promise. Pat clung to him as golden sparks seemed to ignite in her bloodstream, carrying desire to every part of her body.

"Did I hear Pat come in?" Mattie's voice preceded her slow steps down the hall.

Raven and Pat drew apart slowly, their lips clinging, reluctant to part. Her legs felt shaky as Raven helped her off his lap. She was too bemused to do anything but stare at him as he gently smoothed her ruffled hair.

"I thought I heard your voice." Mattie came into the kitchen.

Pat pulled herself together with an effort. "What are you doing out of bed?"

"The doctor said a week, and it's up today."

"Well, even so, you mustn't overdo it," Pat warned.

"Good Lord, child, if I don't get out of bed soon I'm going to weigh two hundred pounds, the way you and Mr. Masters have been waiting on me. I feel real guilty about it." She lowered herself into a chair, wincing slightly. "It's just a blessing that you won't be working yourself to death much longer."

Pat didn't see Raven's sudden tension or the frown that darkened his face. "You aren't going to be taking over for several weeks," she stated. "The doctor was very emphatic about that."

"I know, but at least you won't be doing double duty."

"What do you mean?"

"Didn't you tell her?" Mattie looked questioningly at Raven.

"Well, I . . . uh . . . we didn't get around to it yet."

"Tell me what?" Pat demanded. "What's going on?"

"Mr. Masters has been as worried about you as I have. He said he was making breakfast this morning because you wore yourself out yesterday and it had to stop. He was bound and determined to do something about it, and that's when I thought of my nephew." The older woman looked very pleased with herself.

"What nephew?" Pat felt a prickle of foreboding.

"Sam Walsh, my dead sister's boy—the only relative I have left in the world. I haven't seen little Samuel since he was seventeen, and he must be—let's see." Mattie stared at the ceiling while she figured. "He has to be all of twenty-two now. My goodness, doesn't time fly?"

Pat tried to restrain her impatience. "I don't understand. What's all this about your nephew?"

"That's Mr. Master's surprise. Sam is going to take over your job."

At Pat's sharp exclamation, Raven swore pungently under his breath. "That isn't the way it is at all. He's just going to help out until Mattie gets back on her feet."

"Oh, really?" Pat's back was very stiff as she faced him. "Isn't it convenient that this young man can suddenly drop everything to come here and 'help out.'" She gave it an ironic inflection. "He must have a very understanding employer."

Mattie leaned forward eagerly. "That's what makes it so good all around—Sam is unemployed. The factory where he worked shut down. It's really terrible the way they just let all those people go with hardly any warning," she disgressed. "Anyway, Sam jumped at the chance when we phoned him this morning. He said he was fed up with Los Angeles anyway."

"It's all settled?" Pat was looking at Raven. "You called him without even discussing it with me?"

"You were sleeping," Mattie answered for him. "Besides, Mr. Masters knew you'd have a fit. He wanted to get everything settled so there wouldn't be any arguments. You're going to thank him when Sam gets here tomorrow."

"Tomorrow!"

"Mr. Masters promised him a bonus to do it." Mattie's admiration for Raven's generosity showed in her voice.

"I see." Pat felt as though she had inadvertently walked into a brick wall. She tried not to show the pain. "Well, I'd better start packing."

"Pat, wait!" Raven called.

She kept going but he caught up with her in the driveway. He took her arm when she wouldn't look at him. Holding her forcibly he said, "I was going to tell you but I got . . . sidetracked."

She glared up at him. "I didn't realize that kiss was a consolation prize—or was it in lieu of two weeks pay?"

"You're not fired! Will you please calm down?"

"You hired someone to replace me. What would you call it?"

"Only for a short time. And only because you can't single-handedly take care of this ranch and everyone on it—in spite of what you think. I care too much about you to let you kill yourself trying."

"Don't bother turning on the charm," she said angrily. "And don't insult my intelligence. Mattie's nephew isn't coming all the way from California just for a few weeks work."

"He's unemployed and I made it worth his while," Raven insisted.

"Can't you even be honest with me?" Pat raged. "The whole plan is crystal clear. Sam inherits my job and I move up to the house. In a short time Mattie recuperates and takes over again. I'm left in a vague position somewhere between guest and freeloader. At that point you suggest that I move to New York and become your live-in playmate."

"That wasn't what I—"

She continued without letting him finish. "I'm supposed to accept because I have nowhere else to go, and the three of you get what you want. That's the script, isn't it?" Her eyes flashed green fire. "Well, you can just forget it! I don't need your so-called help, and I certainly don't need your charity!"

She yanked her arm away and would have stalked off but Raven pulled her back, fastening both hands on her shoulders. "If you're through ranting maybe you'll listen to reason. It's true that I want you to come to New York, but I would never try to trick you into it. You're free to stay here the rest of your life if that's what you insist on."

"As what?" she demanded.

Raven sighed. "As caretaker. If Sam works out and he likes it here, I'll have Buck Henley take him on as a ranch hand."

The first rush of Pat's anger had subsided, but she still didn't trust him. "If you weren't trying anything underhanded, why didn't you talk to me about this before you went ahead and did it?"

His hands slid up her neck to clasp under the silky auburn hair. "When I came in last night and found you lying in an exhausted little heap, I couldn't take it anymore, honey. I decided then that I had to do something."

"Well, I'll admit I'd had a rather hectic day, but yesterday was unusual," she protested.

"You bet it was!" He touched foreheads with her, rubbing his nose against hers. "When you're too tired to make love to me, that's *very* unusual."

"You certainly got your revenge."

He straightened up, looking at her searchingly. "You don't believe that?"

She didn't know *what* to believe. Raven had always been straightforward with her before, but he had never made any secret of wanting to change her life. In addition to that, he could charm a charging bull. Was she buying swamp property from yet another man?

She gazed at him doubtfully. "Can I stay on in the cottage?"

"Of course you can!" He linked his arms around her waist, drawing her lower body to his. "I wouldn't have it any other way. Where else would I spend my evenings?"

If only he hadn't added that. All of Pat's waning doubts were rekindled. Was that the only reason he was letting her stay there? Did he really plan on easing her out when the time came, in spite of his honeyed words? It was something to think long and hard about.

Pat was very abstracted that day. She tried to find things to occupy herself away from Raven.

He commented on it that night at dinner. "Where were you all day? I hardly caught a glimpse of you."

"I was working outside. The front gate was coming off the hinges. I had to bore holes for new screws, and . . . oh, a lot of other little things."

"After tomorrow you can delegate those jobs to Sam so we can start spending more time together."

"Yes, I guess so." She folded her napkin carefully.

Raven's tawny eyes assessed her downcast face. "You still don't trust me, do you, Pat?"

"I don't know," she replied honestly.

A wealth of emotions coursed swiftly over his rugged

face—anger, impatience, frustration. But when he finally answered, his expression was impassive. "Well, I'm afraid that's something you'll have to work out for yourself."

Pat's own emotions were in a turbulent state as she did the dishes. Raven hadn't mentioned coming to the cottage later, and she wasn't sure how she felt about it. If he was just using her, it was better this way. Maybe he was even starting to tire of her. That thought brought a pain so sharp that for a minute she couldn't breathe. It was a possibility, though. Nothing was forever. Even now changes were in the wind. Mattie's nephew would be living at the house, and his friends would come to visit. Her refuge was becoming over-populated.

Pat tried not to look at the clock that night, but as ten o'clock approached she was as jumpy as a cat at a dog show. Janus gave her reproachful looks for jumping up from the couch every few minutes. He was trying to sleep on the floor beside it.

By eleven o'clock Pat knew Raven wasn't coming. She undressed and got into bed, trying not to picture the rapture-filled nights in his arms. This was reality, that was a dream—one that was over. She curled up into a sleepless ball of misery.

The coffee was already perking and Raven was in the kitchen when Pat got to the house the next morning.

After glancing at the clock she said firmly, "I'm not late." As a matter of fact, she was early.

"I know. I couldn't sleep so I came in to start the coffee."

"Well, I'll take over now," Pat said briskly.

He didn't move. "Did you sleep well, Pat?"

"Like a baby," she lied.

"One who cries to be picked up and held?" He watched her with golden cat's eyes.

"Not at all. Like a person with a clear conscience."

"I missed you," he said softly.

"You knew where I was." The words came out without Pat's volition. She hadn't meant to give him the satisfaction.

"I didn't think you wanted to see me."

"You were right." She kept herself very busy getting out plates and silverware so she wouldn't have to look at him.

He took the dishes out of her hands. "We have to talk, Pat."

"We did a lot of that yesterday," she answered bitterly.

"Not enough. We're going to thrash this thing out before it grows into a solid wall between us."

"Nothing you can say is going to change anything," she said wearily.

"No, but something I can *do* is. You're convinced that bringing Sam here is part of a Machiavellian plot against you. Okay, when he gets here I'll tell him the job is filled."

"You can't bring a man all that distance and then tell him to turn around and go home!"

"I'll give him a month's pay, naturally."

"What about Mattie? She's been looking forward to having her nephew here; he's the only family she has. And Sam is expecting to start a whole new life."

"It's a dirty trick and I'm sorry about it. But you're the only one who matters." He raised her chin in his palm. "I'll do whatever it takes to make you trust me."

As Pat stared at him, the cold lump in her breast started to melt. If Raven would go to such lengths he must care a great deal about her. How could she have let her own doubts make them both so miserable?

Her eyes were misty as she murmured, "You'd really do that for me?"

"I want to do a great deal more." He stroked her cheek gently. "Don't you know that, sweetheart?"

Pat did know it. Finally all of her suspicions were laid to rest. She gazed at him with such pure love shining out of her eyes that Raven gathered her fiercely in his arms.

"You'll never know how I suffered last night," he muttered brokenly. "I never knew you could actually ache for someone."

Pat rubbed her cheek against his satisfyingly solid shoulder. "Why didn't you come to me?"

"Because my stupid pride was hurt," he groaned. "I told myself I could get along without you just fine." His fingers tangled in her hair, pulling her head back so his warm mouth could slide down her neck. "And toward morning I admitted that I couldn't."

"I'm glad," she whispered, closing her eyes as a shiver of delight ran up her spine.

"How about you?" His tongue touched the wildly beating pulse at the base of her throat. "Did you miss me?"

Pat's smile was tremulous. "Only about as much as I'd miss the sun if it didn't shine."

"My love!"

As Raven's head descended, she put shaky fingers over his lips. "Not now. If Mattie follows her usual pattern she'll be joining us any minute. And if she finds me with a dreamy look on my face one more time, she's going to think I'm coming down with something."

"Or else that you're in love," he murmured.

Pat put a careful distance between them by starting to set the table. "You're right, there's no telling what she might think."

He watched her in silence for a moment. "Let's go on

that picnic today, Pat. I'll have to be back this afternoon to explain things to Sam when he gets here, but we can have a couple of hours together anyway."

Pat looked at him then. "I don't want you to send him away, Raven. I couldn't live with myself."

"It isn't your decision, honey, it's mine. I'll take care of everything. Sam won't suffer by it, I promise you."

"But it isn't necessary now. I realize that I was being unreasonable." She grinned suddenly. "Manual labor can't compare to making love."

He didn't return her smile. "Are you absolutely sure, Pat?"

"Take my word for it—I've tried both."

"You know what I mean." Raven's face was troubled. "I couldn't stand for anything to come between us again."

"It won't," she answered confidently.

He stared at her over the intervening distance. What he saw in her eyes seemed to reassure him. "To get back to that picnic," he said softly.

"Why don't we postpone it until tomorrow? I have to get one of the guest rooms ready for Sam and make out a list of things that need doing. And you'll want to be here to greet him. If we wait until tomorrow we won't have anything else on our minds."

"Except each other." His husky voice throbbed.

Mattie joined them as they gazed longingly at each other. Their feelings were plain to see, but the older woman was too wrapped up in her own affairs to notice.

"I declare, I'm so excited I don't even mind the roadmap that doctor carved down my middle," she said. "Actually, I guess that pesky gall bladder was a blessing in disguise. If I hadn't gotten sick, my sister's little boy wouldn't be coming right here to the house."

"He's an adult now," Pat warned gently. The housekeeper's joy made her glad that she had done the right thing.

"I know. I suppose I won't even begin to recognize him."

"Hasn't he sent you any recent snapshots?" Raven asked.

"Sam never was one for writing—you know how boys are. A card at Christmas and another one on my birthday was about the extent of it. I wouldn't even have guessed he was out of work if I hadn't read in the paper that his factory shut down."

"Well, you'll have plenty of time to find out what he's been doing," Pat commented.

She accomplished very little work that day. Mattie followed her around, recounting anecdotes about Sam almost from the day he was born. The absentminded replies she received didn't slow her down a bit. Pat breathed a sigh of relief when the time for his arrival neared and Mattie went to sit in a chair by the window.

One of the ranch hands had been dispatched to the airport in the estate wagon. In the late afternoon it finally appeared in the driveway.

"He's here! Sam's here!" Mattie called.

Pat joined her in time to see a tall, blond young man get out of the car. He looked barely out of adolescence, with a youthful face, and a lanky body that hadn't filled out yet. He was helping the ranch hand unload several suitcases.

Judging by the amount of luggage, Sam had definitely come to stay, Pat reflected dryly. As Mattie opened the front door he turned to assist a very young, very pregnant woman from the car.

"Sam, come here and let me look at you," Mattie called, unable to wait any longer.

He swung around with a wide grin on his pleasant face, and bounded over to give his aunt a big kiss.

Raven had evidently been watching from the terrace. He walked over to the rather forlorn-looking girl and extended his hand, giving her a warm smile.

Pat was too far away to hear what he said, but she couldn't have anyway over the buzzing of anger in her ears. Raven had succeeded in duping her one more time! He hadn't mentioned that Sam was bringing a pregnant wife! Raven's offer to send him packing had been nothing but a very clever ruse. He knew Pat's sense of fair play wouldn't allow it.

Another convincing touch was that pretty speech about *if* he worked out, and *if* he wanted to stay. It was pretty evident that Sam had been *promised* it would be permanent! He would never have uprooted his wife in that condition for a temporary job.

"This is my nephew," Mattie said, introducing him proudly. "And this is Pat Lee, the one whose job you're going to take." She had no idea how devastating her innocent words were.

Sam pumped Pat's hand enthusiastically. "I'm sure glad to be here. That call from Mr. Masters was like a gift from heaven!"

"I hope you're going to like it on the ranch." The older woman looked suddenly anxious. "It might seem a bit quiet for you after the big city."

Sam put his arm around his aunt's shoulders. "I'm going to love it. I've had enough crowds and concrete to last the rest of my life. Nothing could get me back to Los Angeles."

Mattie's worried look was replaced by a smile as she patted his hand. "You don't know how happy that makes me. Everything's working out just fine, isn't it, Pat?"

"Dandy," she muttered through clenched teeth.

"Oh, Mr. Masters, I want you to—" the housekeeper's words broke off as she noticed the girl Raven was leading toward them.

"This is Sam's wife, Betty," Raven introduced her with a smile.

"Wife!" Mattie stared at the girl and then at her nephew. "You never told me you got married! When did all this happen?"

He laughed uncomfortably. "We've been married . . . uh . . . almost a year now. I've been meaning to write to you."

Since the girl was about seven months pregnant, Pat was beginning to get the picture. Sam's vague reference to a year was probably more like six months—the reason he wouldn't want his conventional aunt to know. Pat's eyes narrowed. Mattie's surprise was genuine, but Raven had certainly known that Sam was bringing a wife. He had just conveniently forgotten to mention it when he was assuring Pat that her job was secure.

How soon would it be until Raven hinted that the cottage would be a perfect place for a couple with a baby? Fury swept Pat's slender body like a gusty wind, although the others were unaware of it.

After her initial surprise, Mattie was in a transport of joy. "To think that you have a wife and a baby on the way, and you didn't even send me a wedding announcement. I could spank you, Sam Walsh!" But her round face was wreathed in smiles.

"Think what a nice surprise it is." Raven intervened tactfully as the young couple looked uncomfortable. "You can all get acquainted after they get settled in."

"You're right, Mr. Masters. I'm standing here chattering away, and this poor child is probably exhausted from the trip."

"No, I'm fine," Betty said shyly. "I would like to get freshened up, though."

"Of course you would. I'll show you your room, and after you get unpacked we'll have a long talk. Maybe Pat will make us some iced tea."

"Hot chocolate's her specialty. I can guarantee that it does wonders for you." Raven's laughing eyes sought Pat's. The stony glare he encountered brought a puzzled look to his face.

"I'll take Betty to her room. You've been on your feet long enough," Pat advised Mattie briefly. "Why don't you and Sam go in the living room?" Without waiting for a reply she led the way to the bedroom wing.

Betty looked around admiringly, peeking into the spacious rooms they passed. "I've never seen such a beautiful house."

"Yes, it's nice."

Pat's irate thoughts were on Raven. That disgusting reference to hot chocolate had certainly been calculated to soften her up. And the puzzled look on his face was a masterful touch. As though he couldn't imagine why she was upset.

"I hope I won't be in the way around here." Betty's soft voice was tentative. "Mr. Masters told Sam that you've had your hands full taking care of Mattie and the house. We . . . uh . . . I thought maybe I could sort of help out."

Pat's mouth was a grim line as she turned to stare at her. They weren't losing any time, were they? "You're not exactly in any condition to take over—yet."

"I can do the dishes, and set the table, and . . . well, all kinds of things. I really do want to pull my own weight."

Pat smiled unwillingly. "You're already carrying quite a bit of it around."

She looked more carefully at the younger woman. Betty Walsh could have passed for a high school student—which wasn't too far off the mark. She couldn't have been more than nineteen. Her long blond hair and big, innocent blue eyes looked somehow incongruous above the bulk of her abdomen. Reinforcing the impression of youth was her diffident, conciliatory manner.

For the first time Pat considered things from the girl's standpoint. It must be very difficult being forced to move someplace so completely foreign to her former life. A place, moreover, where she had no family, no friends, not even private living accommodations. She was at the mercy of strangers. Pat's anger at Raven flared brighter. How could he move innocent people around like pawns, just for his own selfish ends?

She managed to mask her rage for Betty's sake. Pat's voice was gentle as she said, "I'm sure there will be a lot of things you can do to help." She opened the door of a spacious bedroom. "The bathroom is through that door, and there are towels in the cupboard under the sink. If you need anything else just call me."

She had gone back to the kitchen when Raven came in. "I'm sorry about the extra work, honey—the added people for dinner I mean. Is there anything I can do to help?"

"You've already done quite enough," she grated, not looking at him.

"Is anything wrong, Pat?"

"No, certainly not! I have a great deal of admiration for you."

"I'd like to think so, but not when you say it in that tone of voice," he answered quietly. "What's bothering you?"

She turned to face him with blazing eyes. "The fact that I've been such a fool!"

"I don't understand." He looked genuinely perplexed. "Is it something to do with Sam? I thought we'd straightened all that out."

"You mean you thought you'd succeeded in flimflamming me again. Well, you did! That's what makes me so furious. I honestly believed your motives were above reproach. I even believed your word was good, isn't that funny?"

Raven's golden eyes darkened to amber. "No one has ever doubted my word. What promise did I break?"

"None yet, but you'll think of a way." Pat flung a dish towel across the room. "Why are you bothering to keep up the pretense when you can tell that I see through you—finally. It was very clever to let me be the one to insist on Sam taking over my job when that's what you intended all along. Do you really expect me to believe that you'd drag a pregnant woman all this distance on a wild goose chase?"

Comprehension entered his face. "I didn't know she was pregnant. I didn't even know Sam had a wife!"

"Raven, please!" Disgust turned Pat's mouth down at the corners.

"I swear to you I didn't! He never mentioned it on the phone."

"It isn't the sort of thing one can keep secret—not in her advanced state. I imagine it occurred to him that we'd notice when they got here."

"Pat, be reasonable! I was as surprised as you were. I don't know why he didn't tell me. Perhaps because he thought I wanted a single man and he was afraid I wouldn't give him a chance if I knew. Sam was really desperate for this job."

"And now he's got it," Pat said bitterly.

"*No*! I told you I'd find some other place for him on the ranch when the time came."

"You told me a lot of things—whatever worked best at the moment."

"You don't really believe that." He put his hands on her shoulders, looking deeply into her eyes. "You must know how I feel about you."

Pat's face was hard. "It won't work anymore, Raven. For a while you made me forget the way men can lie and cheat to get what they want. I thought my first lesson taught me something, but evidently it didn't. You just gave me a refresher course, and this time I think it will stick."

His steely fingers bit into her soft skin. "You can't—" he stopped abruptly as Betty came into the kitchen.

"Our room is just dreamy." Betty's happy smile faded as she sensed the tense atmosphere. "Oh, I'm sorry. I'm interrupting something."

Pat made an effort to speak normally. "No, you're not; Mr. Masters was just leaving. Sit down and I'll make us that iced tea."

Betty glanced doubtfully at Raven's austere face as he stalked out without a word. She caught the corner of her lower lip between small white teeth. "Mr. Masters is angry about my being here, isn't he? I told Sam we should tell him."

Pat's words of reassurance died unspoken. "What are you saying? Do you mean he really didn't know?"

"We didn't have anywhere else to go," Betty said defensively. "Our money was almost used up and I can't work for a while." Her fingers twisted together nervously. "I know it was deceitful, but we thought on a big ranch like this the baby wouldn't bother anyone."

The hard core of Pat's anger dissolved suddenly. Raven hadn't lied! Her exultation died as she recalled the cutting things she'd said, and the look on his face when he left. Why were there always these misunderstandings between them? It didn't help to realize that she was responsible for most of them. Would she ever break the habit of suspicion that was Carl's legacy?

"Do you think he'll send us away?" Betty's fearful voice broke in on Pat's thoughts.

"No, of course he won't! Mr. Masters isn't angry at you. He's delighted to have both of you here." When Betty looked unconvinced, Pat added, "He often has things on his mind that make him seem rather . . . um . . . abstracted."

Betty sighed. "I hope you're right."

"I know I am. Why don't you go in the living room and visit? I'm sure Mattie is dying to get to know you."

Pat was hoping Raven would come back but he didn't. She kept listening for his step all the time she was starting dinner. In the midst of her chaotic thoughts something occurred to her. Was she supposed to feed the Walshs and Mattie in the kitchen while Raven ate in the dining room? Knowing Raven, she didn't think he would choose to dine in solitary splendor, but it gave her an excuse to go talk to him.

Mattie waylaid her, however, as she passed the living room. Pat had to go in and hear a complete account of the young couple's courtship, marriage, and plans for the baby's future. Sam grinned sympathetically as Pat was forced to sit through the endless narrative.

Finally she stood up. "I have to ask Mr. Masters something before dinner."

"Oh, lordy, with everything that's going on I forgot to tell you. Mr. Masters went out."

Pat looked at the older woman blankly. "Did he say when he'd be back?"

"No, he just said he needed a change of scenery. Maybe he went over to the Camerons to see that pretty little Laura." A knowing look came over Mattie's face. "I wouldn't expect him back too early."

Somehow Pat managed to produce an edible meal,

although she didn't eat any of it. After refusing all offers of help she cleaned up the kitchen and went back to the cottage.

Janus's usual rapturous welcome brought tears to Pat's eyes. He was the one constant in her life and she'd better get used to it. Refusing to indulge in self-pity, she took him for a brisk walk and then returned to take a needle-sharp shower and wash her hair. The unceasing activity helped to blank out thoughts of Raven.

She had just finished blow-drying her glorious mass of auburn hair when the bell rang. For just a moment her heart leaped into her throat. Hope died when she realized it couldn't be Raven. For one thing, he never rang the bell. It was probably Sam wanting to discuss his duties. They'd never gotten around to it with Mattie monopolizing the conversation.

"Just a minute," she called as she slipped into a robe.

The sight of Raven on the doorstep threw Pat into confusion. She could only stand there and stare at him.

"May I come in?" he asked formally. The look on his face wasn't encouraging.

"Oh . . . yes . . . yes, of course." She pulled her robe tighter together as he walked by her. "Where did you go?"

"Into town."

"That's . . . um . . . nice."

He raised a mocking eyebrow. "Cougar Run is scarcely a mecca of madcap mirth. I had several beers at the tavern and shot a few games of pool."

"Did you have any dinner?"

"No, I wasn't hungry."

Pat could sympathize with him. Her own appetite was nonexistent. "I could fix you something."

"No, thanks. I came here to talk to you."

"What about?" Pat's heart started to pound. Raven

looked so stern. She indicated the couch and settled in a chair, a careful distance away.

He sat down and crossed his long legs, completely at ease. Pat could only envy him as her own nerves were running a relay race through her body.

"I've given up hope of ever convincing you of anything, so I'm not going to try anymore," Raven began.

It was as bad as she feared. "Betty told me you didn't know she was coming," Pat said hastily.

"Did you believe her?"

"Of course!"

Raven's smile was bittersweet. "You'll believe a total stranger, but you didn't believe me. Well, it doesn't matter now. I'm going back to New York, Pat. I was going to stay a little longer but my leg is practically healed and there's nothing to keep me here anymore."

Every word was like a mortal blow. She raised her chin, determined not to show the pain. "So you came to say good-bye."

"Partially. Mostly though to offer you a contract." When she looked at him uncomprehendingly Raven said, "Security seems to be the most important thing in life to you. You won't believe me when I say you can stay here as long as you like, so I'm going to put it in writing. My lawyer will send you a copy." He got up from the couch.

She couldn't let him go like this. Pat sprang to her feet. "That isn't necessary, Raven, I do trust you," she said desperately. "I'm sorry about this afternoon."

He sighed. "I'm sorry too—about everything. I thought we had something very special, but I was wrong."

The tiny scar on his cheekbone stood out whitely against his tan. As Pat gazed at the lines of pain in his rugged face, she could almost feel her heart breaking. "Don't go, Raven," she whispered.

He shook his head. "I love you too much to stick around and watch it all go bad between us."

Pat's eyes widened. "You love me?"

"Of course I love you! Haven't I shown you with my lips, my hands, my body?"

"But you never said the words. I thought you only . . ."

He cupped her face in his palms, looking down at her almost sternly. "Are you saying you thought I was only interested in you physically? Didn't you ever listen when I told you I wanted to share *everything* with you?"

Pat's eyes filled with tears. "I couldn't allow myself to hope. I was even afraid to let you know I loved you because I thought it might scare you away."

His hands tightened as he stared down at her with sudden intensity. "Are you telling me the truth? Say it again! Say it over and over again! I'll never hear those words enough."

Pat wound her arms around his neck, raining tiny, frantic kisses over his face and neck. "I love you, Raven. I always have and I always will. Please don't leave me."

"My darling! As though I ever could."

He crushed her in an embrace so tight that she could hardly breathe. All the passion and longing were expressed by his hungry mouth and hard, taut body. After a long moment he swung her up against his chest and carried her into the bedroom, looking wordlessly into her eyes.

He joined her on the bed without letting her out of his arms, as though he couldn't bear to lose contact even for an instant. Pat felt the same way. She ran her hands over his neck, slipping her fingers inside his shirt to feel the warm, firm skin of his shoulders.

"Let me look at you," he murmured. "It's been so long."

When he opened her robe and gazed at her with smoldering passion, Pat felt waves of feeling wash over her. His glance was an almost physical thing. And when his hands began a slow journey down her body, she began to throb with desire. He bent his head to kiss each receptive spot, starting with her taut nipples, then gliding down to dip his tongue in her navel.

Rubbing his cheek against the flat plane of her stomach he muttered, "How could I ever give up such beauty?"

"I was so miserable without you," she murmured, holding his head closely against her body.

"You won't ever be again, my darling." He rolled her into his arms and scissored his legs around hers.

While his lips parted hers in a sensuous prelude, Pat unbuckled his belt and touched him as he had touched her. He was so gloriously masculine, so vibrantly alive under her eager fingers. Her restless hands wanted to explore every part of his splendid male physique.

"You don't know what you're doing to me," he gasped. Springing up for just a moment, Raven tore off his clothes.

Pat welcomed him back with outstretched arms, moving her legs to receive him. He filled her with a throbbing pleasure that mounted quickly to rapture, and then to ecstasy. Each movement was an exquisite onslaught that brought her closer to the summit of all sensation. She reached it in a burst of excitement that gradually dissipated into waves of contentment.

"I love you," Pat whispered at the same moment that Raven said those words to her.

Chapter Nine

$\mathcal{P}$at and Raven made love over and over again that night, as though they had been separated for months.

It was very late when she kissed him and said reluctantly, "You'd better be getting back, especially now that Sam and Betty are there."

He pulled her closer, settling her head on his broad shoulder. "I'm not leaving."

"But Raven, you have to! How will it look?"

He chuckled. "The kids will understand, and Mattie will too once I explain that we're getting married."

Happiness exploded inside Pat like uncorked champagne. Raven wanted to marry her! It had been enough to discover that he loved her, this was almost too much.

Then the problems started to intrude and her happiness faded.

Everything was perfect here on the ranch because they were in a kind of time warp where nothing mattered except each other. Pat would have been content to go on this way but Raven wasn't. He insisted on taking her back to the city where their troubles would start.

To begin with, he didn't even know who she really was. She had told him a limited amount about Carl—but nothing of the attendant publicity surrounding their divorce. How would Raven feel about having a wife who had been an object of ridicule? And that was only *one* of the problems!

He didn't seem to notice her sudden stillness. "Would you rather be married right away here on the ranch, or wait until we get back to New York and have one of those big receptions that nobody but the caterers enjoy?" He grinned. "Not that I'm trying to influence your decision, you understand."

"We don't have to discuss it now," she murmured.

He chuckled. "What better time—or place? I'm offering to make an honest woman of you."

She slid her lips seductively along the strong column of his throat. "All I care about is being a woman."

Raven's reaction was more than satisfactory. His kiss was both tender and passionate. But if Pat had thought to distract him completely, she was mistaken. After a thrilling few moments he returned to the subject.

"So, where is it going to be?" he asked.

Pat concentrated on weaving her fingers through the springing hair on his lean chest. "I'll have to think about it."

"What's there to think about? We love each other and we want to get married. The only question is where." His penetrating gaze assessed her lowered lashes. "You *do* want to marry me, don't you, Pat?"

Her eyes flew open. "Yes, of course!" That part was true.

"Then, what's the problem?"

"Well, we . . . we have things to discuss. You can't just rush into something like this."

"I see." He sat up in bed. "Then, maybe we'd better start discussing them. What's on your mind?"

It always made Pat wary when Raven set his jaw that squarely. The light of love had definitely vanished from his eyes. He might have been presiding over a board meeting.

She pleated the sheet nervously. "Getting married is a serious step. We have to decide all sorts of things."

"Like where we're going to live?" he asked quietly. "That's what's bothering you, isn't it, Pat? The idea of moving back to New York."

There was no use pretending with Raven. Pat's frustration boiled over. "New York chewed me up and spit me out!" she cried. "Don't you understand why I can't go back?"

His face softened as he reached for her. Holding her in his arms and stroking her hair gently he said, "It will be different this time, sweetheart. You'll have me to take care of you."

That was uncomfortably reminiscent of Carl. "I don't need a protector," she said sharply. "I'm perfectly capable of running my own life."

"I would never try to do it for you," he answered quietly. "I want a partner, not a dependent."

Pat's momentary flash of anger died. She knew Raven was only motivated by love. The trouble was that his idea of an equal partner was someone who could hold her own in the glamorous setting that was his real world. Someone like Suzanne Turner, the blonde in the designer jeans.

That's the kind of woman Raven should marry; the kind he'd always gone with. If Pat were to go back to New York with him she would be as out of place as Suzanne was in Wyoming. How long would it be until he started to notice—and how long before other women began to console him? It was much better to have Raven remember her as perfect then to have him find out she wasn't.

Raven watched impassively as Pat wrestled with her demons. He noted the sadness on her face. "Are you still in love with him?" he asked harshly. "So much in love that you're afraid to be in the same city with him?"

"Oh, Raven, no! Carl means nothing to me. I don't even hate him anymore." She realized for the first time that it was true. "He isn't even worth *that*."

Raven stared at her intently. Finally, recognizing her sincerity, he relaxed. "You've never said much about him. All I know is that the idiot was unfaithful. Would you like to talk about it?"

Pat shook her head. "It's a closed chapter in my life—over and done with."

His golden eyes were very penetrating. "I wonder."

It was a subject she had no intention of discussing. Raven mustn't be allowed to get anywhere near the truth. "You really should be getting back."

He frowned. "That means you don't want me to tell anyone we're getting married."

"Not for a while," she murmured.

"Why do I get the feeling that you're just stringing me along?"

Pat's old inability to lie was plaguing her again. "Haven't I shown how much I love you?" she evaded.

"That doesn't answer my question." His voice was

very firm as he said, "I won't let you get away with it, Pat. We're getting married and you're coming back to New York with me, so you might as well make up your mind to it."

"Give me a little time," she pleaded. "I haven't even gotten used to the fact that you love me."

His expression softened. "That doesn't seem possible, but okay, you have two weeks. Mattie should be back on her feet by then, and I really have to get back to work. We'll announce our engagement and set a date for the wedding."

"No! I mean . . . let's just keep this to ourselves for now."

"Why?" His tone was uncompromising.

"Oh . . . you know how Mattie is. She'll make a soap opera out of this. She'll want to know our plans, and she . . . well, she'll make me very self-conscious."

"That doesn't sound like a valid reason to me."

"Please, Raven. I just want us to have this time alone together."

Two weeks was little enough. Even though she always knew their romance had to end, when there was no specific date she could put it out of her mind. It was like knowing you were going to die some day, but not dwelling on it. Now every hour had become precious.

"We'll have *more* time together. Engaged couples are afforded privacy." His smile was replaced by determination. "No, Pat, we're announcing our engagement. I want everyone to know that you're mine."

As she gazed into his adamant face Pat was desolate. She wasn't even to have two weeks to store up memories that would have to last a lifetime. Her idyl was about to end this minute. When she told Raven she couldn't marry him it would all be over. As misery gripped her like an actual pain, she felt tears tightening her throat. She blinked rapidly. Pat despised women who used tears to try to get their own way.

Raven pulled her into his arms, holding her so close that she could hear the groan reverberate in his deep chest. "You win, honey, we'll do it your way—although it's against my better judgment."

"Oh, Raven, you won't regret it!" She raised a radiant face to his. "This will be the best two weeks of our entire lives."

If Pat's conscience gave a slight twinge, it was easy to ignore. It *would* be an enchanted time. And when Raven looked back on it later, he would know she was right.

"I can see who's going to be the boss in this family," he chuckled. "You can get me to do anything, you little devil. I'll even go back to my own bed—but not just yet."

His hands slid down her back to pull her hips closer to his as his mouth closed over Pat's eager one.

The following days were as wonderful as she had promised. With Sam to take over her former chores and his wife to help in the house, Pat was free to spend a lot of time with Raven. She had been reluctant at first to let Betty assume any duties, but the younger woman was persistent.

"I can't just sit around and do nothing," she said. "I'm used to working."

"You're going to have plenty to do when the baby arrives," Pat advised. "I'm told an infant is a twenty-four-hour a day job."

Betty looked worried. "I won't mind, but I hope it won't disturb Mr. Masters."

"He won't be here." Pat gave her full attention to the strawberries she was washing. "As a matter of fact, he's going back to New York shortly."

"Oh, too bad. He's such a nice man—and gorgeous too!" Betty added with a mischievous grin. "I don't know which grabs me the most, that rugged face or that fantastic bod."

Pat's eyebrows shot up. "Shame on you. You're married and pregnant."

"But I'm not dead." Betty laughed. "Why should men be the only ones to appreciate the opposite sex?"

"You're right. Down with men."

"Well, I wouldn't go that far." They laughed together.

As she became more secure, Betty revealed an entirely different personality. She was fun-loving and a complete delight to be with. Pat enjoyed her company tremendously. During the time they spent together she learned that Betty and Sam had been dating since her high school days. They were very much in love and had been planning on getting married as soon as he had saved enough money for a down payment on a small tract house. But the advent of the baby speeded things up.

"We've always dreamed of having our own home," Betty said, looking wistfully around Pat's cottage.

They were sitting in the living room having iced tea. Mattie was taking a nap, and Raven was out on the ranch with Sam so they had some free time, much to Janus's delight. The Great Dane had widened his list of favorite people to include the newcomers. He was resting his massive head on Betty's knee, practically purring as she stroked his ears. Pat felt a slight twinge at his defection. If she went away and left him here Janus would hardly miss her. Except that she wasn't going anywhere. Pat quickly closed the door on any such thoughts.

"Sam's awfully level-headed," Betty was saying earnestly. "Most young couples start off in an apartment, but Sam said all they had to show for it were rent receipts. He said it was better to begin building equity in a house immediately." She sighed. "Our dream keeps getting farther and farther away."

"Not necessarily. The money you save here on rent can go into a house fund."

"Oh, no! Sam's going to talk to Mr. Master's about paying rent as soon as he gets his first paycheck. We couldn't impose that way. It was good enough of him to give Sam a job."

"Do you really think you're going to like living on a ranch?" Pat asked curiously.

Betty's answer was emphatic. "It's heaven already! Sam's always wanted to work outdoors, and there's all this freedom for the baby to grow up in. The only thing that would make it absolutely perfect is if there was another house like this on the property." She laughed. "I don't suppose you'd like to give up yours?"

"No, I wouldn't!" Pat answered, more sharply than she intended.

"I was only joking." Betty looked momentarily hurt. Her feelings mended as she glanced thoughtfully around the living room. "You could make this place into a little doll house with some printed curtains at the windows, and maybe the same fabric slip covering those two wing chairs." Her face grew animated. "I'd be happy to do it for you. If we rented a sewing machine I could run it all up in no time."

Pat had never bothered to fix up the cottage beyond stacking her books in the bookcase and putting out a few treasured knickknacks. Viewing it now through Betty's eyes she saw the possibilities. It could indeed be a love nest for a young couple. The thought made her both depressed and angry. It wasn't her fault that Sam and Betty were forced to live in one room in someone else's house. No one promised anyone a rose garden, she told herself. It didn't help to lessen the guilt.

"It's something to consider." Pat stood up restlessly. "We'd better be getting back to the house. Mattie might be up."

Betty's eyes widened as she noticed Pat's grim expression. The subject was tacitly dropped.

By dinnertime the slight tension between the two had vanished. When Sam and Betty first arrived, Raven had insisted that they all have their meals together in the dining room, overriding Mattie's protests.

"If you think I'm going to be a lonely exile while the rest of you have fun in the kitchen, you're mistaken," he stated firmly. "Besides, Sam would be outnumbered."

Sam returned his grin. "I don't mind being surrounded by beautiful women."

"Watch your step," Raven growled. "Pat's *my* girl."

Raven had kept his word about not announcing their engagement, but his attitude toward her spoke volumes. She gloried in Raven's love, enjoying every touch, every glance, while she had the chance.

The young couple took it for granted, but Mattie didn't. She grew more worried as time went on. One day she called Pat into her room for a private conversation.

The older woman seemed at a loss for how to begin. "You know I'm very fond of you, Pat," she started awkwardly.

Thinking she was going to express her appreciation yet another time, Pat said, "Don't start thanking me again, Mattie. If I'd been sick you would have taken care of me."

"No doubt about that. But sometimes it's easier to

take care of people when they're sick than when they're well."

"I don't understand."

Mattie's neck flushed a dull red. She hesitated, choosing her next words with difficulty. "Mr. Masters is a very fine gentleman, but he's a man, for all that."

Comprehension dawned. "I see."

"Men have certain urges, and women are the ones who have to be strong," Mattie explained carefully.

Amusement penetrated Pat's discomfort. Mattie might have been a mother, telling her pubescent daughter the facts of life. She meant well, though. Unfortunately the older woman would never understand Pat's relationship with Raven. He would just have to start being more discreet, since neither of them wanted to upset her.

"You're perfectly right." Pat tried to sound reassuring.

Mattie wasn't convinced. "Sometimes even the most level-headed woman forgets to use common sense. Mr. Masters is like an exotic bird of paradise. He comes here a few times a year and brings a little glamour into our lives, and then he goes back where he came from. He wouldn't be happy here for long, and we couldn't stand the pace if we got some crazy idea to try and follow him."

The words struck Pat like stones. "I know. Don't worry, Mattie, I understand that better than you do."

Pat was depressed for a few hours, but when Raven came to the cottage that night, future heartbreak seemed worth it. She did warn him about toning down his behavior in front of Mattie, giving him an expurgated account of their conversation.

"I'll try, but it won't be easy." He cupped his hand around her breast, bending his head to kiss the rosy tip.

"If you'd let me tell everyone we're engaged, she'd know my intentions are honorable."

"You promised me two weeks." Pat raked her fingernails lightly over his buttocks.

Raven was distracted, as she had meant him to be. "All right, my beautiful little enchantress," he muttered thickly. "But not a day more. This damn two weeks already seems like an eternity."

When his mouth possessed hers with a dominant masculinity, Pat wished sadly that it *could* last that long.

As Betty and Sam overcame their awe of Raven, the two couples became good friends. They got into the habit of going to the movies together, or watching television, or perhaps playing Scrabble.

"Honestly, Raven, sometimes I can't believe you," Betty said one night. The four of them were sitting around the game table in the den.

He raised a dark eyebrow. "Why is that?"

"You're rich and famous. You must lead a very exciting life in New York, but here you are playing games with us as though you didn't have anything better to do."

"I like your company." He slanted a mischievous glance at Pat. "And I like the simple life. Don't I always turn in early?"

"Now *that* doesn't surprise me." Betty laughed as Pat turned a bright pink.

She called Raven on it when he accompanied her to the cottage a little later, but he was unrepentant.

"If you care that much about appearances I have a ready solution," he remarked.

"You never give up, do you?" Pat muttered.

"It's something you'd better learn about me," he

answered, wrapping his arms around her and molding her to his lean body.

It was difficult to stay annoyed when all of her senses were quickening under his provocative touch. Pat decided that their dwindling nights left no time for arguments.

One morning at breakfast, Raven declared a holiday. "We're going to pack a picnic basket and drive up in the mountains to prospect for gold."

"How neat! Is there really gold still to be found?" Betty's face was animated.

"Maybe not another Comstock lode, but enough to have fun with."

Sam looked uneasily at his wife. "I don't think Betty should be climbing around in an abandoned mine."

"None of us should," Raven agreed. "We're going to pan for gold in the great outdoors. Betty can sit on the bank of the stream while the rest of us wade in."

"No fair, I want to play too," she protested.

"You will," Raven promised. "While you ladies are making lunch I'll go hunt up the equipment and leather boots."

In the general hilarity of packing the car, Janus watched with an almost comical air of sadness. He was seldom allowed to accompany them because they were usually going into town. It was strange—after years of being a city dog, Janus had gone completely native. Whereas before he knew to wait for traffic lights to change, now he considered it his divine right to cross the street whenever he felt like it. Pat was always afraid he might slip the leash and get hurt.

"Don't look so sad, baby." She bent down to put her arms around his neck. "You're coming with us." The dog was immediately galvanized into action, barking and racing around in circles. Pat smiled fondly. "Wait until he discovers all those trees up there. He'll think heaven has a new suburb."

Raven's face was serious. "I've been meaning to talk to you about Janus. I know how much you love him—I do too—but do you think it's fair to take him back to New York? He might not be able to cope with it after leading such a different life."

Why won't you admit that I have the same problem, Pat asked silently. She reached down for a pair of wading boots, avoiding Raven's eyes. "We'll discuss it another time."

He squatted down beside her. "You can't keep putting everything off, Pat."

"Later, Raven, please?"

He looked into her pleading eyes and swore softly. "Okay, honey, but a day of reckoning is coming."

It was easy to put out of her mind when they were having such a good time. The drive into the Grand Tetons was breathtaking, with a new, stunning vista around every bend. Wildflowers carpeted the valley floor in vivid blues and oranges, giving way to shrubs and alpine blooms as they climbed higher. A stream wandered in and out of view, and an unexpected delight was the occasional sight of churning white falls cascading down the mountains. At the higher elevations, giant fir trees cast a deep shadow beneath the snow-capped, looming peaks.

Raven pulled off the road in a clearing bordering a crystal clear river that bubbled over smooth stones.

"It doesn't even matter if we don't find gold," Betty declared. "This is the most divine spot I ever saw!"

"Don't take such a defeatest attitude," Raven advised. "We're going to find enough gold to send the baby to college."

Pat raised her eyebrows. "Invested wisely, that is, for eighteen years at compound interest."

Raven laughed. "I'm surrounded by Philistines. No wonder the Gold Rush was composed of men."

"With a few indispensable exceptions," Pat reminded him dryly.

While Janus bounded off to explore, Raven explained the principles of panning for gold.

"The best place to look is in the middle of the stream, so Sam and I will wade out. You girls can do the panning. The way it's done is to hold the pan in both hands in a level position, partially submerged in the stream. You turn it in a circular movement to let the heavy particles sink to the bottom. Gold is nineteen times heavier than water, and seven or eight times heavier than rock, so the sand will rise to the top."

"How do we get rid of it?" Pat asked.

"After you've rotated the pan until all you can see is sand, tip the pan slightly so the water can wash it away."

Pat and Betty concentrated diligently over the filled tins the men brought, discarding the large pebbles as Raven instructed, and rotating the metal circles vigorously. At first they were disappointed when all they got for their efforts was a residue of black sand. But then Raven took over. He gave each pan one quick spin which separated the grains.

"That's called a 'string of colors,' " he instructed. "Now we can see what we have."

"It's gold!" Betty shouted, for all the world like one of the early prospectors.

"Not what you're looking at." Raven took some tweezers and pointed to some specks of bright yellow. "That's iron pyrite, more commonly known as fool's gold. It looks more like the real thing than gold itself."

Betty sighed. "I knew it was too good to be true."

"You give up too easily." Using the tweezers carefully, he picked up some dull, yellowish grains. "Now, there's your gold."

"You're kidding! That plain-looking stuff?"

He nodded.

After that they worked with even more energy. Not every pan yielded treasure, but by the time they were ready to leave, there was a small heap in the mason jar they had hopefully brought.

"Have you decided on a college yet?" Raven asked smugly.

"Be serious," Betty pleaded. "How much do you think this is worth?"

"At today's gold prices, a nice sum." He grinned suddenly. "Well, at least enough for you and Sam to have dinner in town."

"We're going to split it four ways," Betty protested.

"No, it's all yours." Raven put his arm around Pat, smiling down at her. "Pat and I are rich enough already."

As they were gathering up the picnic things Betty murmured to Pat, "That man is a positive gem. If you let him get away you're crazy."

"I have to round up Janus," Pat said hastily.

The two weeks were almost up when Betty suggested they all go to the weekly square dance.

Sam looked pointedly at her blossoming stomach. "I think that's a little strenuous for you right now."

"I'm not going to dance, I just want to watch. I've never been to a square dance. Couldn't we please, Raven?"

"I'm afraid it's too strenuous for me too. I've only recently mastered walking again."

"Oh, I'm sorry! I didn't think."

She was so sweetly penitent that Raven smiled at her fondly. "I don't see any reason why we can't go, though. You and I can sit on the sidelines while Pat and Sam work up a sweat."

"Ladies don't perspire, they glow," Pat informed him loftily.

"They certainly do—in the dark," he murmured in her ear as Betty turned to persuade her husband. "Ouch!" he yelped when Pat pinched him sharply.

"You're no gentleman," she hissed.

Raven cupped her cheek in his palm, gazing at her with pure love in his glowing, golden eyes. "I'll be whatever you want me to be," he said in a husky voice.

"Sam's willing if you are, Pat," Betty said eagerly. "Is it all right?"

Pat turned her attention to the other woman with difficulty. "What? Oh . . . sure, why not?"

The town hall was decked out for the occasion, and the music had started when they got there.

As she watched the energetic dancers Pat began to have second thoughts. "I haven't square danced since I was a kid."

"I've *never* done it." Sam clearly shared her apprehension. "Shall we just sit on the sidelines with the old folks?"

"I want you to learn so you can teach me," Betty coaxed. "Go ahead, it looks like fun." She turned to Raven for support. "They'll be the best-looking couple on the floor, won't they?"

He chuckled. "Well, at least they'll be the bravest."

In spite of their trepidation, Pat and Sam were soon caught up in the infectious rhythm. They twirled and promenaded, carried along by the sheer momentum of the rapid calls. If they missed a step there was always someone to help them, and they soon got into the spirit of the thing.

When the music stopped Pat found herself hand in hand with a tall, blue-eyed ranch hand who was the quintessential cowboy. His jeans rode low on hard, narrow hips, and his deep tan spoke of days spent on the range. His rugged good looks could have graced a billboard.

"Well, hello!" The blue eyes were alive with interest. "My name's Corey Hawkins, what's yours?" After she had supplied it he said, "I haven't seen you around here before."

"No, this is my first time."

He took her other hand, pulling her slightly closer. "But not your last I hope."

Pat pulled her hands away, smiling brightly. "You never know."

As she turned to go he caught her wrist. "Hey, don't rush off. Can I buy you a drink?"

"No, thanks, I'm with friends. And I'd better be getting back to them." Pat had met Corey's type before. She dismissed him as soon as she turned her back.

Sam had already rejoined the others. He was flopped in a chair, pretending exhaustion. "That sort of thing isn't for a city bloke."

"Come on, you loved it," Pat teased. "I'd forgotten how much fun it is." Her face was animated as she turned to Raven. "It's too bad you couldn't join us." In her enthusiasm she didn't notice that his smile didn't reach his eyes.

"You seemed to be doing all right without me," Raven remarked evenly.

"Pat put her heart and soul into it all right," Sam agreed.

"I must have." She pulled her shirt away from her

damp body. "It's sweltering in here. I'm going outside to cool off for a minute."

Two pairs of eyes watched her move gracefully toward the door. Raven's narrowed as he saw the tall cowboy follow her.

Pat was gazing up at the diamond-spangled sky when Corey Hawkins joined her.

"Did you have a fight with your boyfriend?" he asked hopefully.

"Nothing like that." She hoped he wasn't going to be a nuisance. "I just came out for a breath of air."

"It is warm in there," he agreed. "Maybe we should sit the next one out and get acquainted."

"I told you I was with someone."

"Is he anybody special?"

Her radiant face gave him the answer even before she replied softly, "Yes, very special."

He looked regretfully at the silky auburn hair curling around her slim shoulders. "I should have known a beautiful girl like you would be spoken for. Some guys have all the luck."

"I imagine you have your share of female companionship," Pat commented dryly, starting back to the dance hall.

He followed her inside. Before she left him, Corey took her chin in his palm, gazing down at her with open admiration. "I still say he's a lucky guy."

Raven's face was like a thundercloud when Pat rejoined him. "Come on, we're leaving," he said curtly.

"But why? The dance is only half over." Her bewildered eyes sought Betty and Sam, who looked embarrassed.

"I'm sorry to tear you away from your admirer, but I'm leaving," Raven bit out harshly. "You can either come with me or stay here."

"Raven, you can't honestly think—" her words were addressed to his retreating back. "What on earth got into him?" she exclaimed.

"I think we'd better go," Sam said uncomfortably.

As she accompanied them to the car, Pat's temper started to rise. Raven was obviously annoyed over that macho cowboy's attentions to her, but he didn't have to make a scene. And he certainly didn't have to drag them home like wayward children! Pat couldn't have cared less about staying, but he had no right to spoil the evening for Betty and Sam. Nor did he have any right to dictate to *her*.

She fumed silently all the way home, not wanting to descend to his level in front of the others.

It was a very uncomfortable trip. Raven drove like a madman, without a word to anyone. After making a few attempts at desultory conversation, Sam and Betty lapsed into silence too.

As soon as the car screeched to a stop in front of the cottage, Pat got out hurriedly. Raven slid out of the driver's seat, saying curtly to Sam, "Take the car back to the house."

Pat's reaction was outrage. Raven had a lot of nerve to think he'd be welcome after the way he'd just behaved. She wanted to tell him exactly that, but there were also a great many other things she needed to get off her chest—things that had to be said in private.

She stalked to the door, her slight body rigid with fury. Raven followed almost on her heels, also radiating anger.

The minute the door slammed after them Pat whirled to face him, her eyes spitting green fire. "I suppose you're proud of that disgusting display you just put on!"

His mouth was a grim line. "How about your behavior?"

"I don't know what you're talking about. *I* wasn't the one who acted like a dictator—ordering everyone around to show your supreme power."

"Was I supposed to sit tamely by while you let a strange man fondle you?" he asked coldly.

"Are you out of your mind?" she gasped. "He did nothing of the sort!"

"My eyesight happens to be perfect, even if the rest of me isn't. I know what I saw."

"Then, *you* tell *me*. We were standing in the middle of a room full of people, for heaven's sake," Pat pointed out impatiently.

"What went on when you so conveniently needed to go outside to cool off?" Raven demanded. "Did you make a date with him?"

"That's too stupid to answer."

His steely fingers bit cruelly into her soft skin. "That means you did."

Pat's anger began to seep away as she saw the desolation behind Raven's fury. "How could you even think a thing like that?" she whispered.

His body was taut as he stared at her. "I don't know what to think anymore."

Pat shook her head helplessly. "If you believe I could be interested in another man after all we've shared, then you're beyond convincing."

Mixed emotions warred on his strong face as the truth of her statement seeped in. Finally he groaned, reaching out and smothering her in a fierce embrace. "I knew at the time that I was overreacting but I couldn't help myself. When he touched you I wanted to kill him."

Pat was moved by the depth of his feeling, yet it disturbed her slightly. "Jealousy is a mark of insecurity, Raven," she told him earnestly.

He kissed the tip of her tilted nose. "You're responsible for that. If you'd let me put a ring on your finger everyone would know you're mine."

"*You* know it; that's all that matters."

"Not to me. I'm a very possessive guy, Pat." He picked her up and carried her to a big chair, sitting down with her in his arms. "You can start deciding where you want to be married because I'm not going through another night like this one."

Her body grew tense. "But the two weeks isn't up yet."

He shrugged. "It was an arbitrary time to begin with. Now, where is it going to be, here or New York?"

Pat's mind raced wildly, like a small trapped animal trying to find an escape route. Her long lashes fell as she twisted a button on his shirt. "I've been thinking about it, Raven, and I don't think we should make up our minds just yet."

"There are certain arrangements to be made—the license, that sort of thing," he remarked evenly.

"I know, but perhaps we should wait a little while."

"You don't want to marry me, do you, Pat?" he asked quietly.

"Of course I—well, maybe not right this minute." She got to her feet, hugging her arms around her trembling body. "I just don't see why we can't go on the way we are."

"A long-distance romance? With you here and me in New York?"

"It might be best. When you get back to the city you may find this was only a summer romance after all."

He stood up to loom over her. "Don't lay the blame on me—you're the one who has doubts."

"Can't you see that it's understandable?" she pleaded. "I made one mistake; I don't want to make another."

"If you're putting me in a class with that wimp you

were married to, then, maybe you're right and we don't have any future together," he said savagely.

"I know you're not like Carl. It's only that . . . I need a little more time," she concluded lamely.

"It's just run out." His face was like granite. "I love you, Pat, but I won't be dangled on a string."

She set her chin stubbornly. "And I won't be dictated to. This is my decision as well as yours."

"Then, you'd better make it, because it's marriage or nothing."

"Don't threaten me, Raven!" she flared. "I got along just fine before I met you, and I can do it again."

"That's what you really want, isn't it?" He stared at her with a faint look of contempt in his tawny eyes. "I knocked a hole in that wall you built around yourself, and for a while your body betrayed you. But sex isn't enough to leave your fortress for, is it? Well, don't worry, I won't bother you any further. I wanted more than a bed partner, even if you didn't."

Pat was too stricken to do anything but stare after him as he stalked out the door.

Reaction set in immediately. Raven couldn't honestly believe those harsh things he said? He had to know how much she loved him. Why couldn't he see it her way?

Tomorrow she would have to find some way to convince him, because he was too angry to listen to reason tonight. It wouldn't solve a problem that was insoluble, but it was unthinkable for him to go on believing the worst of her.

For the first time in a long while, Pat cried herself to sleep.

Chapter Ten

$\mathcal{P}$at was so reluctant to face Raven the next day that she invented all kinds of tasks around the cottage to delay their meeting. It was essential that she correct his opinion of her but if she was successful, Raven would again insist on marriage. And Pat hadn't changed her mind about that.

Finally she grew impatient with her own shilly-shallying. She was only prolonging the misery. Squaring her shoulders resolutely, she marched up to the house, trying to act as though this were just an ordinary day.

Betty was alone in the kitchen, cleaning up the breakfast dishes. She had insisted on taking over the morning meal. "Oh . . . hi, Pat." She looked embarrassed. "Would you . . . um . . . like a cup of coffee?"

Pat was about to refuse, but she reconsidered. Raven might join them and give her a clue to his mood. It was just possible that he had spent as miserable a night as she, and be eager to make up.

"I'd love some coffee." After she had poured herself a cup Pat said brightly, "How's Sam this morning? Recovered from all that strenuous exercise?"

"He . . . uh . . . I guess so."

Pat sighed. "This is silly, Betty, pretending nothing happened last night. I know it was sticky, but it wasn't really important. Raven and I are still good friends." Would he help her keep up the fiction?

"Sam and I were hoping you'd work things out," Betty said in a low voice.

"Well, we yelled at each other a lot. I got it all out of my system." Pat tried to smile. "I'm about to go find out if he got it out of his."

"Raven's gone," Betty said quietly.

Pat stared at her blankly. "What do you mean?"

"He caught a plane for New York early this morning."

The sky seemed to come crashing down suddenly. "I see." It was an effort to form the words through her numb lips. "Did he leave any message for me?"

Betty looked as though she were near tears. "No, he . . . he just left."

Pat had a preview of what it was like to be very old; it was difficult to get out of the chair. "I guess I'd better . . . see if Mattie needs anything." For a moment she couldn't remember what her usual routine was.

"Oh, Pat, I'm so sorry! I know how you must be feeling."

Pat doubted it. Even she couldn't believe the sharp pain that slashed her midsection. But the last thing Pat wanted was pity. She squared her shoulders gallantly. "I feel fine. I was just surprised for a minute. I didn't think Raven was leaving quite yet."

"He'll be back," Betty said softly.

"I'm sure he will. Mattie says he pops in several times a year." Pat's brittle tone portrayed the way she felt, terribly fragile, as though she might shatter in a million pieces.

Betty hesitated. "Sam and I used to have quarrels, but it wasn't the end of everything."

"Surely you don't think Raven left because of that silly little argument last night?" Pat tried to appear incredulous.

"Anyone would have to be deaf and blind not to know that you two were in love," Betty answered simply.

Pat couldn't very well deny her own feelings at least, but she tried to make light of the situation. "I'll admit that we were attracted to each other. Raven is a very fascinating man. But there certainly was no grand passion between us."

"The four of us spent a lot of time together, remember? Maybe I should mind my own business, but Sam and I have gotten so fond of both of you." Betty's young face was earnest. "I'd hate to see a foolish misunderstanding spoil something beautiful."

Pat's shoulders slumped as she gave up the pretense. "It was very beautiful," she said quietly. "But it's over."

"It doesn't have to be! Phone him tonight. I'll bet Raven is every bit as miserable as you are."

"That's quite possible," Pat admitted. "But it doesn't change anything—and he'll get over it. There are a lot of things you don't know."

"I know he couldn't keep his eyes off you. No one else mattered when you were around."

Pat's mouth twisted in the semblance of a smile. "You're a big girl now, Betty. You know about sex."

"There was more to it than that," the other woman said impatiently. "You two were like . . . like soul mates. You enjoyed each other's company. Even when we were only watching television, I could tell you were happy just to be together."

Every word was hammering a spike into Pat's heart. She stood up abruptly. "What you saw was a storybook romance. It was very charming but it wasn't meant to be taken seriously." Before Betty could argue the point Pat said, "I'll be down at the cottage if you need me."

The next few days were hell—and the nights were worse. Pat kept waiting for the sound of remembered footsteps, knowing they would never come again. She grew so used to not sleeping that sometimes she didn't even bother to undress, merely lying on top of the bed fully clothed.

The only thing that sustained her was the knowledge that she was right. If Raven was as miserable as she, he would have called. And if he'd really loved her, he couldn't have left.

The letter from Raven's prestigious firm of attorneys was his only communication with her. It came in a legal-size envelope along with a contract making her caretaker of the ranch until she terminated her own employment. As she stared at the document, Pat's pain deepened. Raven was writing finis to their interlude, as he called it; paying her off and slipping back into his old life. It hadn't taken long.

She ignored the instructions to return one signed copy. It was further evidence of the chasm between them that Raven thought she needed a written guarantee. Pat knew it was time to move on. It was self-flagellation to stay on at the ranch where everything reminded her of him. Every corner of the house and cottage were filled with memories too poignant to be borne.

There was another reason for leaving. She really had very little to do. With the best will in the world, Betty had gradually taken over her duties at the house, and Sam was doing better with the outside than Pat could. Mattie's health was improving every day. When she was completely recovered, Pat would be about as necessary as toes on a tuna. It had all occurred exactly as she predicted, yet Pat knew that none of it was premeditated. Things just happened.

Although she had reasoned everything out quite unemotionally, lethargy prevented her from doing anything about it. The very thought of uprooting herself again sent her mind swiveling away from the idea. She would take until the end of the month, Pat told herself vaguely.

The trouble was that the days seemed endless. She was so used to being active. It was the only thing that had bothered her about writing—the long hours of inactivity in front of the typewriter. But against her will she recalled how fast the time had passed then, and how totally absorbed she'd been. Many a night she had worked until the early hours of the morning without feeling a trace of fatigue.

Pat pushed the memory out of her mind. That was a closed chapter in her life, just as Raven was. She would find somewhere else to go, and something else to do. Perhaps she and Janus would just get in the car and drive to another state—when she got around to it.

Pat began to look for things to occupy herself away from the ranch house. Betty's silent mixture of sympathy and disapproval was hard to take. Pat had effectively discouraged her when she tried to reopen the subject of Raven, but there was nothing she could do about her eloquent glances. Mattie was no joy either. Her constant references to Raven's sterling qualities set Pat's already taut nerves vibrating.

One day she wandered over to the bunkhouse and almost pleaded with Buck Henley for something to do.

"I never saw such a demon for work," he chuckled. "I just wish I had a few dozen wranglers like you."

"I like to keep busy," Pat answered lamely.

"Well, I guess you could curry the horses if you're really serious. This is roundup time and we haven't been able to give them more than a lick and a promise. I could sure use the help."

"You've got it." Her eyes brightened at the prospect.

It was painstaking manual labor that Pat attacked with vigor. She used the brushes and curry combs until the coats of the small stable of horses gleamed like caramel-colored satin. Then she polished their hooves and brushed the long, plumy tails, crooning softly in a language they seemed to understand.

When she finished in the late afternoon, Pat gave herself a small treat. She led her favorite, a spirited palomino with a golden coat and a blond tail and mane, out to the riding ring. Mounting him bareback, she galloped the beautiful horse around the track with Janus in joyous pursuit. The sheer poetry of motion exhilarated her, and Pat smiled for the first time in days.

After rubbing the horse down, she put him in his stall and went back to the cottage, feeling pleasantly relaxed.

She shed her rather gamey clothes in the service porch before going into the bathroom to take a shower. As the hot water soothed her tight muscles, Pat could feel her tension lifting. She washed her hair, then stepped out and wrapped herself in a large bath towel while she blew her hair dry. She was gazing absent-mindedly in the mirror at the cloud of auburn hair that drifted around her bare shoulders when a movement at the open door caught her eye. Turning her head, she froze. Raven was standing in the doorway.

"I rang the bell but there was no answer. Then I heard your dryer going," he said.

Pat was in a state of suspended animation. She stared at him unbelievingly as the dryer in her raised hand continued to whip the soft hair around her pale face. Finally she rallied enough to turn the machine off.

"What are you doing here?" she whispered.

"I had to come back." Raven's voice was hoarse.

"Why?"

"That's a silly question." He advanced slowly into the bathroom, putting his hands on her bare shoulders and staring at her as though trying to memorize every feature. "You must have known I couldn't stay away."

Pat's heart was starting to beat again. She tried to ignore its wild pounding. "It didn't seem to bother you for the last two weeks."

"Is that how long it's been?" His hands made caressing motions over her shoulders before skimming the edge of the towel. "It felt like an eternity."

Pat clung desperately to her very real indignation, even though it was rapidly melting under the excitement he was generating. "Don't try to sweet-talk me, Raven. How much could I have meant to you if you left without a word?"

"So much that I was afraid to say good-bye. I knew I could never do it if I saw you again."

"Well, you managed," she said tautly. "Why did you come back?"

"Because it isn't over between us; you know that."

"You're wrong." She struggled in vain to get away

from his destructive hands. Raven's touch was disturbing, raising hungers she had tried to suppress. Her long lashes masked her inner turmoil. "We had fun together, but you mustn't blow it out of all proportion."

"Fun? Is that your word for the nights you spent in my arms, for the way you gave yourself to me totally, letting me become a part of you?"

The memory of those nights made her tremble. It was an effort to keep from throwing herself in his arms, begging him to make her whole again. "It isn't very kind of you to remind me," she murmured, barely audibly.

"I don't want to be kind," he flung out savagely. "I want to carry you to bed and make love to you a hundred different ways until you admit that you need me as much as I need you."

How long could she withstand him? Raven's body was like a weapon, threatening to destroy her defenses. "I don't deny that our . . . that the physical side of our relationship was very satisfactory," she said carefully.

"It's good of you to admit the obvious!"

"You don't have to be sarcastic," she said in a low voice.

"It's preferable to the things I'd really like to say." He jerked her chin up, staring at her with blazing eyes. "Is that all there was for you, Pat? All those things you said when we reached paradise together were part of an act?"

"No! I mean . . . well, you know how it is when . . . " the words trailed off.

"Sure, I understand. It spurs your partner on to greater heights. Was my performance adequate?" he asked bitterly. "Yours certainly was. I even believed all those fevered protestations of love. That must have handed you a big laugh!"

His cruel accusations were flaying her like a whip. Pat

closed her eyes to shut out Raven's withering scorn. A tear escaped and rolled down her cheek in spite of her effort to stop it.

His hand tightened for a moment before falling away. "For God's sake, don't cry! You don't have to trot out your whole bag of tricks for me. I'm going." He turned abruptly and strode out.

Pat followed him into the bedroom, clutching at her towel. It was unthinkable to let him leave thinking such ugly things of her. "Raven!" she called desperately.

The stony look on his face told her there was no hope. Where was the tender lover whose only aim had been to please? This man looked as though he hated her.

"Well?" There was chilling disinterest in his tone.

It told her there was only one thing left to say. "I'm sorry," she whispered.

They stared at each other for a quivering moment. Then Raven's expression softened and he moved slowly toward her, as though pulled by an invisible magnet. He touched the soft cloud of her hair before trailing his fingers over the curve of her cheek.

"I'm sorry too," he murmured.

It was too much. Pat's control suddenly snapped and she flung her arms around his neck, molding her shaking body to his hard, remembered angles. "I can't let you go like this, Raven! It wasn't an act. I meant every word I ever said to you."

He held her off as wild hope warred with deep suspicion. "Is this another trick, Pat? Because if it is, I swear to you I won't be responsible!"

The warmth of his lean body, the strength of the rigid hands that gripped her shoulders, even the male scent of his after-shave, were blessings long denied. All of her pent-up longing was there to see as Pat gazed into his eyes.

"I've never lied to you, Raven." The soft words had the unmistakable ring of truth.

He caught his breath sharply, gathering her in a fierce embrace. "My darling! If you only knew how . . . I thought you didn't care. I was so . . ." Muttering broken phrases he lifted her in his arms and carried her over to the bed.

Sinking down beside her, Raven took possession of her mouth with a passion that was evidence of his frustrated yearning. His tongue probed deeply, staking a masculine claim that stirred her senses. They quickened when he dragged his mouth away and gently tugged at the towel that had slipped down until it only covered the tips of her breasts. He drew it apart, exposing her completely. For a moment Raven just gazed at the slender perfection of her body, his eyes molten with desire.

His avid glance was almost as tangible as a caress. And when he touched her, Pat cried out in delight. Her soft sounds of pleasure spurred him on. Bending his head, he kissed the hollow in her throat, then continued down to the shadowed valley between her breasts. After kissing each aching nipple, he trailed a path of fire all the way down her quivering body.

When a tremor of ecstasy greeted his lips he murmured, "You missed me too, didn't you, sweetheart?"

"You'll never know how much!" Pat stretched out her arms, needing this man as she had needed no other.

His eyes were brilliant with triumph as he gathered her so close that she was like the missing half of him. "I knew I couldn't be wrong about us. You were mine from the moment we met."

"I know." Pat sighed, admitting the incontrovertible. Her fingers fumbled with the knot in his tie.

"Nothing will ever come between us again," he declared fiercely.

His shirt was unbuttoned now and Pat pushed it off his shoulders, shivering at the sensuous feeling of his warm, muscled flesh under her palms. Her eyes were half closed as she raised a passion-drugged face to whisper, "Love me, darling."

"Until the end of time," he promised tenderly. "Our marriage will last forever."

"Don't spoil it, Raven." She was melting in the flames that mounted higher with every caress. "Just love me."

His hands stilled and he raised his head. "Don't *spoil* it? I'm asking you to marry me!"

His harsh tone was a jarring note, intruding on the magic of the moment. She looked at him in confusion. "How can you talk about marriage now?"

"I don't believe you!" Raven raised himself to one elbow, staring down at her incredulously. "When would you like to discuss it? I can't think of a more appropriate time or place than when a man and a woman are in bed together."

Pat's fevered body felt bereft without him. How could he arouse her to such heights and then tease her this way? A surge of anger caused the waves of desire to recede.

"It isn't necessary to be crude," she said coldly. "I'm beginning to think marriage is an obsession with you."

"And I realize now that I was right about you the first time." A muscle twitched at the point of his square jaw as Raven got to his feet. "You don't love me, Pat. All you want is the sexual gratification I can give you. Well, you're going to have to find it somewhere else because I'm through!"

Pat pulled the towel around her shaking body and sat up against the headboard. "Don't talk to me about love! Have you ever examined your own feelings?

What you really want is to dominate me. You see yourself as a latter day Pygmalion. Well, I'm not your Galatea, so you can forget the whole thing!"

"That's exactly what I'm going to do." Raven's voice was low and deadly. "From now on you don't exist as far as I'm concerned."

Pat's anger collapsed as soon as the front door closed after him. How could this have happened, she wondered dazedly? It had been like a miracle when Raven returned and told her he still loved her. Everything had been so perfect. How could it have gone so wrong?

Her desolation deepened as she realized that her heated denunciation had been true. Raven's determination to marry her had become a point of pride. Her refusal not only injured his male ego, it also triggered his combativeness. Raven wasn't used to losing. He was determined to impose his will on her. Or at least he had been. The memory of his rigid face as he flung out of the cottage told Pat that this time it was really over.

In the days that followed Pat continued to tell herself that it was for the best. She even began to make half-hearted plans for the future by buying the out-of-town papers and scanning the classified ads. It was a tremendous effort that she couldn't concentrate on for long. What difference did it make where she went? Raven would come along to haunt her.

One afternoon Pat was lying on the couch reading when Betty rang the bell. They had seen very little of each other because Pat no longer took her meals at the house. Since her shattering encounter with Raven, she avoided everyone's company.

"I hope I'm not disturbing you," Betty said.

There was a look on her face that Pat couldn't decipher, but she put it down to the constraint between them. "Of course not, come on in. Would you like some coffee or tea?"

"No, thanks." Betty seemed to be examining her as though she'd never seen her before.

"Is anything wrong?" Pat asked.

"Why didn't you ever tell anyone who you were?" The words tumbled out.

"You already know who I am." Pat felt a chill of foreboding.

"Not until I read this copy of *World Today*." Betty displayed a magazine she'd brought with her. "There's a picture of you, that's how I knew. I don't suppose I would have connected the name—Patricia Lauren Lee. Why didn't you tell us you were a famous author?"

Pat sighed, ignoring the question. "What does it say?"

Betty opened the magazine and handed it to her. "It's all here, including an interview with your ex-husband." She looked at her friend with discreet curiosity. "You never mentioned him either."

The article was headed: "Whatever Became Of." It was about newsmakers whose star had blazed brightly before being extinguished. The information on Pat detailed the runaway success of her first book, then speculated on her failure to produce subsequent ones. Following that was an interview with Carl. His comments were righteously self-serving:

"Patricia's first book was brilliant. It's a tragedy that she couldn't write anymore. I tried to motivate her, but she had great personal problems. They even led to the breakup of our marriage. At first I agonized over my failure to help Patricia develop her talent, but finally I had to accept the fact that some writers have only one important book in them. She was probably wiser than I to give up."

"That bastard!" Pat's clenched fingers crumpled the page.

"Your . . . uh . . . husband?"

"Do you want to know what really broke up my marriage?" Pat asked tautly.

It was as though a dam had burst. All of the outrage and disillusionment that she thought was safely buried came out in a torrent. There were people who knew bits and pieces of the sordid events, but Pat had never confided the whole story to anyone. It was a relief to unburden herself, and it was better for Betty to know the truth than to believe Carl's lies.

"You poor kid!" Betty was both shocked and sympathetic. "What a rotten experience. No wonder you didn't want to talk about it."

"It's funny, but now that it's all out in the open I feel almost relaxed," Pat remarked thoughtfully. She tried to smile. "Nothing like giving the old skeleton in the closet a good airing."

"You shouldn't have carried this around locked up inside yourself. A stiff upper lip may be very noble, but it would have been a lot better for you to cry on a good friend's shoulder."

"I didn't have any." Pat examined her fingernails carefully. "I don't seem to be very good at judging people."

Betty's eyes were sad as she gazed at her friend. She forced a cheerful tone of voice. "How can you say that? You're up to your ears in friends. There's Sam and me, and Mattie—and Raven," she added deliberately.

Pat got up and went to stare out of the window with her back to the room. "Three out of four isn't a bad percentage."

"Why won't you admit what's perfectly obvious—that the man is in love with you!" Betty fumed impotently. Something occurred to her. "Does Raven know who you really are?"

"No!" Pat whirled around. "And I'd appreciate it if you didn't tell him."

"He could read it in this magazine the same as I did."

"Raven doesn't read that trash." At the look on the other woman's face Pat said, "I'm sorry, Betty, but that's what it is. They exploit people with no regard for how it will affect them. Look at me. I made a new life for myself, and now it's all down the drain. I'll be a local curiosity. Someone's bound to dig up all that dirt about the divorce," she said bitterly.

"People here aren't like that," Betty protested. "I'll admit they'll be interested because you were a famous author, but what's so bad about that?" She looked at her friend curiously. "Did you really give up writing? I thought it was a kind of compulsion, like not being able to stop after eating one peanut." She laughed.

Pat returned a wan smile. "It *is* rather like an addiction. I still find myself drawn to my typewriter, but so far I've been able to resist temptation."

"Why?" Betty demanded. "You have a wonderful gift. Why are you denying yourself?"

"All it brought me was misery," Pat replied tautly. "I don't want to get caught up in that phony world again."

"You don't have to. You could sit right here in your living room and write."

"It isn't that simple." Pat tried to explain. "Your publisher expects you to go on publicity tours and give interviews. You're thrown into the social whirl of cocktail parties and press functions whether you like it or not."

"It can't be that bad." Betty clearly thought it was quite the opposite. "You happened to get in with a bad bunch—courtesy of that flaky husband of yours—but everyone in New York can't be like that. After all, Raven comes from there."

Pat's smile was just a movement of her lips. "I rest my case."

"How can you say that? Raven is a wonderful, kind, generous man."

"Thank you, Mattie Johnson," Pat remarked sardonically.

"I'll admit I was disappointed that he hasn't called, but then, I don't know what went on between you two after the dance that night." Betty hesitated. "Is it possible that you said some unforgivable things and he's waiting for you to make the first move? It's hard to believe that he would just walk out on you after . . . well, you know." Her cheeks were bright with color.

Pat wrestled briefly with her conscience. Betty adored Raven. She could tarnish his image by letting Betty believe he had seduced her, then used a convenient argument as an excuse to disentangle himself, or she could tell the truth. Pat's conscience won. What difference did it make now? She would have to leave here anyway—the sooner the better. Before someone told Raven about the article and he called with either jeers or condolences. Pat knew she couldn't bear either one.

"Raven was here a few days ago," she said in a low voice.

Betty looked bewildered. "None of us saw him."

"He came to see me—and I presume he went right back."

"That must mean you had another argument." Betty sighed. "Don't you know *anything* about men, Pat? If he flew all the way out here just to see you, it proves he's crazy about you. I'll bet if you played your cards right you could even maneuver him into marriage."

"He asked me to marry him before he left," Pat answered tonelessly. "And again the other day. That's what we argued about."

"You turned him down?" Betty almost choked on the question. "Are you out of your mind?"

"I had one husband who didn't love me. I don't need another."

"I don't believe this! A man asks you to marry him and you say he doesn't *love* you?"

"You don't understand. Raven wants to take over my life. He wants to decide where I'll live and what I'll do. When we first met he disapproved of the kind of work I was doing here, then when he found out I was a writer he tried to push me in that direction."

"I thought you said he didn't know who you were."

"He doesn't. We were talking one day—he was always asking me questions—and I . . . he sort of made me admit that I'd done some writing. But I didn't tell him I'd sold anything."

"So what he did was encourage you—give you moral support."

"Well, yes, but I didn't ask for it," Pat replied defensively.

"Don't you see what a good person that makes him?" Betty demanded. "He cared enough to want you to reach out for the brass ring."

"That's what Carl kept pushing me to do." Pat's eyes were bleak.

"There's a big difference. Your freeloading husband was after a meal ticket; Raven only wanted you to fulfill your potential. He doesn't need your money—or your success. Don't you know a secure man when you see one?"

The truth of Betty's statement was something Pat couldn't deny. She had fought against the knowledge, not wanting to admit that Raven was a superior person. Because it didn't change anything. She told Betty that.

"You don't love him." Betty sighed, disappointed but resigned.

"You must know better than that! I wish with all my heart that I didn't." Pat's mouth trembled. "But it would never work. Raven's life is in New York, and I don't want to go back there."

"Now I've really heard everything! How can you be so selfish?" Betty was like an angry kitten, bristling with indignation. "You're ruining both your lives because you once got a raw deal from a blue-ribbon fink. What kind of revenge is it to sulk in a corner? Raven is the one who's paying for it, not you."

"He'll get over it," Pat said in a low voice.

"Will you?"

"No." It was a soft sound of despair.

"What makes you so special?" Betty demanded. "Do you think you're the only one who can feel pain? Suppose you're destroying Raven's life the way Carl destroyed yours? Raven must love you an awful lot to have put up with you this long," she said disgustedly. "He had confidence in you when he didn't even know if it was justified. He gave you trust and encouragement, in addition to his love. And what did you ever give him in return—besides something he could get from any number of willing women."

"That's just the point. There *are* all those other women. How could I compete with them?"

"By taking what's yours and hanging onto it. You've already given up your career for Carl. If he can make you give up the love of your life, his victory will be complete."

Pat stared at the other woman, too startled to speak. She had never thought of it that way. Carl had taken everything she had to give while they were married. Was she still letting him bleed her dry? Pat had never realized what she was doing to herself, nor considered Raven's feelings. Why hadn't it occurred to her that his suffering was just as real as hers? Besides being a prize idiot, was she really selfish?

Betty's face wore a look of satisfaction as she struggled to her feet. "Well, at least I've given you something to think about. That's a step in the right direction. I'll leave you to wrestle with your own private devils." She grinned widely. "Personally, I'm betting on the angels."

Pat remained motionless in her chair. In a gentler way, Raven had tried to tell her many of the things Betty had come out with so bluntly. He knew that Carl was poisoning her life, that she would never be well until she went back to face the problems he had caused.

Without knowing their magnitude, Raven had offered his protection, and she had rejected it scornfully. He had tried to pry her out of her haven for her own sake, not merely his. And when she defied all his efforts, he still cared enough to make sure that her refuge was secure. Was there ever a love so tender? Pat's eyes filled with tears at her own folly.

Was it too late? Her heart started to thunder as she faced the future instead of the past. Would Raven forgive her after all the rotten things she said? Had he written her out of his life the way he threatened? It was a terrible possibility, but Pat knew she had to go to him and chance it.

She ran into the bedroom to get her suitcase from the closet shelf, but her arms dropped as she reached for it. There was no reason for Raven to believe she wanted to resume anything but a physical relationship. She had used evasions so many times. How could she convince him that she was not only ready, but eager to face anything life dealt out as long as she could do it as his wife?

After a long moment Pat's mouth curved in a blissful smile. She went back to the living room and pulled a stool in front of the bookcase so she could reach the dusty typewriter on the top shelf.

"You want to know what happened to Patricia Lauren Lee? She took a slight detour, but she's about to make a triumphal return." Pat's lilting voice was very confident.

Chapter Eleven

Pat worked literally night and day completing the first three chapters and an outline of the book that had been taking shape in the back of her mind. As the words flowed onto paper she realized how futile it was to think she could ever stop writing permanently. Whole pages of dialogue seemed to have been stored in her subconscious. For the first time since Raven left she felt alive and productive.

During those days she frequently forgot meals and only went out of the house to take Janus for a run. Even that was connected with her work. The rutted wagon trails carved in the hard earth kept her in the mood of the eighteen hundreds.

The typewriter was going like a machine gun when Betty paid a visit to the cottage. "What's going on?" Her eyes widened. "I thought I'd give you a couple of days to yourself, but then I got worried when we didn't hear from you."

Pat flashed a big smile. "Everybody can stop worrying about me now. I gave the past a decent burial and I'm out of mourning."

"I knew you'd see the light! You *have* come to your senses, haven't you?"

"If you think writing is sensible," Pat teased.

"You know what I mean. Have you called Raven?"

Pat's smile faded. "No, I'm going to go see him."

"Well, what are you waiting for?"

Pat haltingly explained her reasons. She looked down at the typewriter keys. "I'm dedicating this book to Raven—no matter what happens between us."

"I already know what's going to happen. After he bawls you out for taking so long to get there, he's going to march you off to the nearest judge."

"I wish I could be as sure." Pat's eyes were wistful.

"Take my word for it." Betty dismissed it as an accomplished fact.

"Will you keep Janus for me while I'm gone? I . . . I might be back in a day or two, and I'd hate for him to have to make the round trip. Janus doesn't like to fly."

Betty stroked the dog's back. "I'd be happy to keep him permanently. He's really better off here; you and Raven can visit him."

Pat bit her lip. "Well, we'll see."

Although the book was proceeding in record time, Pat was worried about the days slipping by. She knew Raven wouldn't forget her that soon, but he might get used to being without her. As the pain of separation lessened, he might decide that it was a good thing. The bleak thought made her mouth dry—along with images of how he was consoling himself. Her fingers flew even faster as she raced to finish.

It was two o'clock in the morning a week later when Pat ripped the final page out of the typewriter. She was exhilarated by the knowledge that it was the best work she had ever done—and it was all due to Raven. He had taught her what love really meant, its depth and generosity. She would never have been able to breathe such life into her characters if he hadn't given her the precious gift of his love.

The ride into New York City from Kennedy Airport brought back memories. Pat had forgotten that cab drivers routinely ignored the scientific principle that says it's impossible for two solid objects to occupy the same space at the same time. As her taxi abruptly changed lanes, Pat closed her eyes. Instead of a shattering crash there was only anguished honking from the car they'd cut off.

"The guy must be a tourist," her driver remarked disgustedly.

When the soaring towers of the city came into view, she started to feel a prickle of excitement. There was an undeniable electricity in the air. Everyone seemed to be hurrying to an important appointment. Pat's head swiveled from side to side, watching the people surge across the street, looking in the cleverly trimmed shop windows, absorbing the unique frenzy that was New York City.

Her destination was the Waldorf Astoria. Pat hoped she wouldn't be spending the night there, but it had been only prudent to book a room. Raven might have meant what he said when they parted. Pat had been filled with joyous optimism all the time she was working on the book. On the plane trip her confidence had wavered a little, and when she actually reached the city it began to plunge.

How could she possibly have imagined that Raven would still want to marry her? After the quiet, uneventful days in Wyoming, she felt like a country hick. That was probably the way he'd see her too.

She set her jaw grimly, stifling the urge to turn around and go back. She was through running away. If Raven didn't want her anymore she would just have to live with the fact. It was something she had to find out.

Her hands were trembling as she looked in the phone book for his office number. A receptionist with a pleasant voice plugged in Raven's extension. Pat's throat tightened as she listened to the phone ring. She was so intent on her opening speech that it was a shock when a woman's voice answered. Pat realized at once how foolish it was to expect him to answer his own phone. Of course he would have a private secretary. What she hadn't anticipated was that the woman wouldn't let her speak to Raven.

"Mr. Masters is in a meeting. May I help you?"

Pat's heart sank. How could she bear another delay? "No . . . uh . . . it's personal. I'll call back. Can you tell me when he'll be free?"

"I really couldn't say." The woman's voice was coolly impersonal. "Mr. Masters has a very full schedule today. You can leave your number and I'll have him return your call when he's able to."

"No!" It was unthinkable to sit by the telephone waiting for it to ring. What if he never called? "I mean . . . I'm going to be in and out," Pat finished lamely.

"Then, I'm sorry but I can't help you."

"It's really terribly important! I . . . I'm Mr. Masters's caretaker at his ranch in Wyoming, and I have a message for him."

"I see." There was a wealth of disbelief in the two words.

Too late, Pat remembered that she had said her business was personal. "I really am an employee of his. At the Circle Bar Ranch just outside of Cougar Run," she added, hoping that would lend authenticity to her claim. "Perhaps I can get him at home this evening. Could you tell me his phone number?"

"I'm not authorized to give that out. In any case, it wouldn't do you any good. Mr. Masters will be at the Wentworth Foundation benefit tonight." The secretary's smug tone indicated that Pat would have known that if she were truly an insider.

Pat frowned. The name meant nothing to her, but she vaguely remembered seeing it somewhere. Then it came to her. She had read it on the events board in the lobby while she was waiting to check in. "Is that the dinner dance being held at the Waldorf?"

The secretary regretted her incautious urge to gloat. "There's really nothing more I can do for you, Miss Lee," she said firmly.

Pat hung up the receiver, thinking furiously. The woman's intransigence hardened Pat's resolve rather than discouraged her. Nobody was going to keep her from seeing Raven. The problem was how?

The fact that he was going to be right there in the hotel that night seemed like a good omen. All she had to do was get an invitation. And Pat thought she knew how. Without bothering to unpack, she picked up her manuscript and left the hotel room.

She went out the Park Avenue exit and walked crosstown to Madison where her literary agency was located. It was the reason she had chosen the Waldorf, because the two were close together.

Her reception was everything she could have wished.

She was treated like a long-lost, treasured friend, and scolded fondly.

"Well, it's about time you surfaced!" John Melinkoff, Pat's agent, admonished. "I suppose it never occurred to you that your friends would be worried."

"What's to worry? Can't a person take a little vacation?" She tried to pass it off lightly.

"If that's all it was. But you dropped out of sight without a word to anyone."

She couldn't quite meet his eyes. "It seemed like a good idea at the time."

"It was all that trash in the paper, wasn't it, Pat?" he asked gently.

She gave up the pretense. "I decided the laughter of my so-called friends would be easier to take from a distance," she remarked bitterly.

"How can you even think a thing like that?" He looked genuinely hurt.

"Not you, John—you were sorry for me, no doubt. But pity wouldn't have been any more palatable."

"You have a lot to learn about people," he said sternly. "Of course I'm sorry it happened—I'm sorry there are creeps like Carl Kloster in the world—but that doesn't mean I pity you. Nor does anyone else. We're just glad you finally dumped the clown."

"I feel like such a fool for being taken in that way," Pat said in a low voice. "I was naive enough to think a marriage vow meant something."

"Are you going to kick yourself the rest of your life for being a decent person?" he demanded.

"No, I think I've gotten everything sorted out."

"Was it the article in *World Today*?" John made a sound of deep disgust. "You ought to sue the jerk for everything he wishes he had."

Pat shook her head, a twisted smile on her face.

"Maybe something good came out of it after all." She was thinking of Raven, but John misunderstood.

"You're writing again?" he asked, with a look of satisfaction on his face.

"I think it's the best thing I've ever done," she answered quietly.

John asked a lot of questions which Pat answered eagerly. It was truly like old times—including the constant interruptions.

"This is crazy," he declared when the phone didn't stop ringing. "Why don't we have dinner later on in some nice quiet restaurant where we can talk?"

It reminded Pat of her other purpose in coming. "Not tonight, John. I have a favor to ask."

"Name it," he agreed promptly.

"There's a big benefit this evening for the Wentworth Foundation. Can you get me a ticket?"

John's eyebrows climbed. "You used to hate those things!"

"I know, but this is ¡ . . . I just want to go."

"Well, sure, no problem." He looked at her with a puzzled frown, trying to figure out what was in back of the request. Mercifully, he decided not to ask. "I'll even escort you there myself," he offered instead.

"No, I . . . um . . . this is something I have to do alone."

"I see." It was plain that he didn't.

Before he could change his mind about asking questions, Pat got to her feet. "Just leave the invitation at the desk, will you? I have a couple of errands to run."

He stood up too, giving her a warm smile. "It's great to have you back, Pat. Let's have lunch tomorrow and really catch up." Before she could answer he snapped his fingers. "Doggone it, I've got an appointment tomorrow. How about the day after?"

Pat managed a smile. "Let's just play it by ear."

Until she saw Raven her plans were up in the air. She would continue writing of course, but not necessarily in the city. It was very possible that she would be on a plane out of town tomorrow.

Pat banished the somber thought as she walked across Fifty-Seventh Street to Fifth Avenue. The broad thoroughfare was lined with shops displaying merchandise so fascinating that it took her mind off her problems temporarily. Furs and jewels and exquisite china were displayed without price tags—a sure sign that they were expensive.

When she reached Fifth Avenue, Pat headed for Bergdorf Goodman, where she took an elevator to the beauty salon on an upper floor. She could hardly remember the last time she'd been to a beauty shop, but that day she intended to have the full treatment.

It was an unaccustomed luxury to lie back and have someone else shampoo her hair. It was also strange to have it set in rollers instead of blown dry in the casual style she usually wore. But she had requested an elaborate hairdo.

"You're going to the Wentworth benefit tonight," the hairdresser commented. It was a statement rather than a question.

"Yes, how did you know?"

He shrugged. "Half of the city will be there. It's going to be a real mob scene."

A slight frown puckered Pat's smooth forehead. She had forgotten what a crush those big charity affairs could be. It was possible to go through an entire evening without seeing people you knew were there. Suppose she couldn't find Raven in the mob? Her chin set firmly. She would find him if she had to have him paged over the loudspeaker system!

"Your nails are in really frightful shape." The manicurist's disapproving voice broke in on Pat's thoughts. "What have you been doing with your hands?"

An imp of mischief entered Pat. Raising her eyebrows she drawled in an affected voice, "You wouldn't believe me if I told you, my dear."

"Is this what you had in mind?" The hairdresser touched her finished coiffure lightly, patting a curl here, pulling out a tendril there. He was obviously pleased with the result. "I think it's absolutely ravishing."

Pat looked in the mirror at a total stranger. Her glowing auburn hair was pulled up and back, so it cascaded down in a shining mass of waves and curls that bounced around the nape of her neck. Silky bangs covered her forehead, and little wisps formed coquettish curls in front of her ears. She looked both glamorous and sophisticated.

It was a needed boost to her ego. The assured person looking back at her was the kind of woman Raven was accustomed to, here in New York. If he saw her like this perhaps he'd forget her former uniform of jeans and cotton shirts. Now that she had made up her mind, it was essential that he realize she was perfectly capable of fitting into his life-style.

Pat's next stop was the dress salon where she requested something very special. In the past she had often been intimidated by the haughty saleswomen, but her reception that day was gratifying. The new hairdo and her general air of assurance wrought a dramatic change. In moments she was presented with a wide selection of expensive gowns.

There were several outfits that had long-sleeved black velvet jackets paired with skirts of brocade or gold lamé; very pretty, but not what she wanted. There were also satin charmeuse evening pants, and long, floating chiffon prints—all adequate, but not quite right. Then the saleswoman brought out the perfect gown. It was a simple slip of a dress, white silk organza with a scoop neckline and narrow bands over the shoulders. What made it outstanding were the silver bugle beads that covered it completely in an intricate design of waves and swirls.

Pat's eyes sparkled like the hand-embroidered crystal beads as she gazed at herself in the mirror. Even in her modest opinion she made a smashing appearance. The gown was horrendously expensive and it looked it, yet it was elegant rather than ostentatious. The famous designer whose name was on the label was undeniably a genius. Pat's confidence soared as she stared at her image. The sophisticated woman in the mirror could hold her own with anyone!

"That gown looks absolutely divine on you," the saleslady enthused. "Not everyone could wear it, but you have the perfect figure. I think you made a wise choice."

Pat had a chilling moment of déjà vu. In another place at a different time, a salesperson had said practically the same thing, implying that all her dreams would come true if she wore the right dress. That evening had ended in disaster. Would this one follow the same pattern? Pat tried to shrug off the sinking feeling of impending doom. Nothing was going to go wrong tonight. She glanced in the mirror for reassurance.

After a brief stop on the first floor to buy sandals and a small evening bag, Pat headed back to the hotel.

As the hour grew later, the butterflies in her stomach beat their wings faster. So much depended on that night. At first the time had dragged and she didn't know how she would get through it, but when it was finally time to go downstairs Pat had to force herself. She took a last look in the mirror. The emerald green eyes of the glittering stranger who stared back at her were slightly feverish, but her makeup was impeccable and her coiffure was faultless. Lifting her chin high, Pat closed the door and walked down the hall to the elevator.

As she stood in the entrance of the grand ballroom a few minutes later her heart sank. There seemed to be more people milling around in that one room than there were in the whole state of Wyoming! How would she ever find Raven?

"Are you lost?" The amused question came from a suave man who appeared beside her. "You look rather desperate."

"Only because I feel that way," she assured him. "I have to find someone."

"In this crowd that should be just slightly easier than Diogenes' search for an honest man."

"At least he had a lantern," Pat commented ruefully.

"I wouldn't worry." The man gazed at her admiringly, from the crown of her shining head to the spike heels that enhanced her shapely legs. "Whoever the lucky fellow is, he'll undoubtedly find *you*." When she ignored his compliment, continuing to look over the room with a worried frown, he said, "Would you like to dance? You can cover more territory that way."

As she was about to refuse, the truth of his statement sank in. "That's very nice of you."

"Not really." He led her onto the crowded floor. "I'm really hoping we won't find him."

Pat found it difficult to make the light conversation that was expected. Her eyes kept darting over the dancers, searching for a tall dark man who held the key to her happiness. As they circled the packed floor she began to despair. What if Raven had changed his mind about attending? He wasn't on the dance floor as far as she could tell, and she hadn't spotted him in the milling throng.

Suddenly Pat stiffened. Raven was sitting at a choice table with a view of the bandstand. His handsome face wore a faint look of boredom as he glanced over the room while listening to his date's animated chatter. Suzanne Turner didn't seem to notice. The beautiful blonde looked confident and happy, sitting there with her arm linked through Raven's. They made a stunning couple, Pat had to admit bleakly. His elegant black and white evening clothes were a fitting complement to her sleek perfection.

A wave of futility engulfed Pat. The man sitting at that table was a total stranger. He was about as far removed from the tender companion she had laughed and loved with, as New York was from Wyoming. How had she ever thought she could bridge the gap?

The man Pat was dancing with had felt her tension. He followed her gaze. "I guess you located your quarry."

"Yes," she admitted reluctantly.

"I knew it was too good to be true." He led her to the edge of the floor, holding her hand a moment longer. "It looks like he's been consoling himself in your absence. If it doesn't work out, just remember that I'm available."

She made some kind of reply without even thinking about it. Pat's mouth was dry as she threaded her way between the tables. What was she going to say to Raven? Foolishly, it had never occurred to her that of course he would be with a date. All of Pat's carefully prepared speeches fled, leaving her mind a blank.

Suzanne noticed Pat before Raven did. The blond

woman frowned slightly as though trying to place her. Raven followed her line of vision indifferently, then froze as Pat reached their table.

"Hello, Raven." She forced a smile, turning to his companion. "Suzanne. Do you remember me? We met at the ranch in Wyoming."

"You're kidding!" Suzanne's incredulity wasn't very flattering. "I never would have recognized you!"

"I suppose that's understandable." Pat flicked a glance at Raven. He was staring at her as though in shock—which didn't tell her anything.

"What are you doing in New York?" Suzanne asked.

"I'm here to join my fiancé." The words came out of nowhere, but once they were said Pat knew she had to go through with it. "Would you mind if I borrowed him for a few minutes?" She turned to Raven, who continued to look at her wordlessly.

"What is this, some kind of a joke?" Suzanne asked, her frown deepening.

Pat felt as though she were in the middle of one of those nightmares where one suddenly finds oneself naked in the midst of a crowd. She wanted to run and hide. How could she have made such a fool of herself? Raven's rejection spoke volumes by its very silence. He didn't even care enough to ease her humiliation—although nothing could.

Tears filled her eyes as she turned away. "It . . . I guess it wasn't a very funny one."

"It certainly wasn't." Raven's hand closed around her wrist, halting her progress. His deep voice was vibrant once he found it. "Marriage is no laughing matter. Ours is going to be a very solemn ceremony."

Pat tried to pull away but he wouldn't let her. "Please, Raven," she murmured. "Just let me go."

He put his arm around her waist instead, pulling her

close. Turning to Suzanne he said, "Would you excuse us for a short time? I haven't seen my fiancée in weeks."

"You can take the rest of the night as far as I'm concerned," she replied angrily. "I'm going to join Freddy Wilmore's party."

"You shouldn't have done that." Pat watched the other woman stalk off. "She's annoyed and I don't blame her."

"Because I wanted to have a private word with my fiancée? I don't think that's very understanding." His eyes kept roaming over Pat, taking in her elaborate hairdo and high-style gown.

"She's gone now," Pat said tautly. "You don't have to keep up the fiction."

Raven seemed charged with an inner excitement. "You mean you've changed your mind in the last few minutes? I do believe you've just broken your own record."

Pat could scarcely blame him for making fun of her. She had barged in here tonight and ruined his evening, trying to force herself back into his life after he had told her in no uncertain terms that he was through. But Pat couldn't bear his ridicule.

"Don't worry, I won't bother you anymore," she said miserably.

"I doubt that very seriously." Raven appeared to be enjoying the whole thing.

"I'm only going back to the ranch to pick up Janus," she insisted. "You won't ever hear from me again."

"How is good old Janus anyway?" Raven took her arm, guiding her toward the exit. "Still scrounging as many meals a day as he can get?"

Pat couldn't answer. It was a bittersweet reminder of the day she and Raven had met, when Janus had disrupted his picnic. The virile man next to her now was a far cry from the semi-invalid he had been—how long ago? It seemed an eternity.

When they reached the lobby he said, "Give me your claim check and I'll get your coat."

"I don't have one. I'm staying here in the hotel."

"That makes it even more convenient." He led the way to the elevators.

Pat held back. She didn't want to be alone with him. "We can say good-bye here."

"Don't be ridiculous. Give me your key," he ordered impatiently.

There was nothing to do but give it to him or risk a scene, which wouldn't bother Raven in the slightest. He was only interested in getting his own way.

At least he was silent going up in the elevator, in recognition of the other people accompanying them. Pat stole a glance at his classic profile. Why had he insisted? They had nothing left to say to each other. Was this urbane pose all an act? Was he going to turn cruel once they were alone?

Pat was very conscious of Raven's powerful physique as they walked down the corridor together, although she had no fear that he would hurt her physically. There were so many more subtle ways at his disposal. It was with extreme wariness that she preceded him into her hotel room.

There was a quivering silence after the door closed and they were alone together for the first time. Then Raven reached out and gathered her in his arms with a groan of satisfaction.

"Come here. I want to touch you, and taste you, and smell you." He buried his face in her neck, inhaling the perfume of her skin as he almost squeezed the breath out of her.

Pat clung to him for a moment even though she knew it was utter folly. Why tantalize herself with forbidden fruit? She was only making it harder. She pulled back, using a supreme effort.

"How can I convince you that it isn't necessary to pretend any longer?" she asked desperately. "I saw how you felt about me downstairs."

Raven kept his arms around her waist, smiling down at her as she leaned away from him. "What did you see?"

"You didn't say a word to me! You just sat there, letting me stumble around making an idiot of myself."

"Silly little Pat." His long fingers reached out to pull the hidden pins from her hair.

As the gleaming mass started to tumble around her shoulders she grabbed for his hand. "What are you doing? I spent hours in the beauty shop getting this hairdo."

"What a waste of time." The pins were all out in spite of Pat's attempt to stop him. Raven ran his fingers through the stylized curls, from her nape to her crown, combing out the silken strands until they framed her face softly. "There, that's the way I remember you."

"As a little country girl?" Defeat left a bitter taste in her mouth. All of her efforts had been wasted.

"No, as the most enchanting, unaffected woman I've ever known." His voice was very husky. "Do you want to know why I didn't say anything when you first came to the table? I couldn't. I was afraid you were just a figment of my desperate yearning." He touched her cheek gently, letting his fingertips wander down to trace the shape of her trembling mouth. "Do you know how often I've imagined your face in a crowd? How many complete strangers I've chased after, certain that they were you? You've been in my mind every moment of the day and night—awake or asleep." He pulled her close in a convulsive movement. "God, how I've missed you!"

"You never tried to get in touch with me," she faltered.

"I didn't think you wanted me to. The last time we argued, you ordered me out of your life."

"You still could have tried," she mumbled, even though she knew what he said was true.

He tipped her chin up. "My dearest love, if I'd thought there was the slightest chance, I would have gotten down on my knees and begged. At first I tried to convince myself to take whatever crumbs you offered, but I knew it would never work. I couldn't live with the fact that someday you'd leave me. It was inevitable if you didn't care, and the longer I held on to you, the harder it would be to give you up."

Pat was thunderstruck at what she was hearing. She was the one who had been afraid he would tire of *her*! She touched his face tentatively, seeing the signs of strain for the first time. "We've hurt each other so needlessly. Is it too late, Raven?"

"Only to retrieve the weeks we've wasted. But we have a whole life ahead of us." His hands tangled fiercely in her hair. "You will marry me, won't you, Pat?"

She smiled tremulously. "If the position is still open."

"You're the only one who could fill it!"

Raven's mouth closed over hers with such tenderness and yearning that Pat's throat felt tight. She put her arms around his neck, clinging tightly to give him the reassurance he seemed to need.

He lifted his head to look at her with glowing eyes. "You do love me, don't you, sweetheart?"

"With all my heart," she sighed blissfully.

Raven's kiss was more urgent now, parting her lips with a male demand. His hands moved down her back, arching her body into his. Pat shivered at the wonderful, remembered contact, letting herself become completely pliant in his arms.

Without releasing her mouth he swung her up against his chest and carried her to the bed. Sitting on the edge with Pat cradled in his lap, Raven slid down the zipper of her gown. As the material parted his hand smoothed her back, trailing down to the brief panties that circled her hips. They were the only undergarment she wore.

"Your skin feels like satin," he muttered hoarsely. "You are absolute perfection."

His fingers retraced their sensuous path, sending waves of excitement pounding through her. Pat pressed closer to him, kissing the strong column of his neck. When his fingers slipped below her waistband to weave erotic patterns, she made a small sound of pleasure.

"You missed me too, didn't you, my love?" he asked triumphantly.

"So much!" she breathed, untying his tie and fumbling with the studs in his formal shirt.

His tongue teased the inside of her lower lip while he shrugged off his jacket and finished unfastening his shirt. It flicked in and out of her mouth as he slipped the glittering gown to her waist, then lifted her slightly so he could remove it entirely without ever giving up possession of her mouth. Raven's sensuous hands on her body, his seductive tongue in her mouth, were creating a storm inside Pat that threatened to rage out of control. When he unbuckled her sandals and placed her gently on the bed she held out her arms wordlessly.

Raven's tawny eyes blazed with excitement as he looked at her nearly nude body. His fingertips traced the line of her collarbones, then moved slowly to capture each tightly furled nipple, rubbing his thumb lightly over the small buds.

Pat clutched at the sheet, twisting her body restlessly. "You're driving me wild," she moaned.

"I want it to be good for you, sweetheart." His dark head bent and his mouth glided down her body, trailing a path of fire. He paused to slide her panties down her hips before continuing his fiery exploration. After kissing the soft white skin of her thigh he murmured, "This is what I dreamed about all those lonely nights."

"Please, Raven, I need you now," Pat begged.

"Yes, angel, right now." When he threw off the rest of his clothes she could tell that his passion was as great as hers.

He took her in his arms, winding his legs around hers to mold their bodies tightly together. She was crushed against his hard male contours, set on fire by the intense heat he was generating. The inner flames leapt from one to the other, welding them into one person.

"It's never been like this with anyone else," he groaned. "Tell me it's the same for you."

"I love you, Raven . . . only you." Pat's soft avowal was made with complete confidence. She knew now that this man was worthy of her trust.

"I'll live to make you happy," he declared fiercely.

The roughened texture of his thigh parted her legs as he slid her body beneath his. She was pinned heavily by his weight, sinking deeply into the yielding mattress. He filled her entire world, enveloping her completely. When he surged against her in triumphant possession, Pat shuddered at the force of her own feeling.

She matched his throbbing thrusts, her taut body racked with wave after wave of almost unbearable pleasure. Her unbridled cries of delight were swallowed up in Raven's mouth as he sought to be joined to her in every way possible. His hands fastened on her hips, urging her into an even wilder rhythm that mounted to an explosive crescendo. Golden sparks shot through Pat's body in a twisting spiral that tossed her to the summit of sensation.

Raven's own satisfaction was derived from hers. As she reached her peak he held her protectively, shuddering in her arms with a wordless shout. The release from tension filled them both with a warm glow that brought complete contentment. Pat felt utterly fulfilled. When Raven rolled her onto her side she curled up in his arms, fitting her soft curves to his male angles.

They were quiet for a long time before Raven began to stroke her back languidly. "Where would you like to go on your honeymoon?"

It reminded Pat of the one piece of unfinished business between them. She knew now that it wouldn't matter to Raven; it was just something he had to be told. "There's something you should know," she began.

His long body tensed and he lifted his head to stare down at her. "You're going to marry me, Pat. I won't let you out of this hotel room until you promise."

"That might not be so bad," she teased, relenting when she saw the strain on his face. "Of course I'm going to marry you, darling. I think I would have died if you'd changed your mind," she whispered softly.

Raven's tension fled as he gazed into her adoring

face. "I hope you never have any worry more serious than that." The tender kiss they exchanged erased any possible doubts on either side.

But when he started to deepen it, Pat drew back. "I really do have something to tell you, Raven."

"It can wait," he growled, pulling her close again.

It was a temptation she resisted. "You're the one who told me I shouldn't keep putting things off," she reminded him.

His caressing hands stopped wandering over her body. Raven looked at her searchingly. "Is anything wrong, honey?"

"Not exactly—at least I hope you won't think so. The thing is, I haven't been completely honest with you about my past."

He put his fingers gently over her lips. "You don't have to tell me anything, sweetheart. Whatever you did before isn't important. All that matters is that we're together again."

Pat kissed his fingers before capturing his hand and pressing it against her cheek. She smiled mischievously. "I'm sorry to disappoint you, but I don't have anything lurid to confess. I just didn't want it to come as a surprise when I signed my full name to the marriage license."

Raven's bewildered expression changed to pleased surprise as Pat explained. But when she reached the part of the story that involved Carl, and her eyes became shadowed with remembered misery, he pressed her head against his solid shoulder.

"It's all over with, angel. You're never going to think about him again. I'm going to see to that."

She tilted her head to look up at him. "You don't mind all of the publicity? The newspapers didn't leave anything out. It won't bother you that I was an object of ridicule?"

"Are you kidding? That jerk you were married to is the one who made a fool of himself. He wasn't man enough for you, honey."

"I always thought I wasn't woman enough for him or he wouldn't have . . ." her voice trailed off miserably.

"Listen to me, my love." Raven forced her to look at him. "You're all the woman any man could ever want. He not only isn't worthy of you, he's a pitiful, insecure clown. Any guy who has to keep reassuring himself by sheer numbers, is in real doubt about his manhood. I'm sorry you had to find out in such a painful way, but take my word for it, sympathy was all on your side. *Sympathy*," he stressed, "not pity."

Pat thought about her meeting that afternoon with John Melinkoff and the agency people. They had all been so genuinely glad to see her, treating her like a long-lost friend, not a pitiable victim.

She looked at Raven in dawning wonder. "I almost let Carl destroy my whole life, didn't I?"

"You would have come to your senses in time." He kissed her tenderly.

"Are you sure?" she asked somberly. "It frightens me to think what would have happened if you hadn't come to the ranch."

"You'd have come back to New York and we would have met somewhere, sometime." He cupped her chin in his palm, staring hypnotically into her eyes. "A love like ours was meant to be. It was a heavenly directive on the day we were born. Nothing could have kept us apart, and nothing will ever part us from now on."

Pat's heart swelled with joy as she realized that every word Raven said was true. All of the bitterness and self-doubts were washed away by the miracle of his love.

She smiled through tears of happiness. "I once told you that you were too good to be real, and I was right."

Tiny pinpoints of light glittered in the depths of Raven's golden eyes. As his parted legs wrapped her to him and his hands began an erotic, enflaming journey down her body, he murmured huskily, "You're a hard lady to convince, but I'm going to enjoy proving it to you over and over again."

WIN

a fabulous $50,000 diamond jewelry collection

ENTER

by filling out the coupon below and mailing it by September 30, 1985

Send entries to:

U.S.
Silhouette Diamond Sweepstakes
P.O. Box 779
Madison Square Station
New York, NY 10159

Canada
Silhouette Diamond Sweepstakes
Suite 191
238 Davenport Road
Toronto, Ontario M5R 1J6

SILHOUETTE DIAMOND SWEEPSTAKES
ENTRY FORM

☐ Mrs.   ☐ Miss   ☐ Ms   ☐ Mr.

NAME _____ (please print)

ADDRESS _____ APT. #

CITY _____

STATE/(PROV.) _____

ZIP/(POSTAL CODE) _____

RTD-A-1

RULES FOR SILHOUETTE DIAMOND SWEEPSTAKES

OFFICIAL RULES—NO PURCHASE NECESSARY

1. Silhouette Diamond Sweepstakes is open to Canadian (except Quebec) and United States residents 18 years or older at the time of entry. Employees and immediate families of the publishers of Silhouette, their affiliates, retailers, distributors, printers, agencies and RONALD SMILEY INC. are excluded.

2. To enter, print your name and address on the official entry form or on a 3" x 5" slip of paper. You may enter as often as you choose, but each envelope must contain only one entry. Mail entries first class in Canada to Silhouette Diamond Sweepstakes, Suite 191, 238 Davenport Road, Toronto, Ontario M5R 1J6. In the United States, mail to Silhouette Diamond Sweepstakes, P.O. Box 779, Madison Square Station, New York, NY 10159. Entries must be postmarked between February 1 and September 30, 1985. Silhouette is not responsible for lost, late or misdirected mail.

3. First Prize of diamond jewelry, consisting of a necklace, ring, bracelet and earrings will be awarded. Approximate retail value is $50,000 U.S./$62,500 Canadian. Second Prize of 100 Silhouette Home Reader Service Subscriptions will be awarded. Approximate retail value of each is $162.00 U.S./$180.00 Canadian. No substitution, duplication, cash redemption or transfer of prizes will be permitted. Odds of winning depend upon the number of valid entries received. One prize to a family or household. Income taxes, other taxes and insurance on First Prize are the sole responsibility of the winners.

4. Winners will be selected under the supervision of RONALD SMILEY INC., an independent judging organization whose decisions are final, by random drawings from valid entries postmarked by September 30, 1985, and received no later than October 7, 1985. Entry in this sweepstakes indicates your awareness of the Official Rules. Winners who are residents of Canada must answer correctly a time-related arithmetical skill-testing question to qualify. First Prize winner will be notified by certified mail and must submit an Affidavit of Compliance within 10 days of notification. Returned Affidavits or prizes that are refused or undeliverable will result in alternative names being randomly drawn. Winners may be asked for use of their name and photo at no additional compensation.

5. For a First Prize winner list, send a stamped self-addressed envelope postmarked by September 30, 1985. In Canada, mail to Silhouette Diamond Contest Winner, Suite 309, 238 Davenport Road, Toronto, Ontario M5R 1J6. In the United States, mail to Silhouette Diamond Contest Winner, P.O. Box 182, Bowling Green Station, New York, NY 10274. This offer will appear in Silhouette publications and at participating retailers. Offer void in Quebec and subject to all Federal, Provincial, State and Municipal laws and regulations and wherever prohibited or restricted by law.

SDR-A-1

READERS' COMMENTS ON SILHOUETTE SPECIAL EDITIONS:

"I just finished reading the first six Silhouette Special Edition Books and I had to take the opportunity to write you and tell you how much I enjoyed them. I enjoyed all the authors in this series. Best wishes on your Silhouette Special Editions line and many thanks."

—B.H.*, Jackson, OH

"The Special Editions are really special and I enjoyed them very much! I am looking forward to next month's books."

—R.M.W.*, Melbourne, FL

"I've just finished reading four of your first six Special Editions and I enjoyed them very much. I like the more sensual detail and longer stories. I will look forward each month to your new Special Editions."

—L.S.*, Visalia, CA

"Silhouette Special Editions are — 1.) Superb! 2.) Great! 3.) Delicious! 4.) Fantastic! . . . Did I leave anything out? These are books that an adult woman can read . . . I love them!"

—H.C.*, Monterey Park, CA

*names available on request